RAPIDS

RAPIDS

a novel

TIM PARKS

ARCADE PUBLISHING
NEW YORK

9-06
24.00

FIRST NORTH AMERICAN EDITION 2006

First published in the United Kingdom by Secker & Warburg

This is a work of fiction. Names, characters, places, and incidents are either the work of the author's imagination or are used fictitiously.

Library of Congress Cataloging-in-Publication Data

Parks, Tim.
  Rapids : a novel / by Tim Parks. —1st North American ed.
     p. cm.
  ISBN 1-55970-811-5 (alk. paper)
  1. Alps, Italian (Italy)—Fiction. 2. Kayaking—Fiction. I. Title.

  PR6066.A6957R37 2006
  823'.914—dc22   2005029292

Published in the United States by Arcade Publishing, Inc., New York
Distributed by Time Warner Book Group

Visit our Web site at www.arcadepub.com

10 9   8   7   6   5   4   3   2   1

EB

PRINTED IN THE UNITED STATES OF AMERICA

To all those who taught me
not to be afraid of the water,
and never to fight it.

The following pages are fiction. No reference to any living person is intended or should be inferred. While the place names are real, scenery and circumstance have been somewhat altered to suit the plot. There is no campsite at Sand in Taufers. In particular, the rapids of the river Aurino are not exactly as described. Canoeists beware! This book is not a guide for a safe descent.

A STOPPER

This isn't the right world, he told her. For us. He unrolled a sleeping bag and laid down on the planks. Be strong, he said. Earlier, immediately on their return, they had tried out the stretch downstream from Sand in Taufers. Filthy cities, Clive muttered. Michela looked taller and slimmer in her wetsuit beneath the large backdrop of the Alps, if possible even younger. Filthy Milanese, he insisted, pulling tight his spraydeck. Old misanthrope! she laughed. She was happy. It was right to go, she said, I don't regret it at all, but great to be back.

So it was. They seal-launched from the bank. The river was high. It slid solid beneath the bridge. She knew she loved him and so was thinking only of the practical arrangements: the campsite, the pitches, the food, the equipment. This is the big day. These are her duties. I hope they don't bring any basket cases, she called. Clive was already away downstream. He broke in and out of the swift flow. The merest hint of an eddy was refuge enough. He was so stable on the flood. He used so few paddle strokes, so little energy. Michela darted behind. She was aware that basket case was his expression. She was aware of emulating his deft certainty in the strong water. It's not my element yet. Clive broke out again. His yellow boat slewed to stop with its prow in only a handkerchief of stillness behind the lure of something submerged. The river tugged by. Move off! she called. The current was faster. Make room! He shook his head. He was laughing. The eddy was too small for two. Meanie! Now she must take the rapids first.

Suddenly alone, the river's horizon comes to meet you. There's a certain glassiness to it and as the roar swells the water grows more compact, it pulls more earnestly. The mountains around and above are quite still. Already you are past the point of no return. You must choose your spot. Michela knows the right place, slightly left of centre. But just before the plunge, she sees it has changed in their week away. The river is constantly changing. A rock has gone under. A heavy log is caught in the larger boil of the stopper. Perhaps still in the spell of last week's drama, or half focused on the group that will arrive this evening, she tries at the last second to change her line. She isn't used to leading. It's a mistake. The surface is already curving down. The pull is fierce. She throws in a sharp paddle stroke on the right to avoid the log, tries to straighten on the left. But already she's in the quick of it. Not quite in line with the current, the kayak is sucked abruptly back into the stopper, sideways to the flood.

For a second the young woman allows the elements to take over. A moment's inattention is more than enough. The water pounds on the spraydeck, forcing her head down into the rush. Her helmet bangs on the log. The red kayak spins on its axis. Her face is under now, in the foam. Again the helmet grates. But Michela is calm and lucid. She is always calm when it actually happens, when she's gone below and the world is blurred and swirling dark. She has her paddle gripped tight. As the stopper spins her up, head downstream, she leans out across the water to block the rotation, the bottom of the boat exposed now in the drumming cascade of the fall. At once she's steady, held in the churn of the stopper, but with her face just above water, her arms reaching to scull for support on the troubled surface. The log bangs and bangs on the hull. She's stuck.

There's someone shouting now, but the roar of the rapid is too loud. She glances up. Clive is already there in the eddy she was headed for. He's watching her. He beckons. He's so near. Slide out this way! Her boat is pointing towards him. Beyond its prow the stopper runs on for a couple of yards or so, a line of transparent water pouring over a ledge of rock to spin white beneath the surface. Every piece of flotsam dragged down the river is held there, for hours, perhaps for weeks, turned and turned in this liquid trap. The water flows on, but not the driftwood. Or the coke cans. Or even a dead rat, or sheep. Michela is caught. It's all she can do to keep her head above water.

Just beyond the stopper is the complete stillness of the eddy where she should be, sheltered by a spur of rock. Clive is grinning, beckoning, motioning to show how she can use the paddle to edge along the line of foam. She knows that of course. In theory. But in this position she can't get the boat to move. It won't budge. The underside grinds against the rock and the log. The water drums. And she can't hear Clive's voice either, if only because her right ear is actually in the icy water. The river is snowmelt. I must be strong, she thinks. But now she sees he's about to toss a line. He's passed it round a sapling on the bank and is waiting for her to understand. The throw-bag falls exactly over her arms. She grasps the line quickly with her left, twists it round a wrist, almost loses her precarious balance, then has it passed round the paddle and is gripping tight. Cautiously, Clive starts to tug. He seems to be savouring the resistance of the stopper, balancing the two pulls exactly, the water, the rope. Inch by inch, the boat slides along the ledge of the fall, approaching the eddy. Then it rocks free so suddenly that the girl capsizes and has to swing the paddle wide to roll up, drenched.

Idiot! Clive laughs.

All at once Michela can hear again. The world is calm and still and warm, unusually warm for the mountains. There are flies and river-bank smells. Only a couple of yards away, the roar of the crashing water seems remote and unimportant.

You should see your face, he says.

If you'd led the way, it wouldn't have happened.

You can't always be following me. Actually, you did brilliantly. He's smiling at her, water glinting on his thick beard, his eyes narrow against the sun. It's not easy to come out of a spin. Most people would have pulled the deck and swum.

Why didn't you leave the eddy to me?

There was room for three!

There was not!

You didn't try.

She would have liked to kiss him now, he was so steady with his wet beard, glinting eyes, thick forearms, but Clive is already shifting his boat round hers to move into the stream. By the way, he asked, how do you say eddy in Italian?

I told you, no one speaks Italian in this part of Italy.

I just want to know, so I can sound knowledgeable if people ask.

La morta, she said. You say *entrare in morta*.

With one stroke he was in the stopper. A simple move

4

of the hips lifted the underside of the boat to meet the falling water pouring over the ledge. At once the hull locked in, trapped in the tension between fall and reflux. Now he was in the same position she had been, though facing the other way. It looked easy. With long strokes that seemed to caress the surface of the water downstream of the boat, he moved slowly to the other side and popped out. He motioned for her to try. Michela shook her head and pulled into the flow below the fall. Evidently they would have to start the weaker paddlers further down.

The group arrived towards eight. They had driven all the way from England. Michela was waiting at the gate. Michela loves English people. Michela loves all things English and despite having lived only six months in the country Michela speaks and writes a near-perfect English. The fact that it isn't perfect is a torment to her. You have no accent, Clive explains: To be perfect, people would have to know where in England you come from. Michela comes from Brescia. She doesn't want Clive to learn Italian. It won't be necessary. Not in the South Tyrol. Her destiny is England and English. She feels this deeply. To become truly strong, she must leave Italy. They are only here because English people like to go abroad for their holidays, because the South Tyrol is so unspoiled and beautiful. Is there anywhere unspoiled in Europe aside from the Alps? They are only here for the summers. Then they'll go back to England. I don't like to speak Italian, she told him. I hate my mother tongue. I hate this country. Clive was thinking about other things. When not on the water, he is troubled, concerned. He is checking a kit bag, or looking through paperwork. Michela likes the impression he gives of always thinking, always foreseeing and forestalling some accident. It's an important moment in their lives. This is the first group they have brought here. They have made an investment.

Weren't there supposed to be thirteen of you? The van bounces on the rutted track turning into the campsite. It's a dirty white. The driver hits the horn in celebration. Am I driving carefully? asks a sticker on the back. There's a phone number and the name of a county council. The trailer with all the camping equipment and a couple of personalised kayaks bumps and trundles behind. Then people are spilling onto the grass, shouting, laughing, shaking hands. Mandy, Keith, Adam. Who's got the bloody trailer key? Who's got the duty list? Sugar! A tall chinless man in early middle age is trying to make a call from his mobile. At once Michela is excited, but anxious. The English are never quite the English she would like them to be, the English as she thinks of them when they are not there. One of the men is decidedly paunchy. It's their language she loves. Mandy too turns out to be robust and squat. They are shaking hands. Miserable crick in the neck! the older woman complains. She wears a shabby smock and clutches a digital camera. The boy who runs into her is in his gormless early teens. Clot! Mandy tells him abruptly. Her accent is unmistakably South London. You're on the cooking tent, Adam. Water canisters, please! Out of the e-mail and into the wetsuit, laughs the fatter, older man. I'm Keith. He grasps Michela's hand with both of his. His eyes are glassy and jolly. Mandy takes a photo. One for the website. Weren't there supposed to be thirteen of you? The girl asks again. Two coming separately, Keith explains. Already on holiday somewhere down south. Lucky sods.

The campsite is a cosmopolitan patchwork. The van moves slowly through a chequer of tents and chalets, the clutter of washing lines, cooking equipment, loud cries in Dutch, in Spanish, of children playing ball. Three grim teenagers are

6

sitting around African drums, transmitting a nervous rhythm to the twilight. Suddenly the forests above are black, the mountains stark. We've got the pitches nearest the river, Michela explains. Furthest from the loos, a spindly girl moans.

Speech! Keith announces as soon as the van has stopped. Men and women, kids and kayakers, lend me your lobes! So here we are in Wopland at last. Okay, it's been a long journey, I know, we've had a couple of sense-of-humour breakdowns, it's only natch, but what we need now is maximum co-op-er-ay-shun! It's nearly dark. We're going to have to move fast. From this moment on nobody thinks of themselves until the kitchen tent is up, the van unpacked, the water canisters filled and supper under way. Is that clear? We before me, okay? Thine before mine. Then you can put up your own tents and get yourselves sorted. Remember: this is not, repeat *not* a holiday; it's a *community experience*, right! As soon as we're all done and we've eaten we'll have the evening meeting and plan out tomorrow's activities. Oh, and don't forget to prepare your nominations for Wally of the Day!

As he finished speaking – and an Indian boy was already on top of the van furiously undoing tie-ropes – Michela saw Clive emerge from their chalet. His face more than ever expressed a contained, manly perplexity, a faint smile at the corner of the bearded mouth. Long time no see, he said, shaking hands with his old teacher. Wonderful place you found for us, Keith enthused. As the last light shrank behind the peaks, the valley was suddenly chill. How's the river? High, Clive said. The glaciers are melting. Mallet please! someone was shouting. Mall-et!

Sorry to be so silent, Vince told his daughter. Once again the autostrada had come to a standstill. These are his first

7

words of the drive. The air-conditioning hummed. The girl was changing CDs. Head down, lips pursed she looked at him sidelong, half smiled. What's there to say? she asked. He felt ashamed. You've put up with Florence, he said. Now you get your fun, see some friends. Louise laughed: I *liked* Florence!

Then the car was shaken with an urgent rhythm. May I? She turned it up even louder. He nodded. He hated the music. It was shameful that he had nothing to say to her. Nothing has been said about Gloria. His daughter was staring intently, tapping on her knees. The landscape trembled with heat. For at least a mile ahead the cars glittered stationary, as if a great river sweeping down from the Apennines had solidified in the summer haze. The planet is burning up, he thought. An asset long since amortised. He felt quite untouched, shivery.

Swaying her head, his daughter smiled, still with a faint hint of compassion. She is thinking of her mother, he decided. How can a holiday like this do anything but make us think of her? Yet it isn't really Gloria I am thinking of. He knew that. It was to do with Gloria, but it wasn't her. I don't *see* Gloria. He was suddenly anxious. I don't *hear* Gloria's voice when I remember the things she said. You think of nothing at all, he told himself. But so intensely. Life had not prepared him for this.

The pulse of the music became an obsessive repetition, a hectic running on the spot. The car throbbed. The song went on long beyond the point where you'd heard enough. The traffic stewed. Abruptly Louise turned the volume down: There is one thing though: if we're camping, how am I supposed to recharge my phone? Vince was gripping the steering wheel, willing the cars to move. Dad? Sorry, what was that? How am I supposed to recharge my phone? In what sense? We're camping, there won't be plugs.

8

He looked at her. No idea, he said. He managed a smile. Do without it for a week. Live free. Dad! She shook her head and turned up the volume again. Only now did he notice she was cradling her mobile in one hand, as if expecting some vital call. She has been fondling her mobile all week, he thought. I haven't even made fun of her. All at once the fierce drumming of the car stereo was challenged by the sound of a distant siren speeding along the emergency lane. Somebody has died, he decided. Someone won't be going home.

Michela felt keenly how different tonight's meeting was. Still, she had no presentiment of what was about to happen. Last week she and Clive had slept in the squalor of a *centro sociale* in Milan; more than two hundred people were spread across the floor of an abandoned warehouse. Many were smoking dope. There were angry speeches and chants, which she translated more or less for Clive. Sometimes someone stood up and spoke in English, or French, or German. They were speeches punctuated with slogans that everybody could repeat, whatever their language. Michela wasn't sure if she was enjoying it, but felt keenly that they were right to be here. They shared a cause. Everything precious was under threat. Some final barrier was about to come down, some crucial dam would burst releasing the final great wave of destruction. They must be strong to resist. They must protest. She joined in the chants. There were people of all colours and nations, mainly young, all scandalised. Our world is a scandal, somebody stood to say. Quite probably it will end in our lifetime.

Clive rolled his cigarettes. Despite the crowding, the intense heat, they had managed to make love every night, a slow, strong, silent love. We are two torrents flowing together in the dark, she whispered. During the meetings she sat between his legs. She had never felt more protected. Her man was solid, solemn. Free trade is just the free transfer of wealth from the poor to the rich, a young man explained. Loans are theft! It is criminal to ask for interest payments from the starving! It is lunatic to cut down the forests and burn more and more oil!

People clapped and cheered. Everywhere they went throughout the week they were met by the same impenetrable line of riot shields and truncheons. Police vans blocked the entrance to a square. Helmeted men with teargas launchers sprouted from hatches above. The heat was oppressive. Thirty-eight degrees. On the Thursday they tried to force the cordon round Palazzo Marino as President Bush arrived. They assumed it was President Bush. Usually so calm, Clive heaved wildly behind a thick Plexiglas screen they had made to push against the police. He was beside himself. *Issa!* the Italians shouted. Heave! *Issa! Issa!* Scores of photographers were crammed into a specially protected paddock. Heave!

The crowd surged. Some of the men had balaclavas, or motorcycle helmets. When the police counter-charged, two demonstrators were killed. That is: a barrier collapsed alongside the road and a dozen or so people were forced under the wheels of an oncoming tram. There was a chaos of sirens and scuffles. They had a policeman on the ground. That could easily have been us, Clive shouted. It could have been you! He was angry beyond anything she had seen before. They've fucked everything up, he kept repeating, everything. A rump re-formed across the street by La Scala. Multinational murderers! they chanted. No surrender!

For perhaps twenty minutes the situation was out of control. Michela felt proud of her man. We shall not be moved, he sang. She pulled him away from the truncheons. Dozens were being dragged to police vans. That evening the dormitory was alive with angry debate till three or four in the morning. Thunder rumbled across the city. A teenager with a guitar sang a song: You can't bomb your way to peace, Mr President. His amplifier was faulty. Clive bought some dope. To forget, he said. It was expensive in the strict economy of their lives. They still had equipment to purchase before heading back to the mountains. The jeep needed new tyres. Michela's mother had offered no help. They were poor and in debt. Michela stroked his high forehead, his straggly hair. I am living intensely, she told herself. Let me stroke you, she said as he lay on his back, smoking in the dark. His body was rigid. He is crying, she thought.

But this evening in the South Tyrol, Keith, the English group leader with the glassy eyes, the paunch, invited all the kayakers to say who they were and why they'd come on this trip and what they expected to get out of it. They were sitting in a circle on the hard dusty ground between pine trees and guy-ropes. Only one or two had seats. The others shifted on their hams. Starting on my left, Keith said. He was warm and avuncular. I know most of you know each other, but some don't. He had a fold-up canvas chair with wooden arms. Come on, don't be shy.

I'm Amelia. This was a wiry girl with bony white legs. I live just outside Maidenhead. The accent was moneyed. I did my three-star paddler with Waterworld last month. I love kayaking and can't wait to get some experience on white water. She seemed to have finished, then as if some explanation were required added. Oh, I'm fifteen. All right! someone cheered. Amelia forgot to say, Keith intervened, that she won the Girl Scouts Southern Counties Speed Kayaking competition last year. The girl looked at the ground. Aren't we modest, Mandy shouted. Then her camera flashed.

In a deadpan voice, rolling gum in her mouth, the fat, freckled girl beside Amelia said very quickly: Caroline, fifteen, from Gillingham, hoping to have a good holiday because I love the water and all.

Name's Phil, announced the gormless boy beside Caroline. His eyelids drooped. He too was chewing. Love playing on the water, like, but I've only done weirs n'all so I'm hoping I'll get on something well fast and dangerous. Never been to Italy before. I've done some surf, though. Like off Broadstairs. Wicked. That's it. In the sudden silence, everybody tittered. Phil seemed puzzled. He has a thick lower lip over a broad chin. Then he raised a fist and shouted: Chuck me in the rapids and I'll go for it! Again someone yelled, All-righty, sir! Respect! said Amelia solemnly.

Keith had to intervene: Fun aside, kids, this trip is not about playing. White water is serious. Okay Phil? The first skill we have to develop is looking out for each other. Making sure no one gets hurt. Too true, Mandy said. I want people constantly watching to see that someone else is not in trouble. Constantly, is that clear? You're always checking that everyone else is okay. That's how a group survives when things get dangerous. Never forget that your personal safety depends on other people looking out for you. We don't want to lose anyone.

It was dark now. A small gas lamp was hung on the lower branch of a pine. The next voice to speak came from a lean, chinless man in his late thirties. He was fingering a mobile. My name's Adam. As you probably all know, I'm a level-two instructor at Waterworld. I'm hoping to improve my skills here and move up to level three, though obviously my main job is to instruct those of you who haven't been on white water before. Anyway, I hope I'll be part of giving you all a good and useful time, so that you have something to take home with you. He turned the mobile round and round in his hand.

Thanks Adam.

Already a sort of embarrassed routine was creeping into these introductions, but Keith seemed to savour this, as if the very embarrassment had a social function. Mint anyone? offered the Indian boy. All the youngsters reached. I'm Mark, said one of them, sitting back. The voice was barely loud enough to be heard. Adam's me dad. There was a silence. You could say a bit more than that, suggested the father. I'm, like, seventeen, you know? And I've come to do my best. Is that all? Adam asked again. What am I supposed to say? the boy wanted to know. Even sitting, he was lanky and awkward. His long hair fell on his face. I'm here, like. He seemed belligerent. And I'll do my best. Oh, I love camping, he added.

Tom? Keith put in quickly.

Yes, I'm Tom. I'm twenty-one. This voice was deeper, the face immediately handsome in the dim light. Every feature was even and warm and strongly moulded, the teeth sharp and white, the hair polished, eyes bright. I study at the LSE. Haven't had a paddle in my hands for a few years now, but some other folks let me down for the holiday we were going to take, so at the last minute I signed up for this. Now I'm here I can't wait to get on the water.

Tom didn't say, but he rows for his university, Keith announced.

You all know me, Mandy said. She was opposite Keith. They exchanged glances. This must be the twentieth trip I've been on, and I'm telling you, after you've done all the admin you feel you deserve to be here. I'm the first-aid person and the menu planner, so any complaints, cuts or bruises or special requests this way. I'm also the trip photographer. She held up the camera, pointed it Keith's way, and set off the flash. So if you have to do anything idiotic, do it in front of me so you can look stupid on the website. And here's hoping this trip will be as exciting as all the others.

Three boys spoke now in quick succession. I'm Maximilian, but you're allowed to call me Max. Come to develop my skills and have a shot at my four-star and it's not true I'll be trying to avoid the washing-up. Oddly, this boy was wearing a proper shirt. Emerald green. And proper grey flannel trousers. He sat on his own camp stool. If anybody's heard snoring, folks, it's not me!

No one laughed.

I'm Brian. Same as Max really. Oh, I'm sixteen. So's Max. Come for the obvious reasons: drink, drugs, sex and underwater swimming. The boy stopped and blushed.

Be just like being at home then, Keith said generously.

Sex! Gormless Phil sniggered. Our Brian, sex!

Quiet kids, Adam protested.

I'm Amal. The Indian's voice was embarrassingly high-pitched. I love Waterworld. It's like a family for me. I'm seventeen. I've done plenty of white water in an open canoe – I did the Canadian trip – but this is my first time in a kayak. I'm sure it'll be a doddle.

Bloody open-canoeists, Max said.

Then in the straining light with the sound of low drums still beating in the fresh alpine air and the moths circling the gas lamp, attention shifted to Michela. There was a short pause; it was the first time perhaps that people had had a chance to see what a beautiful creature she is. Her black hair is cropped tight around a white, perfect oval face where the eyes are steady and dark. I'm Michela, but please call me Micky. Me and Clive here have been setting up this trip for you. We've scouted the rivers which are not traditionally much used for kayaking, so we won't have any problems with traffic. We've sorted out what level is what and who can go where. Or Clive has. He's also selected and bought fifteen good Pyranhas and all the equipment, so this is quite a big moment for us. I've mainly been doing things like booking the campsite, accounts, paperwork and so on. We really care about your having a good experience in a beautiful environment, leaving it as you found it and hoping it will change you for the better.

She stopped. Hear, hear! Keith said. You English? Caroline asked. The fat girl was squatting on her haunches, elbows on her thick knees, chin on hands, chewing. Michela hesitated: I'm Italian, she said, and turning quickly to Clive she asked him what he wanted to add.

As the others also turn, they find themselves looking at a powerful man with a thick beard and broad forehead. I was one of Keith's first pupils years back, he says. His thinning blonde hair is shoulder-length. And I survived to tell the tale. Somebody titters. Clive sits cross-legged, hands forward as if warming himself at a trekker's fire. I've always thought kayaking was more than a sport. I mean, more than playing squash or tennis or something. It teaches you to respect nature, to read it carefully and understand it. One day your life may depend on how well you read the river. Then, when you spend time by the river and on the river, you can't help but understand how dull and squalid a lot of so-called civilised life is. That's why Michela and I have been trying to make it our job to get people involved. He paused.

Anything else? Keith asked. Want to give us some kind of idea about what we'll be doing?

Clive still hesitated. It was the first time Michela had seen him address a group. She couldn't imagine he was nervous. The river Aurino, Clive said, or Ahrn as the Germans call it, rises in the glacier above Sand in Taufers. He gestured with a thumb up the dark valley. On the Austrian border, more or less, about twenty miles away. It's what the Italians call a *torrente*, rather than a river. Until Taufers it's fast and wild. There's a stretch there we might try on the last day, with those of you who are up to it, that is. But I'm warning you, you'll have to convince me and Keith that you really are up to it. The water is powerful and there's no space to breathe. Either you make the eddies and break out perfectly or you'll be carried straight down the river and trashed on the rocks. Anyway, we'll start by working the stretches downstream of Taufers. Plenty of interesting rapids, but usually a good space to roll up and generally relax afterwards if you've got the worst of it. Further down, between Bruneck and Brixen, there are stretches where you'll have to deal with a lot of volume. One day we'll have a go on a slalom course on the river Eisack, north of Brixen. That'll be a bit of a drive.

Any waves? Maximilian asked. He has a public-school voice. Stoppers? Phil wanted to know. Holes? So far they had only heard tell of holes.

Plenty of everything, Clive promised. But actually, what I really wanted to say was . . . You see, last week, Michela and I were at the anti-globalisation demonstration in Milan, you probably heard about it, where two people were killed. I don't know, maybe we're still a bit upset. Anyway, I'd like you to know that we feel the work we're trying to do here is part of the same campaign. You know — to help people respect the world before it's too late.

Yes, that's an interesting thought, Keith said. There was a

pause. Adam said: Actually I'm not sure I can go along with that. My own impression is . . .

Okay, okay, Keith intervened. No politics, not on the first night. We're here to help each other and learn about the water. Now, let's have the Wally of the Day nomination before we break up.

It seemed every evening – Michela could never have imagined this side to Englishness – that a small furry toy of vaguely teddy-bear shape called Wally was to be hung around the neck of whoever had done something particularly stupid during the day. The culprit would then have to perform some demeaning act, after which he or she must keep Wally about him until the following evening and be constantly ready to show it on request. Failure to show Wally at any time, even in the kayak, would lead to further humiliations.

Who gets today's Wally award?

Mandy nominated Keith himself for the incredible cock-up he had made reading the map outside Mainz, as a result of which they had gone west instead of east and arrived two hours late. Maximilian proposed Adam for having tied the kit on the roof so badly. A suitcase had slipped onto the windscreen just before Munich. It wasn't me, Adam quickly explained. It was too, Dad! protested the boy beside him. Yes it was! said Caroline. From a strictly legal point of view, Maximilian said, your name was on the duty sheet, Adam, so it was your responsibility. Oh shut up. The instructor was irritated. But the majority voted Keith. Punishment: a performance – Mandy proposed – of Ken Charles, Outdoor Activity Director for Kent County Council, giving his famous awards speech. Keith jumped to his feet. His glassy eyes shone. He is overweight, his cheeks round and red as a child's. He fixed Wally sideways under his chin like a bow-tie and ruffled up his hair. Ladies and gentlemen, he began, in a pompous bass, strutting back and forth. Everybody cheered. If you had but the teeniest inkling of what your dear offspring have achieved at Waterworld this week, you would be agog with wonder. Drinks! Max jumped up to shout. Everybody to the bar for drinks before it closes. Alrighty, sir! Phil was on his feet. No alcoholic beverages for the under-sixteens, Mandy ordered. Is that clear. I promised your parents.

The group moved quickly off through tents and caravans to where there was still music coming from the top of the campsite. Karaoke perhaps. Michela and Clive went with them. Then, towards midnight, in one of the site's chalets where they had lived for some three months now, Clive watched his girlfriend climb into their bed. He was seventeen years older than her. Aren't you coming? she asked. He kept pottering with bits of equipment. There was a spraydeck to mend, a repair kit to sort out. She waited. He was smoking more than he usually did. The room was rough wood with only the barest necessities. They had to share the outdoor bathrooms with the rest of the site. What's wrong? she asked. You just sleep, he told her. Then he said: What a prick that guy Adam is! Can you believe we're going to have to spend the week with a chinless wonder like that. What's wrong? she repeated softly. You can just see he's a prick, Clive insisted. A tight-arsed prick. Bet he's an estate agent or something.

Michela waited. Clive continued to potter about the room. Now he was sorting out clothes. This isn't the right world, Micky, he eventually told her. Not for us. He had found his sleeping bag in the big cupboard. Be strong, he said. Squatting, he unrolled it on the floor. She sat on the bed and stared. They had been lovers for two years. What are you doing? she demanded. I've been thinking about it a lot, he said. His voice was low and tired. We can't sleep together anymore.

She sat still. He was fiddling with the zip on the bag. Bastard thing! It had snagged. He wouldn't look up. What did I do? she asked. Her voice quavered. What's happening? Clive wouldn't speak. He had coaxed the zip past its snag. Slowly, as if he were squeezing into a new kayak, he sat down on the floor and put one leg after another into the sleeping bag. You hit the light, he said. The switch was just above the bedside table. Michela threw back the bedclothes and stood to grab a dressing gown hanging from the door. She pulled the waistband tight. What 'ave I done? There was an edge of disbelief in her voice. She felt sick. What in the name of God 'ave I done? She was standing over him. He lay face up, but his eyes were fixed on the ceiling. Nothing, he said. It's me. You haven't done anything. Look, don't worry, Micky. Everything will be just the same, the kayaking and the camp and the money and so on. But this isn't the world for us.

Don't slam the door! Vince stopped the car. It would wake people, he said. The need to respect others seemed to have snapped the driver out of his unhappy reverie. He let the car roll along the dirt track, passenger door still open. Louise trotted beside, making little forays among the pitches to check the vans for the Waterworld logo. It was almost two a.m. The autostrada had been jammed for hours. The sleeping campsite was illuminated only by the neon glow from the bathroom block. Everything was tied down and zipped up. Where are they? Louise rushed off between two tents again. Sweeping slowly round the corner at the bottom of the site, the car's headlights picked out a slim figure in silhouette sitting beneath a pine, back bent, face in hands. Vince touched the brake and the passenger door swung forward.

If he leaned back a little, he saw a head of dark hair framed against bushes. *Mi scusi*, he began. Dad! Louise came running, then tripped and fell heavily. Vince climbed out. Don't yell! They're over there! The girl was dusting herself off.

Are you looking for the English kayak group? The seated figure had got to her feet now. A young woman offered a wan smile of welcome. I'll show you to your pitch.

Vince parked beside a screen of trees that sloped steeply down to darkness. The night was quiet, but you had a distinct impression of the proximity of moving water, of a strong pull beneath the stillness of the branches. They haven't left you much room, Michela apologised. Heaving out their camping stuff, Louise tripped again. A torch shone out through orange nylon beside them: If this tent collapses, a posh voice announced, you'll hear from my lawyer!

Vince was surprised that the young woman appeared to be staying to help. You weren't waiting up for us, I hope? he said in a whisper. But Louise had the giggles now, trying to sort out tangled guy-ropes. Maximilian, or perhaps it was Brian, was making an obscene shadow play with torch and fingers on the tent wall.

Kids! Don't wake everyone up, Vince hissed.

I'm Michela, the woman said. I'm responsible for arranging things this end. But please call me Micky.

Oh come on Dad! Louise was laughing helplessly. We're on holiday! The girl's solid body had turned to jelly. We're supposed to be having fun. She laughed madly.

Michela took the guy-ropes from the younger girl's hand and untangled them. She seemed to know exactly how their tent was to be put up. The ground's too hard to push the pegs in with your foot, she warned. Go to the kitchen tent, there's a mallet just inside on the left.

The kitchen tent was a big, hut-shaped canvas structure open at both ends. Inside, between a dozen cardboard boxes with provisions, Vince's torch flashed over two figures asleep on the floor, in separate bags but face to face. Vaguely, he took in the sharp fine features of the one girl, the dull heavy jowl of the other. When he returned, Michela already had the tent up. Louise was complaining she had put the door at the wrong end. Don't look, Dad, she said some time later when they were undressing. It was cramped inside. They were lying on their backs, barely a foot apart. What? Don't look! Of course, sorry. That Max is so stupid, Louise complained. She huffed and puffed, turning this way and that for a comfortable position. Vince lay still.

Half an hour later he had to get up to pee. This was what he always hated about camping. Two zips to undo, shoes to find, struggling to your feet in damp grass to pick through the guy-ropes. Gloria loved it, he remembered. I always refused. In Florence, he had taken Louise to an air-conditioned, four-star hotel. The weather had been torrid. Here instead the night was chill and smelt strongly of pine resin; the sky was solemn with stars. But he didn't raise his head. As he arrived at the bathrooms, the urinals all flushed of their own accord under ghostly neon. I hate campsites, he thought. Why had he come?

Then walking back – it must be three a.m. at least – he saw that the young woman was still sitting where they had found her earlier. He hesitated. He had forgotten her name. She was hunched among the pine roots, face in hands. Somewhere nearby a clock chimed. Perhaps she was expecting another late arrival. There was a church tower just outside the entrance to the site. What if I'm not up to it, Vince worried, crawling back into his sleeping bag. He was a weak kayaker. Before the most ordinary outing he felt a shiver of fear. Maybe that was why he had come.

Then four hours later everybody was woken by a wild clanging of bells. For this is how the day always begins in Sand in Taufers. Christ Almighty, Louise yelled.

A WAVE

The first thing is padding up. Michela stands beside Clive while he gives his little lesson. The course that they have been advertising in canoe clubs all over England is called An Introduction to White Water: Five Days in the South Tyrol. A year ago, Vince Marshall would never have dreamed of coming.

You have to be tight in the cockpit. Okay? This isn't the Thames Estuary. Tight tight tight. The perfect fit.

Like sex? ventures a voice. Brian has a fuzz of red hair, a small snubbed nose, droll expression.

Actually no, not like sex at all, says Clive patiently. He is wearing a khaki cap. The girls are giggling. As somebody might know, if he had a minimum of experience.

Cru-el!

With sex, Clive continues in his measured sensible voice, two entities move constantly in relation to each other, *n'est-ce pas?*

Two what? Phil demands.

Michela's hand is just touching Clive's as he speaks. Vince, who hadn't been paying attention, is suddenly caught by this. He stares.

There is a certain amount of lubricant, Clive insists, with only a faint smile beneath his beard. Of give.

I do beg your pardon, Mr Riley, but what time of day is it? Mandy asks.

Two what! Phil whispers to Amal now.

Whereas if you're properly padded up in your kayak, kids, there should be *absolutely no movement at all*. Got that. None. You and the boat move welded together in the water.

May I venture to say, then – Max's facetious voice pipes up – that this is more like the male member's relationship with a condom.

Oh do shut up! Adam complains.

Only hazarding an ay-nalogy, smirks Max.

Anal? Phil demands.

I said, shut up! Adam insists. Let's remember some basic rules of decency.

Well, the condom would certainly be a more accurate description, Clive acknowledges wryly.

Let's just get on with it, can we? Adam is a scout leader. His son is watching him.

My sentiments entirely, says Amelia. For a second she keeps a straight face. She has pretty freckles round a prim nose, long straight black hair. Then all the adolescents burst out laughing. Even the fat Caroline. Even the older Tom.

Oh, I'm going to pee myself, Louise gasps. Vince now notices that his daughter has the top of her wrist pressed into her mouth.

Kids! Keith steps in. Kids, concentrate! If someone wants their four-star paddler this week they'll have to do more than crack jokes.

Wally! Phil shouts. Where's Wally!

Keith is aghast. Oh no! Eternal damnation! Then the older

man reaches into his open shirt and conjures the little effigy from his armpit. Fooled you!

Clive invites Michela to sit in a boat on the grass at his feet. They have lifted one of the Pyranhas down from the trailer beside the chalet. She's wearing jeans. She unlaces her trainers, puts a hand each side of the cockpit and slips in. The boat is a bright new blue. They have bought them with a loan. Clive squats down beside her. His beard, just greying from red, is close to her cheek. His blonde hair flows out of his cap in the manner of the American pioneer.

How are the feet?

Loose.

The footrests – gather round, kids – have to be so tight that the upper part of the thigh is jammed, I repeat, jammed under the cockpit here.

Clive puts a strong hand on her knee and pushes it laterally, then waggles it hard back and forth.

Too much give. See?

Michela shoots a glance at him.

They are a couple, Vince tells himself. He can't concentrate.

Michela gets out and Clive shows the others how to adjust the footrests. The trick is, set it so it's as snug as can be, right, then tighten up one more notch. Okay? Tight as possible. And then *again* one more. That's the secret. If it's not uncomfortable, it's not right. It has to hurt. At least at first.

Michela gets in the boat again. They are in the small clearing in front of the kitchen tent. Now she has trouble forcing her knees under the cockpit edges. She wriggles, smiles, grimaces, eyes closed, eyebrows lifted. Youch! It is another expression she learned from Clive.

If condoms hurt that much, a voice mutters, I'll do without.

Adam twists his head. He seems to be appealing to Keith to put a lid on this.

Brian's freckled face assumes a saintly glow.

I believe that's why the Pope is so against them, Max remarks boldly. The boy is wearing a broad-brimmed straw hat, as if at some public-school picnic.

Rock the boat, Micky, Clive is saying. Please, watch carefully everybody. Rock it from side to side.

Sitting upright, Michela leans to the right. She wears a white T-shirt that leaves a hand's-breadth of stomach visible. Vince looks away. Above the tents and the coloured clutter of the campsite, he lifts his eyes to climb solid slopes rising steeply through gleaming meadow and dark pine to shreds of bright cloud that drift among barren walls of rock. The instructor's voice fades. Then, further above, even in this month of August, Vince sees patches of snow shining distantly to cap dizzying cliffs of dark stone, gritty corrugated peaks. He breathes deeply. You're on holiday, he tells himself. To the north a tiny cable car crawls up the gigantic back of the mountain.

See how the body moved first, Clive explains, *before* the boat? Did you see that? All at once the voice is louder and insistent. Did you? Vince turns and finds Clive's eye on him.

It is absolutely essential that you take this on board.

Michela shifts her hips, raises a knee, so that the rounded hull of the kayak gradually tips while her torso remains upright. Clive thrusts a hand between the girl's thigh and the edge of the boat. That's the space we've got to pad out and eliminate. Okay? Any give between you and the cockpit, and the sheer fact is, as soon as you're in serious water you're going to be trashed. Which means of course that someone else is going to have to take time out to rescue you. Most of all, remember − now he raises his voice −

please, all remember: to do an Eskimo roll successfully in white water, you and the boat have to be one thing, moulded together. Okay? The boat *is* your arse.

Oh me dearie! Max exclaims, tugging on the brim of his hat.

Clive upturns a big cardboard box full of black poly-styrene blocks in plastic wrapping. Everybody was to pair up, get the boats off the trailer, set footrests, then help their partners to pad up, cutting the blocks to the right width.

You can use an ordinary knife for that. There are tubes of glue when you're sure you've got it right. Oh, and do it in your swimming kits everybody. Make it tight. That way it'll be even tighter when you've got your wetsuits on. I want you to feel like you're in a vice.

Vice is nice! Brian immediately joked. Nobody laughs. There is a general sense of anxiety. It's time to choose boats.

Louise was already paired off elsewhere. Vince saw Caroline grab her friend Amelia. Adam was giving his son useful instructions.

Us oldies should stick together, Mandy said, taking Vince's arm. Keith's brought his own boat, she explained. A mauve costume clung to her shapeless body. She has a round face, short hair dyed coal-black and carelessly cut. The two joined the bustle by the trailer. As they lifted a boat down, Vince was aware of being physically weaker than he would have wanted. Mandy sat in the kayak on the ground. They worked at the blocks of padding. I'm such a fat old sow, she was saying. She had strong wrists and forearms. And she said: Oh by the way, Adam told me about your wife. I'm so sorry.

Thanks, Vince acknowledged.

How has the girl taken it? she asked.

He pressed the foam block between her thigh and the

27

boat. She pulled a face. For all its rotundity, her flesh was solid. I really wouldn't know, he said.

Yaiiii! Towards ten-thirty a scream exploded on the water. Even before Amelia had her spraydeck on, Keith thrust her boat off the bank from behind and Clive, standing in four feet of still water, spun her upside down.

The first thing, kids – Keith now shoved Max off before the boy could grasp what was happening – the first thing, once you've got yourselves as tight as can be in your boats – I hope your ankles are killing you – is to make bloody sure you can get out of them in an emergency. Right, Phil? Another boat splashed in. Clive promptly capsized it.

From the dark water a red helmet popped up. Yaiii!!! Amelia shrieked. It's frigging freezing! It's ice!

You forgot your three slaps on the hull, Keith told her. Nobody comes out of the boat without banging three times on the hull. Otherwise how is a rescuer supposed to know that you're not still planning to roll up.

Then it was Vince's turn. The boat slid off the grassy bank and out across the water. It was a quiet spot downstream from the campsite where the river spread out in a slow curve across flat pastureland before taking the next dive. The nose of the kayak hit the water. Even before Clive could grab it, Vince leaned over and capsized. The shock of the cold water on his face was extraordinary. He was suddenly wide awake, forced into presence. Because he had secured the spraydeck and was watertight, he waited a moment, hanging upside down in the cockpit, to feel the full effect of the river's chill on face and hands. The water was unusually bright and clear after the estuary. He could see his fingers, even the pale gold of his wedding ring, as if in a swimming pool. Okay. He slapped three times without urgency on the sides of the boat, then reached for the tab on the elastic deck. The tab wasn't there. Why not? His hands felt rapidly round the rim of the cockpit. Everything was perfectly visible. The black deck, the blue boat. But he had secured the stretch-rubber top with the release tab tucked inside. In two years of kayaking he had never made this most elementary of mistakes.

Now he banged again on the hull. Another boat must have followed him. Clive was turning it over. He sensed noise and laughter and people scrambling out of the water. He was underneath, unseen, shut away. If he'd come in with his paddle he could have rolled up. But he hasn't. People can't hear, they can't see. I could die, he suddenly thought. He started to claw with his fingers, trying to pull the elastic from the cockpit rim to expose the tab and pull the deck. Nothing. Did they imagine he was showing off staying under so long? He put both hands on the cockpit, tried to pull his knees to his chest to force the deck off. It wouldn't pop. They are made not to pop. It is new and stiff and tight. Then he threw himself violently from side to side, twisting his head for air, shouting into the water, banging on the side of the boat. There was splashing all around. Firm hands grasped him and turned the boat. As he came up, blue-faced, he was looking straight into Adam's grey eyes. The man was shaking his head like some disappointed schoolmaster.

Wally! his daughter yelled. Dad's going to be Wally tonight!

What a fool! Vince shouted. He was furious. I'm such a fool! Damn and damn. He was taken aback by the violence of his own reaction. The youngsters were watching him. Respect, someone said.

Holding his boat on the other side, Michela said quietly,

Better in fun than when it's for real. This was another thing that came from Clive.

The sun was hot, as it had been all summer. They used the slack of the meander to get used to the boats and paddles. Clive had bought good paddles of a new nylon material, light and fast. Altogether it was a big investment. The instructors checked that everybody could roll. Capsize, kids. Go for it. Only Tom had difficulty. It was strange that such a strong, apparently expert boy should be the one to fail. In his eagerness to breathe, he tried to bring his head up too soon. Your head is the last part to come up, Keith repeated. But everybody knows this. Amelia and Louise stationed their boats beside his and gave advice. Tom is so handsome, a slim, straight, powerful young man with a good jaw, deep eyes. He tried again. His head struggled out of the water too soon and sank back. Amelia prodded her boat against the red hull. Tom felt for the bow and pulled himself upright holding that. His strong torso came up, dripping water, his fine face clouded with annoyance. Don't worry, Louise chirped. It took me ages.

Meantime the younger boys were turning their boats over and over in every possible way. Phil capsized, passed his paddle from one hand to the other over the bottom of the boat, head under water, then rolled up. All the time he was chewing gum. Can you do a helicopter roll, Bri? A reverse screw roll? Mark, Adam's quiet son, seemed particularly expert. Look at this one, Dad. He rolled up with the paddle behind his head. Adam watched. Anyone can do that kind of thing in calm water, he said soberly. In calm water anyone can be an expert. Amelia knew how to roll her boat with just her hands, no paddle. You sort of sway your body, like, from one side right to the other, she explained to Vince. He shook his head. It seemed impossible. I don't panic, Tom repeated to Keith. Really I don't.

I used to be able to do it. Swimming away from his boat, his young manliness seemed to be deserting him.

The kayaks spread out across the meander, tipping over and popping up.

What about the other side, Clive approached Vince.

Sorry?

Can you roll the other way round, with your paddle on the other side?

Never tried. As soon as Vince was alone, his mind lapsed back, not so much into thought, but a sort of intense, wordless inner paralysis. There are moments, Clive explained, in white water when it's only possible to come up on one side of the boat, because of the current, or you're stuck against a rock maybe. Vince tried it. He tipped over. Under water, instead of thrusting the right hand forward and across to his left side he did the reverse. His paddle felt for the surface. He pushed the arms far up and away towards a glow of daylight. It is strange how different it feels making a movement you know well, but with the other side of the body. He is disorientated. Like writing with the left hand. Or walking arm in arm with someone you're not used to. Concentrating, upside down in the glacier-fed water, he pulled the left arm through a wide arc and leaned his head back. To his surprise the boat turned, his body came up. For a moment it stopped, it seemed he might fall back. Vince thrashed with his paddle and suddenly he was upright. He felt proud. He had done the right thing to come on this holiday. Clive was sceptical. See if you can do that in turbulence, he said.

They picnicked. On the bank people peeled off closed smock jackets with tightly sealing rubber cuffs and necks. Everybody has strips of neoprene hanging off them, or wet T-shirts, or towels round their necks. It is uncomfortable. At the back of the Kent County Council van where the sandwiches have been stored, Vince found himself beside Michela. There are cheese sandwiches and crisps and melting chocolate, bottles of water. To his surprise, the Italian girl came to sit beside him on the grass. She had pulled down the top of her wetsuit so that the shoulder-straps hung round her thighs. Vince felt vaguely embarrassed by the thought that his daughter would see them sitting together. But this was ridiculous because now all the adults came to eat in one group, the adolescents in another. Your daughter is relieved to be out of your company, he thought. I am relieved too. They would never live together again.

Clive said how hard it was to predict river levels with this global warming. The glaciers retreated each year. The hot weather came too soon. This summer more than ever. The full melt was on you before you expected it. By now they were paddling on the snows of centuries back, the blizzards of the Middle Ages. There were more thunder-storms, perhaps, but less of the same steady release of the winter's snow. The river could be bony or even dry before you knew it. It's amazing they do nothing about the green-house effect, he went on. What was the temperature in Milan during the demonstration the other day? Thirty-six degrees? Thirty-eight? No wonder people went crazy.

He was sitting on a rock beside Michela. She leaned her back against him. I can't believe, he insisted, how enthusi-astic they are when car sales are up. Keith nodded, eating. The world cooks and dries up and they worry about car sales! There was a silence. Mandy was rubbing sun cream into her shoulders. I should take a picture, she said. You wonder, Clive went on, if they will ever really open their eyes before something major simply forces them to.

Like what, Adam asked coolly.

A drought, Michela said at once. A flood.

Well, which? He had a wry smile.

Vince was not following. His eye had again been drawn upward to the hugeness of the mountains above them. The majesty of the place was crushing. It appeased some obscure desire in him. At the same time he was intensely aware of the young woman, of the fact that her belligerence now, saying something about multinationals, was to do with her being together with this bearded instructor, this strong capable man. Suddenly, he was stumbling to his feet.

We've bored Vince to death, Keith said.

Hearing his name, he managed to turn. He shook his head. Not at all. He tried to smile. Just need to cool my feet in the water. He had kept his wetsuit on.

The climate changes anyhow, Adam was saying. This whole thing is being exploited by people who have an axe to grind and time on their hands.

Vince sat on the upturned hull of his boat with his feet in the water. It seemed impossible that he would get through these days and months without asking someone for help. He watched the youngsters throwing themselves in the water. You hold an important position, he reminded himself. In a major organisation. For some reason he had a recurrent image of a needle penetrating the skin between his fingers. It would bring relief. It would dissolve the pressure in his mind. Then Tom insisted on swimming right across to the opposite bank. He was a strong swimmer. He had been the weakest in this morning's rolling lesson. Louise, Brian, Amelia and Caroline were trying to follow.

Your buoyancy aids! Keith arrived at a run. He was yelling. No one in the water without buoyancy aids! The swimmers protested. We must keep an eye on them, the group leader told Vince. There was a hint of reproach. Out! He raised his voice. It's a question of insurance. There are rapids round that bend.

But we're here, Amelia complained. You can't accuse us of being round the bend!

Caroline wallowed beside her. Respect, she said.

Out of the water at once, Keith insisted.

Wally! Show Wally!

I'll show Wally when you get out.

Only as they came out on the mud did Vince realise that one of the boys had a club foot. The red-haired lad with the sly face. He had trouble getting to his feet. It was a serious malformation. I've forgotten their names, Vince told himself. He breathed deeply.

Crazy as it may sound, we now paddle upstream, Clive told them. Remember, no one said this was a holiday. In about quarter of a mile, we get to some white water and we can have our first go at a wave. But getting there is going to be a sweat.

Hear that, Phil? Keith asked. Neoprene jacket unzipped, the man's paunch was in evidence.

Doddle, the boy said. On the back of his helmet he has a skull and crossbones and the words, Don't follow me!

Clive smiled. Okay, basically, the thing to do is to use whatever slack water you can find, in the eddies by the bank, or behind the rocks midstream, to keep moving upstream. It's an exercise in reading the water. Anyone in despair, there's a path behind those bushes on the other side. You can always carry the boat.

There was a minute's unpleasantness pulling the damp wetsuits back on, a minute's sleepiness, perhaps. The day was clouding over, as so often in the mountains at noon. It was muggy and chill by turns. There were midges and dragon-

34

flies. The air hummed. As soon as Vince was back in his boat, paddle in hand, life seemed possible again.

All right, Mark? he asked Adam's son, when they were on the water. He knew that name.

Fine, the boy said. He had an earnest, slightly vacant face. Just me feet going numb. Like having your legs jammed up yer arse.

You look good on the water, Vince said.

Tell me dad that!

No sooner had they rounded the bend, upstream, than the river narrowed. The water began to flow more swiftly. The boat wobbled. Wake up, Vince told himself. There was a constant gurgling. He was concentrated, nervous. Lean back when you break into the stream from the eddy, Keith warned. Lean back, you're crouched! You're tense. How can your shoulders work like that? Relax.

The kayaks zigzagged, gaining in the slack water behind rocks and spurs, fighting to cross the swift flow in the centre. Show your butts to the stream, everybody. Make the river carry you across! Vince rested behind a boulder. His eyes moved over the water ahead. From brown it had turned black. Perhaps that was the sky growing darker. There was no time for the landscape. He looked for the flat swirling of water that marked the lower part of an eddy.

Break into the current with the hull scraping your rock, Max! Clive called. Scraping it, I said!

I'm Brian, the boy complained. Max is the fairy.

Bugger you, Bri.

See what I mean!

Vince watched. Brian then the boy with the club foot – concentrate – Max the blonde lad who had worn the straw hat. He was surprised to find how well he was doing. Never in his life had it been so difficult to get through a

35

day, or even a single hour. There had been weeks and months of misery. But now, when you spoke to someone for a moment, or managed to cross a big rush of water and hide behind a low rock, then a little time passed unnoticed. He felt a sense of achievement. Life was flowing again. I'm doing fine, he thought. By the end of the holiday, I'll be cured.

But now there was a more serious obstacle. They were trapped behind a spur. You fight up the cushion of water, Clive explained, then, at the critical point – don't worry, you'll sense it – you throw your weight forward and paddle for it like crazy.

Vince's paddle caught on the rocky spur. The water rushed towards him. I'm gasping. I'm sweating like a pig. He hung on the surge of the current, fought it, paddled wildly, then was carried down, had to struggle just to get back in the same eddy. Meantime, all the others had passed. He was last.

Try again, Clive told him. The key is the angle when you enter the flow. Vince tried and failed. The strokes weren't powerful enough. Or weren't placed right. He sensed the strain in his shoulders.

Just keep working at it, Keith said patiently. He had come back for them. But you have to believe you're going to make it. Use your shoulders, not your wrists. Punch the stroke through.

The sheer fact is, Clive laughed, there's a difference in the ratio of strength to body weight between us and the youngsters. We adults sink deeper. We're heavier. They just try and they fly.

Between *me* and the youngsters you mean, Vince said grimly. Suddenly he was again telling himself he shouldn't have come. I'm making a fool of myself. He should have stayed home to wait out this mental state. To wait till he became himself again.

Go for it!

Vince looks hard at the solid curve of water coming down from above the spur and doesn't understand how all the others have done it. Even tubby Caroline. He throws himself at it again. He gives it everything. The left side of the bow grazes the rock. He lifts the left edge to meet the current. The boat is pushed to the right. Paddle like crazy, someone is shouting. Now! Weight forward! Now! Vince paddles. One stroke goes in with surprising power. It feels different. He's done it. He's on top. It wasn't even that difficult. Now he just has to fight to the slack by the bank to avoid being carried down again.

Mandy is there, her head among the branches of a willow. Waiting for my heart rate to come down a little, thank you very much, she laughs. Even on the water she has the camera attached to her jacket, apparently waterproof. She squints at the little screen. You're red as a lobster! This'll be good. Vince's skull is pounding under his helmet. Did it! he finally finds the breath to shout. Did IT! He punches the air. He is overreacting.

At that moment a red hull swirled by, a kayak floating upside down. Immediately alert, congratulating himself on the fact, Vince broke from the eddy to meet it. They must look out for each other. That was the rule. But even as he pulls into the current, swept back towards the rush he has just climbed from, a paddle breaks the surface beside the hull and in a second the boat has flipped right side up. Phil is grinning gormlessly, chewing, nose dripping under a green helmet. Vince crashes into him as they go down the rush by the spur together. See that! There's a flurry of water and paddle strokes. The boy seems to do everything instinctively. See that tail squirt I did! I was bloody vertical. No sooner are they back in the lower eddy than Phil climbs the rush again, apparently without effort, and is gone. Vince is exhausted. After one failed attempt to get back to Mandy, he paddles the boat the other side of the rock and over to the bank.

There's a heavy smell of dank vegetation here, exposed willow roots with water flowing through them, a buzz of flies. Vince pulls his boat up on the bank, then flounders, looking for a break in the nettles. Now there are raindrops pattering all around. His foot sinks into black mud. Hey! Clive reappears in the eddy behind the rock. You should tell me if you're getting out. He's irritated. Otherwise I'll be worried we've lost you. I'll go searching downstream.

But how could Vince have told him, if the others were all ahead? The path squeezes through dense woodland. On his shoulder the heavy kayak knocks against trunks and branches. It's dark here among the trees and there's a dull roar of water coming from up front. Or is it traffic on some road? Now the rain pours down. Summer storm rain. The boat knocks against his head. He has to crouch to get the thing through a thicket. The ground is broken. The earth smells strangely warm and resiny. Stumbling into a small clearing, he almost bangs into a low makeshift hut put together with blankets and tarpaulin, blue nylon string and hunks of driftwood. On a sheet of cardboard in the mud by the entrance, a thin, heavily bearded man jumps to his feet. Vince stops. Immediately, the man waves a bottle and begins to speak excitedly.

Capisco niente. Vince says. *Verstehe nicht.*

The small man is gesticulating, perhaps warning him. His eyes are red. There's an unpleasant smell. His jacket looks as if it too might have been pulled from the water, like the driftwood of his home. There are fish-heads lying in the mud. The man goes on shouting. In his early forties maybe. Or older. His eyes are fierce.

Verstehe nicht, Vince repeats. He turns and pushes on. The man screams after him. He hurls his bottle into the bushes over Vince's head. Vince finds the path, and after five or six paces the trees open up on the river bank. He sees the rapids and again the hull of a boat floating upside down. Blue this time. The boys are playing at breaking into the stream with the tail edge dipped towards the current. The back of the kayak is forced deep into the water, the nose lifts in the air. Tail squirts. Phil's boat rears up like a mad horse, or a motorcycle raised on its rear wheel. For a moment, the boy holds it there, yelling Yahoo, alrighty! The boat collapses back on top of him.

Vince watches, his face tense.

The river here is squeezed through a gap of only four or five yards then immediately opens out with big turbulent eddies swirling against each bank. A stone ledge stretching halfway across the flow at its fastest point causes the water to drop in a deep trough that then curls up into a tall, steady wave. Adam is showing the girls how to break from the side of the river and surf on the crest of the wave. The water is high and fierce and Caroline refuses to try. She has hooked an elbow round a sapling on the bank. Not my bag, she says, chewing. Adam repeats the same movements, simple and mechanical. Unlike the boys, he seems to take pleasure not in the thing itself, but in knowing how to do it, the control, the communication of technique. He is reassuring, but cold. Amelia ventures into the trough of the wave. The little girl seems so small in her long green boat, so hesitant. For a few moments the wave holds her, then the boat is tossed out like a cork.

Too cautious, Louise misses the trough altogether, spins round when the bow hits the crest of the wave, almost capsizes but, seemingly unconcerned, regains the bank. Vince is proud of her.

At the same time, over and over, the boys throw themselves into the turbulent stream, pushing to the front of the eddy, ignoring any queue the others have formed. Brian with his club foot has an uncanny balance in the boat. He never capsizes.

You selfish brats! Mandy yells. She is dragging her boat out of the water having failed to roll up. She shouts at Max and Phil as if it were their fault. You've got to watch out for each other!

Clive and Keith are sitting a few yards down from the action, ready to help any swimmers. The Indian boy Amal is also playing helper. He has an air of pleased diligence about him.

Try it, Mark, Adam invites his son.

Me arms are aching, the boy complains. I need a rest.

It doesn't require any strength, Adam insists.

I'm well tired, the boy repeats. I got pins and needles. He won't do it.

Vince reaches the top of the eddy. So how do you do this? he asks the instructor.

Okay. Adam holds his boat. You put your nose in the current, pointing upstream and just a little across. You break into the flow and lift your right knee to give a hint of an edge. You shouldn't even have to paddle if you get it right.

Vince is nervous. He is facing a rush of water such as he hasn't seen before. It foams, silver and black, over the stones, moss-green here, marbly grey there. He recalls the bearded face of a few moments before, the alcoholic shouting in German, throwing his bottle. What if I get it wrong, capsize, hit my head on a rock?

Go, Adam says. Don't shilly-shally.

As he shifts his boat out of the eddy, Vince finds it suddenly drawn towards the submerged ledge over which the water is surging so powerfully. He is being sucked upstream and under. This is quite unexpected. How can I be pulled upstream?

Lean back! Adam shouts.

Vince tries to correct, back-paddling, but this has the effect of sending the boat careering sideways, rocking violently. A mountain of water piles down on him. Vince tries to raise the edge of the kayak to meet it, but it's too late, he is down. His head hits the foam.

The experience is quite different from any other capsize he has known. You are no longer in slow water with time to reflect. You are in the quick of it – this is life – eyes open but blind. An icy flood rears and tugs and swirls. The paddle is being dragged away from him. He can't push it to the surface. It won't move, it's trapped against the boat. He tries the rolling motion anyway. The boat half turns. His head breaks the surface. For a split second, comic no doubt to the onlooker, he can catch a breath. He has a vague impression of the world rushing by. Someone's shouting. Then he's down again. Now the helmet scrapes, again he fights with the paddle, again fails to right the boat. This time his fingers find the release tab. The spraydeck pops. The freezing water floods the cockpit and he swims out. Hold on to your paddle! Don't let go of the boat! Turn it upright. As his head breaks the surface, Keith is already there with a tow-sling and a clip. And you forgot to bang on the sides!

All afternoon they keep at this. It's today's lesson. Very soon they are in three groups. There are those who take few risks, happy with what they can do; those who seem to have no trouble with anything – the elect – and then those who will keep trying and trying though almost always beaten.

Time and again Vince approaches the top of the eddy. Fascinated, he watches how others – Michela, Amelia and

Louise now too – penetrate the current and glide across to the wave apparently without expending energy or taking risks. How is this? There is some hidden place, it seems, between eddy and flow, between the soft grey water milling on shallow stones and the fast dark stream pouring into the wave, some place where the river can be unlocked. A secret entrance. You're admitted directly to the heart of things. You're privileged. You can sit on the wave in a miracle of exhilarating speed and reassuring stillness. This mystery is denied to him. The entrance isn't there when he approaches. The explanations – do this, do that – don't seem to correspond to the experience.

In the eddy, Michela brings her boat alongside his. She is laughing. She seems happy. She shows Vince exactly the point of entry, the movement of the paddle and hips. Clive will come round, she has decided. It's so fine to be near him. He is so strong. Those deaths in Milan have brought on a crisis. It will pass. Speaking English makes her feel cheerful. He gives me strength too. Relaxed and determined, she tells the older man to go with the flow. Don't fight it, she says.

Vince grips his paddle. The rain pours on the rushing water. Unnoticed above, the mountains have dissolved in cloud. And take it easy when you capsize, Michela repeats. You're hurrying. There's always more time than you think. Imagine you're in a swimming pool.

Dad, don't overdo it, Louise shouted. You've got to drive me home, you know.

On the fourth attempt, having once more capsized without reaching the wave, Vince rolls his boat upright in the worst of the turbulence. The paddle is suddenly in the right place. He arches the arm, moves his hips and with no effort at all there he is, tossed out on a boil of water, disorientated, floundering, but up, breathing. Things could still go right.

Last night, Keith was saying later, I asked everybody to introduce themselves. But then, as you know, there have been two late arrivals.

It was raining still, but uncannily warm. They had trailed the boats back to camp. They had strung up lines between the trees to hang the equipment. At least if it doesn't dry, the rubber won't stink. They had showered. The Louts had cooked. The three teams are the Louts, the Pigs and the Slobs. This had been young Max's idea during the trip out. A spirit of healthy emulation, he said in his precocious little lawyer's voice from beneath the straw hat. Now they were all crowded into the kitchen tent in the light of the gas lamp. Across the site the French boys were drumming under their awning. Occasional thunder rumbled over their heads. The church clock has just chimed eight. It was time for the evening meeting. Sitting in his canvas chair again, Keith wears a permanent smile of self-congratulation.

Louise?

Yeah, I'm Louise, Vince's daughter said. You all know me anyway. Fifteen. Chatham Grammar. Not cool, I know, but there you are. I'm here because I love the water and the company.

All right, Brian clapped.

That's all. She was trying to catch Tom's eye.

Verdict on today? Keith insisted. There was something evangelical about the man.

Great. Really. Learned a lot. Apart from having Phil push in front of me about every two seconds in the eddy by the wave.

Yes, a Wally nomination coming up there, I suspect. Vince?

43

Sorry?

Could you introduce yourself?

Vince still doesn't understand. His mind has been captured by the drumming.

Let people know who you are. A few words.

Someone sniggered. It was a beat that seemed to go round and round in rapid circles.

Yes, of course.

He was standing by the entrance of the tent. Michela noticed that his eyes were clouded, his mouth always slightly open.

Well, I work in a bank.

There was an adolescent groan.

Vince smiled. Right, he agreed. Very boring. Anyway, probably some of you will have known my wife, my wife Gloria, since she was an instructor with Waterworld until a year or so ago. He took a breath. Anyway, after . . . after what happened, well, she had booked a place on this trip, and I just thought I would . . . He couldn't go on. The drums pattered.

Vince's wife, Keith cut in, was national sprint champion in her age group at Henley, when was that, Vince?

Vince was staring at the lamp-lit faces under canvas.

1998, Adam said.

In the night, he opened the fridge and she was crouching there inside. He wasn't surprised. The fridge was her domain. I can live for ever here, she told him. He was looking for eggs to scramble. What else can I cook? He took them from her hand and closed the door, then went back and opened it again. There was something I should have said. She didn't seem cramped. She was in her gym kit. No need, she said. Her smile was condescending, like a mother's. There's something I want to ask, he insisted. Don't keep the fridge door

44

open, love, you'll waste the cold. She smiled. You're wasting electricity, love. There's something . . . It's precious. Close it. He closed the door. But he was in the flat in London, not at home. Gloria never comes to his London flat. The fridge is tiny. There's something I have to ask. He rushed across the room to tear the door open. The fridge, as always in his flat, was empty. Gloria! He shouted. Gloria!

Dad, you're snoring! From her sleeping bag, his daughter woke him. The girl was sitting up. They were unnaturally close in the tent. She seemed eager to turn away.

I'm sorry. He lay still on his back. The ground is uneven and uncomfortable. But it's not that. The blue canvas flickers from time to time with the torchlight of people heading for the bathrooms. Did I make myself come camping as a punishment? he wondered. Vince put his hands behind his head. His body ached. The day on the river has exhausted him. Then, as always after these nightmares, in the alert, sleepless mood they induce, he played over the sudden last moments of his marriage, the end of life as he had known it. Vince, I'm dying, her voice says. She has called his mobile. He is just climbing the stairs from the Underground at St Paul's. I'm dying. I've phoned nine nine nine. I'm paralysed. It's a stroke. I'm sure. I know the signs . . . It must have been at that point of the call that he had shouted, Gloria! He had stopped in the crowd. People were pushing past. It was early morning at St Paul's. He was standing still, rigid, in the hurrying crowd. Gloria, for God's sake! My head is filling with blood, she cried. Oh, I'm dying Vince. I'm so, so sorry.

The curious thing, as he let each evening's tears fill his eyes, was the clarity of her voice in his head. Freed from the crackly quality of the mobile on the stairs outside the Underground, it spoke directly in his head. I'm paralysed. It's a stroke. The change of tone from her normal matter-of-fact, rather bossy self to something piercingly intimate could not have been more marked. Oh, I'm dying Vince, I'm so so sorry. It was as if right at the end it hadn't been her, or rather it had been her *at last*, someone he had never known. My wife. His mind was caught there, turning and turning in this unexpected maelstrom. Why had she said she was sorry? Why did he feel so ashamed? Very soon, I must become someone else; Vince knew that. He couldn't break out of this churn of thought. After six months, it was a wonder he hadn't already drowned.

A RAPID

At breakfast Tom joined the adults, rather than the children. Those bells! The young man seems in turns uncertain of himself and aggressively assured. Vince had been woken ten minutes before the morning ringing by the arrival of a text message on his daughter's phone. They stood in the mud by the kitchen tent. Who pays the bloke to get up so early every day? Adam was shaking his head. Mandy wanted to know how on earth Michela had learned English so perfectly. She had only been in the UK a few months. She hadn't even studied at university. With the grass damp, people ate standing up. Tea in the pot! Keith announced. I was born in the wrong country, the young woman laughed. The sun was just touching distant peaks, but the valley lay in shadow. The church tower was topped with a gleaming bronze onion dome, quite new obviously.

Neither of your parents speaks English, though?

I would never have learned if they did. It's hard to explain, I always knew from as soon as I could think, I should have been English.

Too much of a class act to be a Brit, Tom said earnestly. Oh thank you so much! Mandy objected.

Michela wasn't eating. She looked at the young man without seeing him. Too much to do in a world that's too ugly, Clive had said last night. Once again he had insisted on the sleeping bag on the bare floor. It was a punishment. Again she had walked out after midnight and sat on the roots of the big pine tree above the group's pitch. In a tent the other side of the track a man and woman were murmuring in a language she didn't know. She sat with her spine against the damp bark. Why now? Why had he chosen this of all moments?

Again, sometime after one o'clock, she had seen the thin, older Englishman head for the bathroom. He sneezed twice. That was the river in our noses. He is carrying a burden, Michela thought. She drew into the shadow so he wouldn't see her. She thought in English. She would not use the language of her father and mother. She would not let Clive see her cry. I must be strong, she decided. If you want to go back to your mum, Micky, he said from the darkness as she pulled the door to, I'd understand perfectly. We could sort out the money side. She waited some minutes before answering. She undressed and got into bed. I'd rather kill myself, she told him.

Her man did not watch as she undressed. He knew her body. He knows how avidly she makes love. The room was dimly lit from a lamp outside. It smelled of bare wood and river kit. A good smell. I checked my e-mail this evening, he said finally. He had driven into Sand in Taufers. They're talking of chartering a plane for Berlin. Will you come?

Of course, she said.

He had not looked as she undressed, but now, over cornflakes, Clive was watching Michela carefully. Vince caught the man's intense gaze and knew he was in love. For months, he thought, I keep noticing people in love. It was almost the only thing he did notice.

But you have a pretty high position, don't you? Adam was speaking to him. He named one of Britain's major clearing banks. The tall instructor was already wearing a wetsuit, the shoulder-straps hanging at his side. I mean, you're one of the big guns, aren't you? He seemed extremely respectful of Vince, eager to get to know him. His hair was neatly combed, his receding chin closely shaved. Clipped to his belt, a waterproof case held his mobile.

Well . . .

I remember your wife saying something.

He only pretty well runs the whole bloody bank! Louise arrived hungry. There was a bag of Chocos she was after, under Tom's elbow. Move over macho! The girl wore no bra under her T-shirt.

One shouldn't exaggerate, Vince began.

Oh, come on Dad! You know you run it.

Adam seemed to be expecting a response. I imagine, he insisted, that someone like yourself has to be in touch even while you're away. I mean at certain levels of responsibility . . .

But now a new noise captured everybody's attention. There was a tinny jingle. Oh no! shrieked the young Max, his straw hat tipped back. On the table in the kitchen tent, beside the milk carton, a white hamster, about a foot high on its hind legs, had begun to beat a tin drum. Legs and paws moved with mechanical grace, while the solemn head made slow turns from side to side. A recorded voice in his innards crooned:

I think I love you, but that's what life is made of.

Amelia and Caroline were bent double with giggles. The

big girl grabbed Phil. Was it you? She had to pull off the headphones of his Discman.

And it worries me to say, the voice crooned on, that I've never felt this way.

Who stole my hamster? Mandy demanded. The bristly white muzzle was hilariously wise. The voice was that of some twenties vaudeville entertainer. Picked up in a service station, the toy had been a constant joke on the long journey from England. Amal was grinning broadly.

Do you think I have a case, the hamster sang, won't you tell me to my face?

Who's been in my tent? Mandy insisted. This is a happy British holiday, Vince told himself. I must participate. Adam smiled sardonically. Who was it? Mandy shrieked. Everybody was running around, giggling. Who stole my hamster? Guilty! Keith peeped a ruddy face from behind Michela's pine tree. Was it possible, Vince wondered, that the group's leader and their administrator had something going together? You cheeky bastard, Mandy made a half-hearted dash. Nosing in my stuff! Oh a serious impropriety! Max shouted in his most camp voice. Photograph! someone shrieked. One for the website! When Vince turned he saw Michela was hurrying away to the trailer where the boats were loaded and locked up. How lithe she was. You are under a spell, he told himself. It was an expression he would sometimes use at work to describe this or that commodity or currency. Coffee is under a spell. There's no other explanation. The dollar is under a spell. But now Tom was saying politely, Mr Marshall, actually I was wondering—

Vince, I'm called Vince.

Sorry, I was wondering if I might pick your brain on money supply at some point? There are a couple of things they've been teaching us at university that I really don't understand.

Listen, don't talk about my work, Vince told Louise quietly as they gathered their kit together for the day's outing. His cag was still damp. She couldn't find her towel. She was sure she'd left it on the line. Please, he said. They fussed about the fly-sheets. It bothers me. What else is there to talk about with you, Dad? she asked. You never do anything but work. He asked if the message she had received this morning had been from her cousins. No, she said. She smiled very brightly. Adam had promised her she could charge her phone on his car charger.

They already had the boats on the water before the sun climbed over the mountainside and poured its warmth into the valley. This time they ran the section from the camp-site to the village of Geiss. Never do anything but work, Vince is thinking. His daughter's words have soured his morning. Yet he hadn't called the office so far this holiday, as his colleagues no doubt expected. He hadn't even read the papers or listened to a radio. Quite probably they are trying to contact him. He hadn't turned on his mobile. He hadn't bought a car charger. He had no idea what the market was up to. For thirty years you give your whole life to something, he thought, you build up a solid career; and then in the space of a couple of weeks, it's forgotten. I have lost my daughter, Vince told himself. This holiday is confirm-ing that loss. First in Florence, now here. I have lost all sense of purpose. All I notice is people in love. From what you tell me you are clinically depressed, his brother-in-law had advised him. Jasper worked in that field. He ran a psychi-atric clinic in South London. You should be on drugs, he said. Vince was afraid that drugs would cloud his judgement. It was a difficult moment in foreign equities. It is always a difficult moment. He had stopped performing after Gloria died. He knew it. He knew they knew it. Why had he let Louise go to live with her cousins? I have no home now. Suddenly, Vince feels a grating under the boat. Wake up! The kayak is broadside to a bank of pebbles rising from below the grey water. The river slides forward with a strong steady pull. He should have seen the tell-tale rippling on the surface. It's too late. Vince finds himself being turned over in only six inches of rapidly flowing water. His shoulder bangs along on the stones. Wally nomination! Phil shouts. Phil has the creature tied round his neck for his behaviour yesterday. What a fool! Vince curses himself. He is livid.

Only a few minutes later, Clive orders: Stop paddling everyone and listen. There are still patches of early-morning mist rising on the calmer stretches of the water. The boys are splashing each other. Listen up! Adam complains. It seems to irritate him that Clive and Keith won't impose discipline more firmly. Mark, I said listen! he tells his son. Stop paddling.

The fifteen kayaks with their bright plastic colours drift on the glassy surface. The thin mist is luminous and the water wide and apparently tranquil, pressing steadily forward. Three ducks are flapping along the bank in front of them. Faint in the distance from beyond the trees is the repeated beep of a truck reversing, in some quarry perhaps. Brian giggles, Mysterious!

Shush!

Leaning back, arching until her helmet rests on the deck behind, Michela gazes upward. Among high white clouds, the tall mountains slowly revolve. It's dizzying. The current is turning the boat. The high rocks seem precarious. They will tumble down. A buzzard swoops above the tree line and the girl feels as if she herself has fallen from there. She is still falling, the mountains turning. It's so calm. She doesn't believe what has happened. She is living an intense swan-song of adoration and denial. She has given herself completely to Clive. My family is behind me. I will go anywhere you go, she told him last night. She lets her hands trail in the water and the chill climbs up her fingers to wrists and forearms. You know I can't go home.

Then Vince hears it. Beyond the still-beeping truck, a low roar emerges, a dark line floats up on the auditory horizon. At once the water takes on a new urgency. They are gliding past narrowing banks of steeper and steeper stone. Alrighty! Phil breaks the silence. River-left! Clive shouts. He is paddling backwards, facing the others. As he tells them what to do, he is sensible, steady, entirely manly. But Michela recognises the hint of impatience in his voice, the energy restrained. He wishes he were in another era, exploring virgin territory, commanding soldiers. She loves this in him. Kayaks are plastic toys, he complains when he is depressed. There's nothing *necessary* about them. They're not natural. One evening he asked over and over, Do you understand, Micky, what I mean by something being *necessary*? Clive is old never to have settled; she knows that. She saw the mad intensity of his eyes at the demonstration in Milan.

Keith is shouting names and numbers. He has to yell now over the roar of the rapid, swollen with yesterday's rain. Amal five, Amelia six, Louise seven. They must follow Clive's line. Three boat-lengths apart. Don't get too close.

One by one the kayaks drop below the horizon. Each hull with its bright colour slips suddenly away, then the helmet. Louise's helmet is white. Number seven is gone. Next to last, with only the expert Adam behind him, Vince dips into a slalom of rushing water and rock. The acceleration is dramatic. For the first time he finds himself actually looking downhill, in the water. No time to be frightened. The boat is flung to the side. The boulders come very fast. Vince steers and turns and braces. His mind is absolutely concentrated, his body is wired and reactive. Suddenly, a boat is blocking his path. Mark is pinned against a boulder to one side of the narrow central chute. The water is piling on his deck. He's shouting. Vince crashes into the boat. Mark is bounced free, but capsizes in the rush. Somehow, Vince does something instinctive, some strange banging of paddle on water, an unexpected elasticity of ageing hips, that keeps him upright in the race. Now he is plunging down into the terminal stopper. The water is frothing. Paddle! a voice shouts. From the eddy behind a rock, everybody is shouting. Paddle hard! The churning white water grabs hold of him. The stern is pulled down, as if arms under there had clutched him. They want him under. *Paddle, for Christ's sake!* Vince paddles and the boat rears and pops out. Safe.

Vince enjoys, then, as on waking every morning, about two or three seconds of complete contentment. He fights his way out of the white water. He sees his daughter's radiant pink face. She is rafted up against Tom in the eddy. My daughter is bursting with excitement and happiness! Their first real rapid. What a rush of adrenalin! Then after this flash of pleasure, the dark returns, with an awful inevitability. You give everything to work, Gloria would say. You have no other life. Bizarre phrases come to his mind. I am *excluded*. He wants to shout the words. Gloria excluded me. I'm so so sorry, she said. What did she mean? Vince is boiling with rage. Whipping the boat round as he crosses the eddy-line, he sees only now that the instructors have passed a rope across the river at the stopper and Clive is in there pulling out Mark. I forgot the boy. I forgot him! Mark is retching. His face is white with panic.

That evening everybody began to drink. The afternoon had been uncomfortably warm and Keith insisted on splashing and playing the fool and putting everyone in a party spirit. How could the idiot get himself pinned in a grade-two rapid? Adam kept repeating of his son. Three more rapids were run without incident. In the spaces between, Amal insisted on pairing up with Vince and chattering in his queer, high-pitched voice. His father had died ten years ago, his mother was obliged to work all hours in his uncle's shop. Waterworld is like a family to me, he repeated two or three times. Amelia had been his girlfriend when they were both on the Canadian trip. She was nice. That was open canoes. But they had agreed to split up.

You run a bank, don't you? he said. They were paddling the last tame stretch to Geiss between high banks of brushwood. Your wife taught me once, he explained. My two-star. She was the one with her hair in a bun, right? And she worked in a hospital. That's right, Vince said. Good teacher, Amal said. Very strict. Didn't let you get away with doing things even slightly wrong.

It was curious how good-looking the Indian boy was, with bright dark eyes and high cheekbones, and how completely the shrill voice and over-eagerness to please undercut this attraction. My brother Vikram is handicapped, he said. He can't kayak except in those special day-out things they give handicapped people, you know. Louise is improving, though, Amal said appreciatively. She has a great hip-flick. Vince felt oppressed, the day was really too warm. Everyone was dipping hands and arms in the water to cool off. He couldn't decide whether to call the office the following morning perhaps. He couldn't see any way forward, only his old self, his old life. Wally, Amal was explaining, is supposed to be the spirit of a drowned paddler, you know. He protects us, like. But only if we protect him. Is that so? Vince managed. That's why it's so important not to lose him, Amal said. The older man wanted to scream.

Then, checking the duty rota back at the camp, Vince read: PIGS, *Wednesday*, <u>Shopping</u>. See list. In twenty-five years of marriage, he had hardly shopped at all. Perhaps I let Louise go, he wondered, because I was scared of shopping. Team! he called. Hey! Pigs! He assumed the joking voice everyone else was using, the holiday voice. We're on shopping. In the car, team! We'll use mine. He had Amelia, Tom and Max.

Do you know where to go? Tom asked. We can't buy this lot at the camp shop. The list stretched to two pages. Micky! Sitting in the passenger seat the young man buzzed down the window. Michela was standing in the no man's land between chalet and tents. Micky! Vince moved the car a few yards. She crouched by Tom's window and gave directions. I can come, if you need help, she offered. Oh, us Brits have a long tradition of bossing about the natives, Max assured her. He was wearing his straw hat, a yellow cotton shirt with button-down collar. As they drove up the rutted track, Vince watched the young woman bob in and out of the mirror. He didn't like the way she called herself by a boy's name. It seemed wrong. Nice girl, Tom said. The young man's powerful hands rested on his knees. For a Wop, Max agreed. She's Clive's girlfriend, isn't she? Amelia reminded them. By the way, can someone give me the shopping list? Sure, Vince said. Am I the only one, he asked, with a pain when they rotate their elbow? Amelia leaned forward between the seats: Tom, why don't you choose the beer and all the crisps and snacks? That'll save time. Me the whisky and bog paper, sang Max.

Beyond the campsite, a fast road ran through an area of warehouses and light industry. Timber milling, it looked like, building materials. Ahead, where the valley narrowed above the cluster of the small town, a castle dominated the scene, a *schloss*, shamelessly picturesque on a tall spur of rock with the dramatic mountain gorge behind. It was hard not to feel you had seen it in some film. How old is your daughter, Mr Marshall? Tom suddenly asked. I mean Vince, sorry. Fourteen, Vince said. I'm almost sixteen, Amelia remarked. You *are* not, Max objected. Only three months! You could be dead before then! the boy shouted. Max, please, Vince begged. Age is so much to do with how you behave, though, isn't it? Tom said sagely. Badly! Max shrieked. Shut up, the girl hissed.

Then they were in Sand in Taufers: swept streets and big square Austrian-style houses, all with the same steep roof, the same wide, pine-fronted balconies, the same fierce geranium displays blazing in the early evening light. Everywhere there were *Zimmer frei* signs and gift shops, a general impression of regimented colour, authorised souvenirs. Posters in three languages proclaimed a festival of traditional horn music. A photograph showed a bearded man in lederhosen blowing into a horn at least six feet long, resting on the ground in front of him. The little supermarket, when they found it, was called EuroSpin, its windows plastered with international brand names, credit card signs. It was curious, Vince thought, how nothing seemed unfamiliar anymore, excepting one's state of mind, perhaps. He found it strange how at ease he felt with these kids.

A stiff little man in a white coat, his eyes bloodshot, turned from stacking Nestlé's snacks. *Guten abend*, he said throatily. Velcum to mai umble 'ome, Max whispered. Are we in Italy or what? *Guten abend*, Tom replied politely.

Vince found a trolley. Remember, everything we get is for fifteen, okay? Almost at once the youngsters were giggling at the sausage section. Great curved turgid things wrapped in red and yellow cellophane. You don't see these in England. *Wurst und wurst!* Amelia cried, picking up a particularly obscene example and waving it at Tom. The shopkeeper shifted from the doorway to keep an eye down their aisle. You choose, Amelia was telling the boy.

The store had the cluttered shelves of a restricted space trying to satisfy every need. Again the attendant moved as they rounded the end of the aisle. Ve arr being voched, Max whispered. Everything Vince chose – there were sandwich things to get and chicken pieces for this evening's dinner – Amelia asked Tom if it was right. Don't you think we'd be better with long-life milk? She had straight black hair clipped in a fringe above a puckered, solemn forehead and at a certain point she contrived to pick up a can of peeled tomatoes that Tom already had his hands on. The young man studied the labels intently, until, to everybody's surprise, Max walked straight down the aisle and addressed the shopkeeper in fluent German. He spoke for at least a minute, with some expression, gesturing at the shelves. The stiff man smiled, took him to the meat counter, then another shelf. That's the sauce for the chicken casserole, the blonde boy said. His shirt seemed freshly ironed, likewise the white cotton trousers. The spuds are round the corner. Brilliant, Vince told him. I did French, Tom advised Amelia. He took her by the elbow.

Vince bought sun cream, matches, a roll of duct tape and a second tray of beers. Actually, we don't need those, Tom said. We've already got a tray. But there are thirteen of us, Vince explained, fifteen with Clive and his girlfriend. Seven or eight are under age, Tom pointed out. Oh come on, Max protested. This is piss beer, this Kraut stuff. Most of us were swigging stronger stuff than this before we could walk. Mandy said no, Tom insisted. Amelia couldn't make up her mind whether to support him or not. I have to get something for Caroline's chapped lips. Does your dad let you drink? Vince asked the girl. She wore a short skirt over thin, coltish legs. Sometimes, she said. Aping the adult, she folded her arms, shifted her weight. I believe Mandy actually signed something, Tom was saying now. He seemed genuinely concerned that a rule might be broken. We could add a tray of Cokes, he suggested, for the kids.

Vince gave the black wallet with the Waterworld kitty to Max and told the boys to carry out the boxes. Then he invited Amelia back into the shop and with his own money bought two more trays of beer and various goodies: marshmallows and skewers, in case they made a fire, and three bottles of sparkling wine. Since we're the Pigs, let's be pigs, he announced. He felt cheerful. You're a tempter, Mr Marshall, Amelia laughed. Vince, he again insisted. Why couldn't they use his name? You don't call Keith Mr Whatever, do you? Bags I the front seat, Max rushed. Tom and Amelia were quiet in the back.

No! Mandy said. No drinking! No, no, no! Keith overruled her. The group leader seemed extravagantly, even brutally merry. Suck on that. He gave a can to Caroline, another to Amelia. Adam was evidently irritated. He gets like this, Mandy shook her head. Soon he'll be flirting with the under-sixteens. It's only beer, Keith insisted breezily. Drink, he told Mark. You're not on the river now. A holiday's a holiday. Even when it's a community experience, Amelia chipped in. And if you want to be really English – Keith handed another can to Michela – you'll have to get in training. You know the British government's thinking of introducing an alcohol test for citizenship: ability to imbibe five pints a day, five days running. A working week, no less, Brian observed. Mark took his beer and sat on the ground beside Amal. The boy had barely spoken after his accident at the rapid. On the table in the kitchen tent, the hamster began to beat his drum. I think I love you. Oh no! the children groaned. Turn the beast off! I think I hate you, Phil laughed. Vince couldn't help noticing the way he and Caroline leaned on each other as they sat.

At the meeting, after the casserole, Louise nominated her father for Wally and the vote was unanimous. Only an idiot could capsize in six inches of water. Public humiliation! Keith demanded. On his third beer, Vince was nervous and pleased. I am becoming part of the group, he thought. But what was the punishment to be? Something really degrading! Louise shrieked, can in hand. Gloria had never let her drink. Uncle Jasper's family was even stricter. You decide, Mandy told Caroline. Vince had seen how carefully the older woman brought in everybody. There would be no faces missing from the website. The big girl grimaced and chewed, then looked to Amelia. There was an old complicity between the two. They burst out laughing. The Chicken Song! Both struggled to their feet, stood side by side in the tight circle of the tent, where the gas lamp was throwing shadows as the twilight faded. Caroline was almost a head taller than her friend, her thighs heavy, wrists and ankles thick, her manner timid, but when she began to dance there was a mad energy and unexpected elegance to her. Incongruous together, the two girls kicked their legs, flapped their arms. I'm a chubby chicken, ready for the chop, they'll cut my pretty head off, stricken, plop, but still I run around and kick 'em. Hop Hop! The girls pulled faces, lolled their heads, broke one one way and one the other, running round the group kicking at people.

Pathetic! Brian and Max shrilled. Naff!

I have to do that? Vince asked.

You're getting off lightly, Mandy told him. She smiled indulgently. Everybody was looking.

With the actions or without?

He took his place in the centre of the circle. Michela is watching me, he saw, and my daughter. Vince danced, Vince who never danced. He was wearing corduroys and a thin sweater. I'm a chubby chicken, he sang. He heard his voice singing. He and Gloria had never danced. He tried to do it well. He was absurd. Gloria did every kind of sport, but didn't dance. It was strange at fifty to be making yourself so ridiculous. I am director of all overseas accounts, he told himself. The kids were giggling. He tried to remember the words. Ready for the chop! The others were clapping and as he made to kick at them, they jumped to their feet and dashed out of the tent. Rise, Sir Wally, Keith said, dropping the creature over his head on a piece of string. Thou must take care of he who protects us. Pathetic! Phil shrieked.

And they went up to the camp bar. On a low stage a local band were playing music for karaoke. There were people of all ages and from all over Europe, Austrian bikers and ageing Dutch nature lovers. The tables were spread over a wide terrace. The kids disappeared, Amelia and Louise dragging Tom with them. It seemed there was an internet café up the road. Everybody has a life elsewhere, a message to send. We'll need you to order the drinks, the girls protested. Tom turned a lingering glance to Michela, but the young woman never noticed. Mark was boasting to Louise about something he had done on a previous expedition, in an open canoe. He has started to talk again. Only Amal stayed with the adults. The boy seemed eager to agree with everything everyone said.

How the twit could get pinned in the world's easiest

rapid, I do not know, Adam repeated, taking his seat. Leave the kid be! Mandy cried. She ordered a round of large beers from the waiter. And no, I'm not being inconsistent, she turned on Keith. It's fine when it's us and not the kids whose mothers I've promised. The man brought half-litre glasses. Some middle-aged Germans were trying to sing 'Maggie May'. Maggie I vish. Drink up, and stop fussing, the stout woman told Adam. My new cag is giving me a rash, Keith complained. Bottoms up.

The music grew louder. A group of Spanish children were playing hide-and-seek among the adults. Vince got the next round. It was years since he had had more than a couple of beers. A strange excitement was fizzing up. Unasked, he started to talk about the man he had seen on the river bank the other day, in the ramshackle hut. Every river has one, Keith said. People who've dropped out and they're just drawn to the river. The river is life, Clive said rather solemnly, sheer life. Michela was beside him. Oh, they're just alkies, Adam objected. He kept playing with his mobile, apparently sending and receiving text messages. It's just easy for them to get driftwood and water by the river and you can crap off the bank. They leave a lot of rubbish around. Shouldn't be allowed. He tapped on the keypad.

The bloke threw a bottle at me, Vince said.

There you are.

Clive began to speak about a man he had got to know by a river in the Canadian Rockies. This guy had lived there for years in brushwood shelters, hunting and selling pelts, sleeping in animal skins. After a rainfall he could tell you exactly when the river would rise and how much. To the inch. He even knew when a tree had fallen into the water upstream or a cow. The birds and fish behaved differently.

Oh I find that very hard to believe, Adam said.

Let's karaoke, Keith interrupted. Come on. Let's ask for some oldies. Be sentimental. But Mandy had launched into an intense attack on someone or something. It's all either technical, she was complaining to Amal, like, we all have to do every stroke in the regulation BCU style; or commercial, you know, if we take an extra instructor, we won't break even, or if you have an end-of-season party, you'll lose money. I must have missed something, Vince thought. His eye had settled on Michela's slim wrist as she poured some of her beer into Clive's glass. They were sitting round a large white plastic table. Clive was drinking a lot. He had rolled himself a Golden Virginia. They will make love later, Vince told himself. He looked away. Adam was consulting his mobile again. The man doesn't see, Mandy was explaining, that that's not really what people are after. They don't come to Waterworld for that. Or not *only* that.

Who are we talking about? Vince asked Keith. Amal was nodding in agreement. Ron Bridges, Keith told him. District Superintendent, Kent Sports and Recreation. The boss. He lowered his voice: Mandy applied for the job, but they wouldn't give it to her.

And the thing is – the squat woman was almost shouting – I don't know how or why, but we never finished a year in the red till he came along. Can you believe it? I remember Sylvia saying, Soon we'll have lost as much as the film *Waterworld*, remember? Hollywood's biggest flop. He's been a bloody disaster! She slammed her beer down, wiped her mouth. People want to have fun, don't they, and to feel their life is being given some sense – she was evidently repeating things she had said before – in a group together, you know? Out in nature. They want excitement and friends. You can't persecute them just because they can't do a reverse-sweep stroke exactly the way the British Bloody Canoeing Union prescribes.

Keith stretched his arms: Attaboy, Mandy!

You should have seen, she shrieked, the list of instructions he gave us for this trip. The length of that list! We wouldn't have had any fun at all. We'd have spent the whole time practising low braces in the first eddy.

Adam again clicked his mobile shut. Still, you do have to teach the strokes right, and you do have to break even.

Of course you bloody do, of *course* – the woman leaned forward across the table. But that's not *the point* of it all, is it? It's not *why* we do it.

Adam began to object, but a beep indicated the arrival of another message. The missus? Keith asked, with an arching of bushy eyebrows. The mistress? Mandy echoed.

What sad minds! Adam shook his head. He began to tap out a response. Across the table, a dangerous expression of scorn had settled around Clive's lips. He rubbed the knuckle of one thumb back and forth in his beard across his chin. There is no *one* way to do any stroke, he began very deliberately. It's a question of *attitude*. Vince for example knows the strokes. You tell him what to do and he does it. But his attitude's wrong.

Vince asked: How?

Clive half smiled. He bit the inside of his lip. Watch Amal, he said.

Me? The dark boy sipped his beer and looked at them over the glass. I don't know anything.

No, tell me now, Vince said. Explain. Then I can work at it.

Keith chuckled: Clive's right, watch Amal, then you tell us.

But I only started kayak last year, the boy protested in his oddly high-pitched voice.

Oh you've been on the water since as long as I can remember, Mandy said approvingly. You're a natural.

I'll watch him too, Michela told Vince. I'm constantly thinking I must be doing something wrong.

Again Adam snapped his phone shut. Your problem is— he began.

Don't! Clive cut in. He'll learn better watching Amal.

Since it's my problem— Vince began.

Wally! Keith cried. Produce Wally or prepare to face total humiliation.

Present and correct, Vince pulled the little effigy from his pocket. He smiled. He liked Keith.

It'll all sort itself out, the leader reassured him, in good time. It's an intuitive thing.

But Adam wouldn't leave be. This mysticism is silly, he said. It's a way of giving yourself airs. Like stories of riverside alcoholics with uncanny powers of divination. Why don't you tell him he sits too far back in the boat? There's no great philosophical wisdom to kayaking. It's the same with the anti-globalisation stuff, to be frank. People want to feel they have a good, semi-religious cause – save the planet, and so on – because then they've got an excuse for breaking things and causing trouble. They release a bit of energy and imagine they're saints.

The chinless man said all this in a relaxed, even cheerful voice, as if it was hardly a criticism at all. At once Michela was frantic.

How can you say that? she demanded. Do you have any idea how many people are dying of hunger while their governments are forced to spend the money that could save them to pay back loans to Western banks?

Not the loans, Clive cut in. He was leaning forward on his chair, smoking intently. Not the bloody loans, the *interest* on the loans. The interest! It's scandalous. I'd feel like a worm if I didn't do something about it. I wouldn't feel human. I'd die of shame if I didn't get involved. You don't have to go *looking* for a good cause these days. The miracle is that some people manage to hide from them. They sit in their air-conditioned offices and pretend the climate hasn't changed, while the rest of the world roasts.

Adam said calmly: If somebody asks for money from a private organisation, what is that organisation supposed to do, give it them for free?

But there are whole continents dying of AIDS, Michela pleaded. She seemed on the verge of tears. Because the drug companies don't want to lower their prices.

That is true, Mandy observed. She mentioned a TV programme.

What a petty morality! Clive cried. A petty, petty morality! Like the money-lender demanding his pound of flesh when the victim and his children are starving. As if we weren't all part of the same human family.

Ask the September 11th people about that.

All we are saying, Keith began to hum, is give peace a chance! He placed his beer mat on the edge of the table, flipped it in the air and caught it. Chill out, folks. Let's talk about tomorrow's paddle.

Why don't *you* explain to them? Adam suddenly said, straight-faced. He twisted his lean neck and turned to Vince. You understand it better than anyone here.

I think we could do with an expert opinion, Mandy agreed. Clive snorted.

Keith sent half a wink that invited Vince to calm the waters. Waiter, he called. He pointed to their beers. It was after eleven now. The three youngsters on stage with their keyboard and rhythm machine were trying to persuade someone to do the Macarena. Two Scandinavian children obliged, then two couples in swarthy middle age. Slavs perhaps. Above the open terrace, the sky had cleared and was seething with stars.

Bit of a far cry, Vince tried hesitantly, from my kayaking problems, isn't it?

Actually, perhaps not, Clive said in a knowing voice. Maybe not at all.

Oh come on, Adam laughed. If you treat everything as a deep and mysterious secret we won't be able to talk about anything at all.

Vince saw Michela's hand gripping Clive's now. He sighed. He pursed his lips. I've been involved, of course, in negotiating and renegotiating loans to Third World countries. What can I say? Actually the bank directors do think a lot about the human consequences of their decisions. It's a complex situation.

What's complex, Clive cut in, about people dying of hunger? You should be ashamed of yourself.

Ease off, Clive, Mandy said.

By the way, Keith put in, check out those Wops! A pair of young Italian women were wriggling back to back. The band played with more enthusiasm.

On the other hand, Vince went on, as a bank, our primary responsibility, inevitably, is towards our shareholders. He stopped: I wish we were discussing my paddling problems.

Perhaps we are, Clive said.

Oh *come on!* Adam looked up from his phone. Michela was grim. She took the tobacco herself now. Her fingers were trembling.

When we've finished, I'll explain, Clive insisted.

Okay, Vince said. I'll give you a typical example. So, a large organisation, maybe even a country, asks us, in consortium with other banks most likely, to extend them a loan. A big loan. We know that this country needs money to develop its economy and improve its people's lot. So we agree, having negotiated certain collateral of course and despite the fact that we are accepting a lower rate of interest than usual. The client is creditworthy we tell the shareholders. Then something happens. The government changes. There's a drought. They start a war. They make a disadvantageous contract with some multinational commodities set-up. The currency market shifts. They spend the money on arms. All of a sudden we have a debt crisis and our shareholders are looking at losses. Now the question is, how far can we be charitable on their behalf? That's not why ordinary people invested their money in our bank.

All you're saying, Clive said. He had to raise his voice because the music was louder now. All you're saying is that the normal, comfortable mechanisms for accumulating fortunes have broken down. Tough bloody luck. But when you're looking at kids with swollen bellies and maggots in their lips, there's only one real question: How can I help?

Vince hesitated. A fourth beer was before them.

And how have you helped, Adam cut in. He had a light, sardonic smile. What have you ever done?

Come on, Adam, Keith said. Chill.

From what I gather you go to a demonstration and shout your head off, but then at the same time you're setting up your own little business in the tourist trade, which is what kayaking is in the end.

Adam's even voice was barely audible above the throb of inane music. The Italian girls had attracted others to the dance floor. The instructor had a hint of a smile at the edge of his mouth, as if what he was saying were not offensive at all. When I teach kayak, he went on, two evenings a week on the estuary, I do it free, for underprivileged kids, in my spare time. You're making money and pretending you're involved in some cause to save the world.

There was a very short pause. As in a collision on the road there was a split second in which everybody realised that they were involved in some kind of accident, without yet knowing how serious.

Enough, let's talk about tomorrow's paddle, Keith said determinedly. I was saying to Clive, I think it might be time to split up into two or three groups around ability levels.

Clive had climbed to his feet. He reached across the table and slapped the chinless man hard across the face. Clive has a knotty, powerful arm, a solid hand. Adam fell sideways against Amal. The boy held him. Something clattered to the tiled terrace floor. The phone. A beer glass had gone over.

Prick!

Michela stood and pulled him back, put her arms round him.

Clive! Mandy shrieked. For God's sake!

He pushed the girl away, stepped backwards knocking over his chair, and walked off. Michela fell back and burst into tears, crouched by the table. Stupid, she was shaking her head. Stupid!

From their scattered tables the other campers were watching. One of the Spanish children was hiding behind Mandy's chair. Amal picked the phone from the floor and wiped the beer off it with the front of his T-shirt.

Since those people were killed, Michela got out, in Milan, he's been so tense. She stifled her tears, sat on a chair. Vince was in a trance. He felt exhilarated, upset. Only now did he notice there was beer dripping in his lap.

If he's broken my phone . . . Adam began. But the mobile was already beeping with the arrival of another message.

I'd better go and talk to him, Keith stood up.

Later, it turned out that Adam's sister-in-law in Southampton had given birth to a healthy little boy. They should have been celebrating.

KEITH'S ROCK

Vince watched Amal. This was the Rienz below Bruneck, a broad brown swirl of summer storm water rushing and bouncing between banks thick with brushwood, overhung with low, grey boughs, snagged in the shallows with broken branches that vibrate, gnarled and dead, trapped by the constant pressure of the passing flood. A hazard.

Amal sits alert and relaxed in his red plastic boat. They are ferry-gliding, crossing the river against the current. The Indian boy waits his turn in the eddy, chatting with the others. The boats rock and bang against each other. Someone is humming the hamster song. Then one firm stroke and the prow thrusts into the flood. The leading edge of the boat is lifted to meet the oncoming water. The current is wild and bouncy, not the steady strong flow of the narrower torrent, but the uneven tumbling of scores of mountain streams gathered together in the lower valley and channelled into a space that seems to resist their impetuous rush. The water piles on top of itself. It comes in waves, fast and slow.

The hull of the boat lifts. Amal has sunk his paddle on the downstream side as brace and rudder. Without a further stroke, the diagonal steady, the trim constantly adjusted, the kayak is squeezed across the flood and, without apparent effort, slides into an eddy against the further bank. The boy sits there steady, helmet wreathed in willow twigs. What is he doing that I can't?

Vince is familiar with the notion that kayaking is an activity where words, instructions, will take you only so far. In her first bossy excitement at having finally persuaded her husband, two years ago, to take up a sport, Gloria had given Vince a book, the BCU handbook, that taught all the strokes. There were diagrams, photographs, tips. Vince studied them. The stroke that most concerned him then was the Eskimo roll. He hated the embarrassment of having to swim out of his upturned boat and be rescued, perhaps by a twelve-year-old girl or a sixty-year-old man, on the muddy shore of the Thames Estuary.

But text and diagrams were not enough. He who understood the most complex accounting procedures at a glance, who oversaw the foreign activities of one of the world's top ten financial institutions, could not get his mind around the co-ordinated movement of hands, hips and head that would take you from the upside-down position, face blind and cold in the slimy salt water, to the upright, sitting steady again, paddle braced in the wavelets, the stinging breeze in your eyes. Even when he learned the movement, when he began to come up nine times out of ten, it was still as if some conjuring trick were being performed, something subtracted even from the most attentive gaze, an underwater sleight of hand. Only that now it was being performed through him. Whatever his motives for starting the sport, he knew that this was the reason he had continued, not the health advantages his wife nagged him about for so long, out of love, no doubt (she feared the businessman's thrombosis), but this stranger business of his body having learned things that his mind would never know, the idea of access to a different kind of knowledge; and, together with that, an edge of anxiety. There was always the tenth time when you didn't come up and didn't know why. All at once, he found he needed this excitement.

Vince! It was his turn. He paddled to the top of the eddy and out. Do I have the angle right? The boat was tossed up, thrust sideways. Now he was paddling like mad on the downstream side to keep the angle. The further bank was slipping by. Already he was downstream from Amal. He was working, sweating in the heavy jacket with its double layer of rubber. I'm inefficient. I'm messy. The hull scraped on a thick branch poking out in a swirl of brown water. For a second Vince was unnerved by the sheer volume of the water piling at him, so muddy and broken. Finally, he fought his way into an eddy a good fifty yards down from the Indian boy.

What do you think is wrong with my paddling, he had asked Louise last night in the tent. After the ridiculous argument between Clive and Adam, there had been a long and tedious conversation with Mandy about her divorce and difficult teenagers – she seemed determined to compare notes, as if a separation could be compared with a bereavement – and when at last he had managed to get back to the tent he had lain in his sleeping bag, waiting for his daughter's return. In the shadows, a glint caught his eye. Something yellow. He switched on the torch. On her copy of *The Lord of the Rings*, in the corner by her pillow, Louise had lined up the contents of her cosmetics bag. A thin oval bottle was catching the light. There was a yellow liquid inside. Suddenly the idea of femininity was intensely present in the soft curves of the glass, the pale colour of this cheap scent. Beside it lay a puff of pink cotton wool. Vince thought of Michela and Clive. They will be in each other's arms. My daughter won't want to share a tent with me next year, he decided.

Crouching to push between the flaps, Louise stumbled. Sorry, Dad. Were you asleep? It was past midnight. He told her about the argument: So then Clive just leans across the table and whacks him one, I mean, really hard! What idiots, the girl said. I'd never go for an older bloke like that, if I was Michela. They're in love, Vince said. He's not that old. Sitting on her sleeping bag, the girl had put on a long night-dress and was removing things from underneath. It was something her mother had always done. Love! the girl snorted. She even sounded like her mother. Well, Tom isn't exactly your age, Vince suggested. Louise giggled. She was brushing out her hair. I'm only doing it to piss off Amelia. Suddenly she was indignant. The way she's acting, you'd think he was already her property! Vince asked: Now you've seen me for a couple of days, what do you think is wrong with my paddling?

Don't be boring, his daughter said.

No, tell me, I'm getting obsessed.

Probably that's the problem then. With sports, the more you think about it, the more you screw up. Phil is such a prick, though. She was studying her toenails with the torch. He kept downloading these dirty pictures and trying to get us to look. Honestly. Then there's the fact that you never wanted to do it in the first place.

What?

Kayak, silly. You only started because Mum forced you. God knows why. And you only came on this trip to be on holiday with me. Probably you'd rather be at the office.

But now I'm here, I want to forget the office, he told her.

God, I'm exhausted. I've got a blister on my thumb. She threw herself back on her sleeping bag. This is so bloody uncomfortable.

Lying in the dark – his daughter had started to tell him some news from her cousins, something about her having to change room while they decorated – Vince thought back to that odd period when his wife had absolutely insisted he try this sport. There had been an atmosphere of crisis in the family, but with no substance, as when the market crashes without even a rumour of bad news. Perhaps that was why he had finally agreed. It seemed so much more important to her than he could understand. He began to take lessons Saturday afternoon, out on the estuary. But not long after he started, Gloria had stopped. You don't want me always telling you what to do, she said. She concentrated on her tennis. In the blue dark of the tent, Vince announced: I've been thinking it would be nice to live together again, next term, Lou. Me and you. His daughter didn't reply. Are you asleep? A patter of rain had begun to fall on the tent.

Vince followed Amal down the river. Whatever it was he was supposed to learn, he thought, had to do with the boy's calmness. His muscles were perfectly relaxed as a wave smacked into the boat. When he slalomed between stones, the upper body swayed in supple response. This is something more easily observed than emulated. Ahead, Tom was thrashing with determination. He is trapped into being a man to the girls. Amelia, Louise and Caroline were always beside him, pestering, giggling, offering themselves. Mark tagged doggedly after them. Vince rather likes Mark. Adam was precise, steady, executing textbook strokes. Phillip looked for every opportunity to turn his kayak on end, spin it round, force it over a rock and into the stopper behind. The skull and crossbones are visible on his helmet. Max and Brian were splashing each other. But Amal seemed to flow around the obstacles like the water itself. A safe pair of hands, Vince had begun to repeat to himself as he paddled. A safe pair of hands. More and more he would allow his consciousness to be submerged in the rhythm of the repeated phrase. Don't fight the water, go with it. Don't fight, don't fight. Behind him, Michela performed every manoeuvre as if it had been learned, very correctly, only moments before. She is a determined disciple in the wake of her guru. Clive has said not a word today. He is stony, silent, embarrassed by last night's madness. From bend to bend, eddy to eddy, they descended the river in a plastic line until, shortly before lunch, Keith injured himself.

Let's learn something new, kids, their leader shouted. Tail dips, Keith proposed. His eyes had their glassy brightness. We're late for lunch, Adam objected. People are getting tired.

Okay, so what we're going to do is to use this rock to push the tail under the oncoming current where it pours over.

The rock was about two feet across with the current pressing hard all round. Keith allowed his boat to be drawn up the eddy, then turned it and paddled backwards so that the tail of the boat was pushed under the water pouring over. The effect was immediate. First the stern was sucked down, into the oncoming rush, then quite suddenly the whole boat was forced vigorously upward and forward as if launched from a catapult.

Wey hey! Keith shouted. It was a pantomime of adolescence. With the exception of Mark and Caroline, the kids were enthusiastic. Cool! But Clive was shaking his head, arms folded in resignation on his paddle. Vince was torn between his interest in the manoeuvre itself, and his awareness that both of yesterday's antagonists disapproved. They don't want their sport to be a game.

Should be able to go vertical, Keith announced, if you get the entry right. He repeated the performance. His face glowed with a sort of second youth. This time, as the tail was sucked under, Keith let his heavy, paunchy body go right back with it. The boat rose, higher and higher until it seemed to stand still a second, vertical on its tail, then toppled backwards into the rush. Oh yeah! The kids clapped. Ace!

With enviable ease, Keith rolled up at once. He had hardly been under water a second. But he let out a loud cry. Across his wrist was a long deep gash. Swinging the paddle, he had caught a rock edge, or something very sharp. More than two inches of skin had opened up wide, ragged, deep and red. Keith stared. Oh! He was bleeding profusely. Already Adam was beaching his boat in the shallows. He had a first-aid kit under his seat. Blood was pumping out of Keith's arm. There were squirts of it. Eventually a bandage was found. They tied it tight. But the man must go to hospital. Suddenly the day has a purpose.

The main group was left to eat their lunch while four boats raced down five miles of busy river to the get-off point where the minibus had been parked: Keith, Mandy, Michela, Vince. The two men with coaching qualifications must stay with the kids. Keith had been adamant about that. Those were the BCU rules. He looked the two of them in the eyes. Clive is in charge, he said.

Hurrying down the river, with no plan for playing or learning, just one goal, to get the man stitched up, Vince finally found himself at home on the water. The sudden purposefulness made it easier, and the trust they had put in him. The bow swept into the current. He paddled. He reached determinedly for his strokes. The river was swollen, but straightforward. Perhaps I am a canoeist, he decided. They smacked into a wave train. He laughed. His face ran with sweat and spray. But Keith was evidently in pain. The bandage was soaked in blood. The man was gritting his teeth. Mandy was scolding him for always taking risks, showing off to the kids. How could he have known? Michela objected. She was panting. It was one in a million to catch a sharp edge like that.

At last they were paddling across a low lake at the bottom of the run. A storm of ducks rose from the water. Keith and Mandy were already approaching the beach, the get-out point. The air was humming with flies. Vince had waited to let Michela catch up. He was elated by the speed of the descent. Okay? She looked at him, flushed with effort, eyes shaded beneath black helmet. Exhausted, she said.

Course, if I go to hospital, Keith complained, they'll tell me I can't paddle for the rest of the week. He was up front in the minibus. You're bloody well going, Mandy told him. She had a proprietorial manner. You'll need stitches, I'm afraid, Vince said. Keith blew out his cheeks and sighed. Photo of my war wound, please, he asked.

With Michela to interpret, the injured man was left at the hospital in Bruneck, while Mandy and Vince drove back to the campsite to get a car. It was ten miles up the valley. What Keith was really worried about, the woman explained, was the last day, the stretch of river above Sand in Taufers, the grand finale of the trip; he wouldn't be able to be there, which meant Clive and Adam running the show together, who hated each other. Keith played the fool, but in the end he only did it for the group. He was totally dedicated.

Vince was driving. Well, the combatants seem to have agreed a truce today, he said. It was the first time he had driven a minibus. Actually, I can't help thinking Clive is right really. At least in general. I mean, when one of us gets hurt, like now, we immediately rush to help. But we don't do anything for people we don't know.

Nor do they for us, the woman said sensibly. She was still wearing wetsuit shorts, and a soaking T-shirt on a stout body. The thing is there's helping, she said, and there's shouting about helping.

It was mad to hit him, Vince agreed.

No, but apart from that, don't you think, it's all very well him having this cause and so on, we all agree with it, but in the end it's easy rushing about and chanting at demonstrations. Clive's never had to deal with things like a divorce, or you losing Gloria like that. He's always worried about people on the other side of the planet.

Can't blame him for not having suffered a catastrophe, Vince thought.

All I'm saying is, I judge a bloke by his personal life, what he makes around him, not his ideals.

He looks like he's got something pretty nice going with Michela, Vince said. He glanced in the mirror.

I've seen him the same way with half a dozen others.

Really? Well, good for him, I suppose.

Turning towards her a second as he spoke, he found the woman looking at him quite intently. Her chubby right knee jerked up and down under her hand. I think blokes like yourself, she said quietly, I mean who've been husbands all your lives, don't understand men like Clive. And vice versa. You're chalk and cheese. But women understand. They have to. Look at Keith, for example, married too young, then has affairs, everybody knows, but won't leave home, like. He has his responsibilities.

Doesn't sound like my idea of being a good husband.

He's stuck at it, Mandy said. While Clive is always talking about universal justice.

And Adam? Vince was aware of a social circle drawing him in. Perhaps, having lost his wife, he should become part of the Waterworld community. He would go to all the club's events. He could gossip and be gossiped about. Except, of course, that there was nothing to say about him. What have I ever done?

Adam's wife's handicapped, Mandy said. MS. No, handicapped's the wrong word. She shot Vince an enquiring glance. Actually, I think your Gloria looked after her in hospital.

I'm really sorry, Vince said. I had no idea.

Campsite! Mandy shouted. Don't miss the turn.

They crossed the bridge, passed the church, trundled down the track between the tents in the bright sunshine. Mandy took over the driving seat of the minibus to head back to the river and pick up the group. Vince went to get his own car to return to the hospital. This was what he'd been brought along for. Fifteen minutes later, on impulse, trapped behind a tourist coach on the narrow, bendy road to Bruneck, he opened the glove compartment of the car, found his mobile and turned it on. There were no messages. Then, driving, he called the office. It was strange. In a matter of seconds he was in touch with London, with reality. His secretary was a small Chinese woman in her fifties. Of course you're needed, she told him, but everybody's agreed to wait till you're back. That would be Monday. So nothing urgent? he asked. It'll be urgent on Monday, Mr Marshall, but not before. She asked him if he were having a good break. It was blistering in London, she said. She couldn't remember a year like it. He told her he felt immensely refreshed.

Vince drove past stacks of timber, sawmills. The sun was fierce. There was an open yard full of wooden weathercocks, machine-carved, life-size crucifixes, curious trolls. We come

79

here to play on the river and have no contact with the locals, he thought. A lean old man in a broad-brimmed hat and blue overalls was scything the steep bank above the road to the right. Quite probably he had never been on the water that raced through his valley. Is it really possible I'll be back in the City on Monday? Vince was conscious of enjoying the drive, of deliberately looking out for everything foreign and unusual: the wide wooden balconies, the gothic script over shops and hotels, the weathercocks, the hay hung on wooden trestles up steep slopes, the little children in leder-hosen, the onion domes of the churches. Did I ever belong to anything aside from the bank? he wondered. Was I part of any community outside the office? Important decisions were being taken without him. I mustn't miss the turn to the hospital, he worried.

They're seeing him now, Michela looked up and smiled. The waiting room was a mix of tourists and locals, sitting round the walls, flicking through provincial newspapers, international glamour magazines, nursing wounds and coughs. Two or three men kept glancing at the tall Italian girl in her neoprene shorts and white bikini top. Only since Gloria's death had Vince become acutely aware that he had never been with any other woman but his wife. He had never 'picked up' a woman. They had found themselves, he and Gloria, in adjacent rooms in Durham university dorms. It would have been hard to establish a moment when either deliberately chose the other. By a process of happy osmosis they had married. If you removed that boulder, Keith had been talking to the group yesterday about reading the river, which way do you think the water would go? How many things downstream would that effect? Suddenly Vince is in trouble again. With a determined effort, he asked the girl:

How many of these groups will you be getting then?

Sorry? Michela looked up from a magazine.

Will you be having another group right after ours?

Four altogether. We have a week's break after this one for a demonstration in Berlin. Then one after another right through to the end of August.

And then?

How do you mean?

I suppose you have some other job.

We'll go back to England, do courses there through the winter. In England the only real white water is in winter. Here it slows up when the glaciers stop melting. She laughed: We must look crazy dressed like this.

Me more than you, he said. He was wearing a grey thermal top and swimming shorts. She raised an eyebrow.

Being so much older, Vince explained.

You're younger than Keith.

And you won't miss anyone in Italy?

No, she grimaced.

There must be someone.

I hate Italy.

All the English love it.

She turned to him. Suddenly she was wry and sophisticated. You want to know? Everybody seems to think I'm such a mystery. I'm not. Just that all the Italian I heard before I was ten was my parents arguing, hating each other and me. Understand?

I'm sorry, Vince said.

But the girl wouldn't let him off the hook. And when I was in my teens it was my mother on her own telling me she didn't want to live anymore. She regularly took overdoses. The hospital, the stomach pumps, at least a dozen times. Okay? Got the idea?

Vince sensed the girl was trying to crush him by the

81

completeness of this disaster and the sarcastic lightness with which she spoke of it. There was nothing he could reply. He looked at the young woman, her short glossy hair, tall neck, smooth olive cheeks, lips parted, eyes clouded. She thinks I'm inadequate, bland. Michela smiled rather sourly: I watched Disney films and read comics in English. English was escape for me. It was another world. Does that make sense now? Has the mystery dissolved?

Vince still couldn't see how to reply.

She eased off: Then just when things are looking promising, Clive goes and makes a scene like that last night.

Did he apologise?

Not yet.

Might be wise, Vince said quietly.

It's not up to me to tell him what to do. She was sharp again.

Actually, Vince went on, I agreed with him, you know, in a way . . . with what Clive was saying. In the end, it's a position you can only respect.

How do you mean?

Well, that as communication speeds up and the countries of the world come closer to each other, it gets harder and harder to avoid the impression that we have a responsibility towards those who are suffering.

If you bloody well agree, why don't you do something about it?

Like hit Adam?

Oh don't be funny. She was scathing.

Vince was finding this difficult. To agree with someone, he said, doesn't mean that you share their passion.

They were sitting side by side on green plastic seats in what might be any waiting room in Western Europe. She was holding a copy of the Italian magazine *Gente*, leaning forward, feet tucked under the chair, girlish and belligerent. He realised he had adopted the condescending voice he found himself using so often with Louise. He didn't know how else to speak to someone so young.

Well, it sounds like an excuse to me, she said. I mean, what would it take before someone like you actually did something about the state of the world? Would some huge natural catastrophe be enough? Or would it have to happen right in central London before you woke up? Will people never see what's going on?

Before he could answer, she started to tell him that she admired Clive so much because of the intensity of this concern he felt. Only he couldn't find a channel to express it. Do you understand? They went to demonstrations and so on, they had to. But it didn't *achieve* anything. Clive really means it, she insisted, when he says we want to use these kayak trips to get people to think differently about the world, to notice that the glaciers are melting, that the planet is being ruined. Obviously we have to make enough money to live, but that's not why we're doing it.

Vince listened. As she spoke, the girl grew more and more fervent. She is pleading, he thought. Her whole face was animated. Her urgency was beautiful. Other men in the room were watching. You can't split up the world, she was telling him now. You can't care for this and not that, the Third World's problems, but not global warming or GM foods. Do you see what I'm saying? It's all part of the *same* campaign. There's a right and wrong behind . . .

Keith emerged from a tiled corridor. His arm was in a sling, his bearded face was pale, but he was smiling. Only eight stitches, he told them, and an order to do absolutely nothing for a month. Great. Now I need a drink.

They found a café in the centre of Bruneck where Vince

noticed that Keith flattered the young woman in every possible way, winking, joking, passing remarks, until at last she relaxed and accepted an ice cream laced with rum and Keith said in all his experience he had never heard of anyone getting such a deep wound from doing a simple roll in an apparently innocuous patch of water. It was as if there were an open switchblade just under the surface. Waiting for me! Kismet! he laughed. Or kiss me, as the case may be. His eyes are twinkling.

Michela hadn't understood. Keith launched into an explanation. Vince's mind began to wander. The café tables around them spread out over a recently renovated square of fresh porphyry cobbles and clean stone-and-wood façades. A lot of money is being invested here, Vince thought. It was a big collective effort, to capture the tourists, but also to maintain their identity. There were baskets of hanging flowers and, beside the café door, a large wooden troll carved from some gnarled tree trunk with a face at once grotesque and madly benevolent, pipe in warped lips, hat on a knotty head, axe held in crooked fingers. Not unlike the drunk with his shack down by the river bank. Oh Vince! Earth to Vince! Have an ice cream as well, mate, Keith insisted. It's great with rum. You paddled brilliantly, by the way. Huge improvement. Come on, the others won't be back yet. Yes, have an ice cream, Michela joined in. She smiled with a long spoon in her lips. Come on, Ageing Mr Banker, enjoy yourself. You look like you don't enjoy yourself enough.

Where's Wally? Phil demanded.

Vince couldn't find the thing. He searched everywhere. He was upset. I can't believe how seriously you're taking it, Louise said. It's only a cheap toy. Mark came to their tent to tell the girl she was supposed to be helping with dinner. The Louts are on. Vince just couldn't find the stupid puppet. He was sure he had tied it to his cag.

Vincent has lost Wally! Phil shrilled. He ran from tent to tent. Wally missing believed drowned! Re-drowned! Stock market'll be tumbling, Adam remarked. He was hanging out the wet kit. Wally wasn't on Vince's cag, nor in his dry-bag. Enormous fines, the chinless man insisted, shaking his head, smiling wryly, if only to pay the increase in our insurance premium. A grave breach of trust, Max mocked. Unspeakable punishments. There were decades of literature on Wally, Keith said. He was a mythical figure, a patron saint of river communities, the archetypal paddler. Went over Niagara, Mandy joined in. His disappearance presages disaster. Vince looked everywhere. The boat, the minibus, the tent. There'll have to be a funeral, Amelia announced solemnly. Ask not for whom the bell tolls. Someone who's lost Wally, Caroline announced, has to buy a substitute and wear it for the rest of his life. She tried to hold a gloomy face, then burst into giggles. It was time to eat spaghetti bolognaise.

We have a new feature on the landscape, Mandy announced as the meal was finishing. Let's drink to Keith's Rock, a remarkable underwater geological feature discovered by the Yorkshire man Keith Graham. There was applause, and a toast: To Keith's Rock! but immediately followed by a chant, from all the children, Where's Wally, Where's Wally? They were sitting in a circle on the ground, their plates on their laps. The sun had long since gone behind the mountain beyond the town, but the evening was still bright, the air warm. Then Michela stood up from beside Clive and came round the circle to whisper in Vince's ear, They've stolen it, silly. They're teasing you.

May I say a word? Vince asked. He cleared his throat.

Pigs, Slobs, Louts. He paused. It is with regret that I must inform you that while the eminent discoverer Mr Graham was in hospital after the christening of his remarkable rock, I was unfortunately obliged to go to the police station, to report a, er, serious theft. Indeed a kidnap. Wally, a character, or rather a spirit, a haunting presence, whom we all agree, I think, is the ghostly heart and soul of our community, without whom, etc. – Wally, or at least the effigy he is obliged to inhabit following his untimely decease, has been taken from us and is presently being held against his will. Now I must warn you all that the Italian *carabinieri*, if not the Austrian *Polizei*, will be arriving in just a few moments to question everyone and search all the tents. The criminals face summary execution. You have just a few seconds to own up.

His daughter, he noticed, was smiling. Then suddenly Wally was flying up in the air in the middle of the circle. The tiny bear wore a small red and white scarf. Who had it? Who stole it? It fell without a bounce beside a stack of dirty plates. Nobody owned up. The creature was awarded then to Max who had forgotten to replace the drain plug in his boat after emptying it at lunchtime and had almost sunk before he realised what the problem was. I shall cherish our patron paddler and protector, he announced, more carefully than has my predecessor. Oh aren't we affectionate, Brian said. His prede-what? Phil demanded. As on every evening, the boy had returned his food almost untouched.

Serious note now folks, Keith interrupted. Serious announcement to finish the evening. No doubt word has got around that our two illustrious instructors had a bit of a barney yesterday evening. About politics, would you believe? Politics! Brian groaned. What's that? They've made it up, of course, but from now on, the rule is, *no discussion of politics* for the rest of the trip. Okay? Anyone caught discussing anything that could remotely be considered to be political will be obliged to run round the whole campsite in just their underpants. Yes, please! Max shouted. Oh shut up! What matters here is us, our paddling, learning to help each other, making the group work. Is that clear? Any outside or personal interests, however noble, must be sacrificed to those goals for as long as we're together. Now, tomorrow will be a half day; we're going to drive out to a slalom course for the morning and do two or three runs to sort out who will be able to do the tough trip on the last day. Then it's rest time for the afternoon. You can go into town or take the cable car up to the glacier.

The Pigs were on washing-up duty. Amelia and Tom stood side by side at the big sinks outside the bathrooms. You've left a bit, the girl complained. She had tied her hair in a ponytail. It's a mark on the plate, Tom said. In the plastic, look. They bent their heads over it. No it isn't. Yes, it is. They nudged elbows and pushed each other and giggled, both clutching the plastic plate. Beneath the inevitable straw hat, Max made faces to Vince. I think I love you, he began to croon, but that's what life is made of. The boy did an excellent imitation of the hamster's mechanical movements, imaginary microphone in one hand, drumstick in the other. It's a manufacturing defect, can't you see! Tom shouted, but he let the girl hold his wrist. They were tugging, laughing in each other's eyes. And it worries me to say that I've never felt this way. Max dropped his tea towel over their heads. Idiot, Tom yelled, but the economics student seemed perfectly happy with the situation.

Someone tapped Vince on the shoulder. Dad? Louise had put a skirt on, and a short top. She wore earrings. Can I have some money to go to the bar? Just behind her, Mark was hovering nervously, a polite smile on his face. Handing over a note, Vince felt old and disorientated. The Pigs were now occupying three sinks with piles of dirty dishes and the kids doing nothing but fool around. Come on team, he told them, let's get going and do it properly. Tom. Amelia! Come on now. When Amelia started carrying the plates back to the kitchen tent, Tom suddenly became earnest again and asked Vince how far it was really possible for a government to establish the true volume of the money supply. A professor at LSE had shown them an unbelievably complex calculation. Discovering the exact quantity of the supply was largely irrelevant, Vince said. What mattered was to establish whether it was going up or down, which actually was all too easy. Ooh, I know, Max laughed, I know!

Afterwards, weary of company and conversations, Vince went for a walk around the large campsite on his own. A Jaguar with Dutch plates was parked in front of a luxury caravan. Through the window he glimpsed an elderly couple and, on the table between them, a goldfish in a bowl. He stopped and looked again. Why would anyone drive from Holland with a goldfish? A tiny child on a tricycle circled a waste bin. Somewhere out of view Italian voices were singing to the accompaniment of guitar and accordion, while behind the surface buzz of the site, thunder rolled faintly in the peaks.

Vince looked up. The glacier beyond the castle was obscured by mist. Shining from behind the nearest mountains, a last flare of summer light had turned the vapour to bright milk above the sombre gorge below. It was like some of the skies they had seen in old paintings in Florence, Vince thought: cosmic drama above tortured saints. He stopped. There was no passion between myself and Gloria, he said out loud. To his left was a low tent with a large motorcycle beside it. A haggard woman in early middle age sat cross-legged in black leather pants, smoking, reading a thriller. The thunder came louder. Was that what she meant when she said, I'm so sorry? He began to walk again. The week in London – all work – year in year out; the weekend, full of domestic chores. There was no passion, he repeated. He stepped aside for a car carrying four bicycles on its roof. But does that matter? There's always something so stupid about passion, Vince told himself. That girl, he thought, is more intelligent than to say those things she said to you. As if the world's sick could all suddenly be healed. She says those things, he thought, to be in love.

Come on, a voice interrupted: You haven't got Wally to talk to now, you know. Adam was beside him. Loos are cleaner this side of the campsite, he explained. Want a walk? It's going to rain, Vince said. So we'll get wet, Adam smiled. He suggested they climb the hill behind the group of houses at the entrance to the site. There was a church poking out from the woods above, perhaps half a mile away and a few hundred feet higher. There must be a path. But what if there's a storm? Vince worried. We'll get drenched, Adam said equably.

They walked quickly, out past the camp shop and bar, the larger church in the valley that rang its bells every morning. Finding a signpost, they struck off up the hill and were soon among thick pine trees. You were talking to yourself, Adam repeated. Getting old, Vince said. The chinless man seemed in good spirits. He said how wonderful the air was here. He worked in insurance, he explained, policy design, risk calculation, dull stuff. What did Vince think about the government's plans for new banking regulations? Watch it, Vince objected. We'll be running round the site in our underpants next. He didn't like the way people kept insisting on his professional life. Oh, I'm not about to whack you round the chops if we don't agree. Adam stretched the corner of his mouth and touched it gingerly. Bloke's a primitive. Well-meaning, but primitive.

Vince said nothing. This is an attempt to make me an ally, he thought. The path crossed a meadow, then was back in the wood again. Odd this thunder, he observed, always there but always far away. It's up on the plateau, Adam said, at seven thousand feet. You know? Different world. After a while they heard the sound of water splashing on stone. It was getting nearer. In the twilight, beneath the dark-green pines, they stood on a small log bridge over a stream that fell towards them down mossy black rock. Adam chose this moment to say how sorry he had been about Gloria. He really should have come to the funeral. We taught a couple of courses together, you know, a few years back. Then we did the Ardêche trip of course. She was really kind to my wife when she was in hospital.

Thanks, Vince said.

Gloria was a wonderful woman, Adam insisted. So full of energy. She gave her time so generously.

Vince had heard this description of his wife from various sources. We'll get caught walking down in the dark if we don't hurry, he said. But Adam wanted to press on. They were almost at the church. Your main problem with your paddling, he began to say, is the way you sit too far back in the boat, as if you were afraid. Apart from breaking in and out, you're usually safer leaning forward, in the attack position, reaching for it.

The path climbed steeply and was stony now and damp. The air had taken on a cool, sweet smell. Vince was wearing sandals and his foot slipped. Eventually they reached a low wall; a gate led into a churchyard with just a few dozen graves. Neat lines of black wrought-iron crosses stood at the head of thin rectangles of shale. In the centre of each cross was a photo of the deceased, a name, some dates. When they both stopped a moment by a fresh grave, smothered in yellow flowers, Adam rather cautiously asked Vince where he had had Gloria buried. She was cremated, he said. I scattered the ashes in the estuary. Oh. Adam seemed taken aback. I really should have gone to the funeral, he repeated.

The church itself was closed. Opposite the door, beyond the graves, a bench looked out across the valley. They leaned on a low parapet. Down below, the road from Bruneck to Sand in Taufers streamed with headlights, but above, the slopes were already colourless and vague with just here and there, high, high up in the forests opposite, an occasional solitary light: some lonely *baita*, a family with their cattle on the high meadows. Strange being so cut off, Adam murmured. With sudden intuition, Vince announced: You know what the last thing Gloria said to me was? His voice was hard and angry in his throat. I am so, so sorry. He was almost croaking. Those were her last words. She had just a few seconds to speak – she phoned me, you know, she knew she was dying, she recognised the symptoms and managed to phone – and that's what she said: I'm so sorry. Turning, he found Adam staring at him in alarm.

It had begun to rain. The drops were clattering on the tents when they got back. Vince went to the bathroom then lay on his sleeping bag to wait for Louise's return. The rain came harder. It drummed on the kayaks roped to the trailer, on the kitchen tent where Phil and Caroline had begun to kiss. Adam was also lying alone, concerned that his son was late, thinking about that moment in the graveyard with Vince. I miss you so much when I'm away, he texted his wife. The bedridden woman sent a reassuring reply. Sarah's baby was doing fine.

The thunder cracked louder now. In the chalet just beyond their pitch, Michela and Clive had been talking round in circles. You just want me to leave, don't you? she repeated. No, I need you, he said. We're in this business together. We invested the money together and we'll have to pay it back together. He began to talk about an e-mail he had received from Diabolik, one of the members in their militants' news group. There was to be a big demonstration at the American airbase in Vicenza. Some people were going to break in and sit on the runway.

The rain fell harder on the roof. Michela watched her man as he spoke. She had made herself a camomile tea. Her stomach was unsettled. He had insisted on whisky. He was smoking. Come to bed, she said softly. He shook his head. The river will be rising, he said. He picked up the book he'd been reading. *The Case Against Nestlé's*. Then the thunder cracked right overhead and the rain fell with loud slaps against the windows.

Towards three a.m. those who had managed to sleep were woken by a wild clanging. The church bell, not a hundred yards away, had begun to ring. In boxer shorts, pulling a plastic waterproof about him, Vince ran squelching from his tent and banged into Mandy. Did it mean there was going to be a flood? There was something gothic about the woman in her white nightdress in the teeming dark. She was fighting with an umbrella. The guy-ropes need tightening, he said. She clutched at him and almost fell. The nightdress was soaked. It was odd to feel the embrace of her body, the heavy breasts.

The church bell rang and rang. Four or five people had already abandoned their sleeping bags for the big kitchen tent. Phil claimed he would be rained out if it went on. Is it a warning or what? He would have to sleep here with

Amelia and Caroline. Then Michela appeared. Above long tanned legs, she wore a heavy mountain oilskin. She was smiling. Listen up, everybody. It's just a habit here that they ring the bells when it rains really hard. She had come to reassure them. The noise of the bells is supposed to break up the clouds. Certainly breaks up any hope of sleep! Why would it do that? Vince asked. She smiled at him. She had a way, he understood, of seeming seraphic beyond her age. I've no idea, she said. It's a faith they have here, a tradition.

Borrowing an umbrella, Vince made his usual trip to the loo. As always the urinals mysteriously began to flush as he approached. It should be reassuring, this sense of being integrated into the world's sensible automatisms. Your arrival is foreseen, you are provided for. Faith in what? Louise demanded, when he crawled back between the fly-sheets. She had been reading a text message. The little screen glowed. The bell rang incessantly. The rain was trying the quality of Gloria's old tent. Gloria loved camping. There were beads of water running along the seams. I know he acts a bit of a loser, but he's sweet, Louise said of Mark. It's his dad on at him all the time that makes him shy. Oh, it turns out they knew Mum quite well, by the way. She visited his mum who's stuck in bed or something. His dad plays in the same tennis club. I know, Vince said. After a moment he asked, Who's the message from? None of your business, Louise laughed.

They were lying on their beds while the rain drenched the fabric above them and the bell clanged on. Funny, Louise eventually said, her head on her hands, the impression Mum made on people. Mark says he liked her a lot. It was the first time in ten days together that she had spoken to him about her mother. I suppose we all make different impressions on people outside the family, Vince said cautiously.

Suddenly, his daughter began to cry. She lay still, crying quietly. Vince leaned across and put his hand on her forehead, stroked her hair. To his surprise, she didn't push the hand away. It was a pleasure to feel the soft hair under his fingers, the warm skin.

Later, after the rain eased off and the bell stopped, he lay awake, listening to distant voices, the clatter of drops blown off the trees, rustling fly-sheets, zips. He imagined the Italian girl unzipping her waterproof. Clive would be embracing her. Gloria, he whispered. He wasn't jealous. Many evenings he went to sleep this way. The rehearsal of that final phone conversation, then the quiet mouthing of her name. Gloria. In Excelsis Deo, she liked to add primly. But he couldn't hear his wife's wry laugh in the dripping tent with his daughter gently snoring. There was no passion, he whispered. For a moment he imagined getting up again and going to the window of their chalet. You are sick, he thought, Vince Marshall. Sick.

KATRIN HOFSTETTER

Max had hung Wally from the brim of his straw hat. The talismanic bear swung from side to side at every bend. Mandy insisted that everyone buckle up their safety belts. No exceptions! The slalom course was almost thirty miles away. People had slept badly. Caroline had cried off altogether. Don't you think 'sort out the men from the boys' is a pretty sexist expression, Brian was enquiring of Clive. I mean, women don't even get a look-in. Anyway, the boys are usually better than the men, Phil boasted. It was the drooping eyebrows that gave him such a gormless look. Oh you think so too, do you, dearie, Max cried. The minibus pulled its trailer along the Bruneck–Brixen road. Amelia and Tom had their heads bowed over the BCU's manual of correct recovery strokes. They seemed seriously absorbed. Vince felt his stomach tight. He had had to crap twice before departing. The course has sections that are grade four, Amal told him solemnly. That means there's only one line to take through the rapid and you have to get it right. Or kaput! The Indian boy smiled. Why do I feel so determined, Vince wondered, to be on this suicide trip tomorrow? What do I have to prove?

About four hundred yards of river had been carefully reorganised to present more or less every troublesome white-water feature: a stopper, a hole, a couple of daunting waves, rocks in the most trying places. Being dam-fed, the water levels were fairly constant. Criss-crossing over the river was a system of wires from which perhaps forty slalom gates were suspended so that their red- or green-and-white posts were just clear of the water. But this extra subtlety, the weaving back and forth in a set course among obstacles, was for the long, slim slalom boats, the experts. All you have to do, Clive explained earnestly – but he in particular had slept little and badly – at least for the first two runs, is to show me that you can break out of the current at every single eddy on the course, then break back in again without any trouble. Okay? We go down in groups of four. At the bottom you get out and carry your boats back to the beginning again. Keith will be stalking the bank taking notes and giving advice.

Vince ran his fingers round the rim of the cockpit to check that the spraydeck was sealed. The tab was out, ready to pull. He was with Mandy, Amal and Phil. At once he sensed he would have felt safer in a group with one of the two instructors. The water rushed down, grey and gleaming, to where they sat ready on the low bank. But of course, not to be with an instructor was a compliment. The pour-overs were larger and fiercer than any they had run before. There were places where even a small mistake would lead to getting pinned against a rock. It's years since I did something as tough as this, Mandy muttered. She was checking the strap on her helmet. Slalom courses are always a doddle, Phil said knowledgeably. They've taken out any sharp stuff you could hurt yourself on, haven't they? Nobody ever gets killed. He seemed disappointed. You lead, Vince told Amal. The Indian boy launched himself from the bank.

Pointing upstream, Amal ferried from the bank to the first rock and signalled to Vince to follow. First his finger indicates the person who is the object of the message, then the place he has to arrive at. As Vince moved out, Amal was already leaving his small refuge to drop down behind the first spur. One by one the group followed. First in the eddy, then back into the flow and through a fierce stopper. Take it close to the left, Keith was shouting from the bank. He had his arm in a sling. Right against the rock! The rocks are your friends!

Vince raced down. The deceleration as you punched into the eddy, raising the bottom of the boat to the still water, was fearsome. At the third he misjudged and was pulled over by the inertia. He rolled up on the second attempt. It was freezing. The cold gripped his head. He was excited. He signalled to Mandy to follow and broke back into the current again. As the least likely to come to grief, Phil was at the back to pick up anyone who got into trouble.

Certainly beats banking, Vince told Mandy at the bottom when they'd completed the first run. Once again, the concentration required and the physical effort had cleared his mind of all pain. You looked good, Mandy said. She had taken a couple of photos from eddies. Pretty dull, Phil thought. He wanted to play in the big stopper. They heaved the boats onto their backs and trudged up to the top.

On the second run, Amal tried a ferry-glide just below the stopper. It has a hole as well! Keith warned them from the bank. It's grabby. They are behind a spur of rock looking upstream into a fierce churn of white water beneath a drop of about three feet. A cold spume fills the air, causing small rainbows to form in the bright sunshine. The world has a glitter to it, a powerful presence. Everything is immediate. Just downstream of the white water, the surface is irregular and turbulent and there must be a point – you know this – where if you push too close to the froth, the backflow in the stopper will begin to pull you in. The boat will sink and spin in the soft, oxygenated water. But to make it over to the eddy that Amal has spotted way on the opposite bank, you can't let yourself drift too far down. You must ride close to the stopper and its deep white hole. Amal steers his kayak out into the stream. His ability to set the angle and edge of the boat is uncanny. With no effort, he glides across.

Vince follows. He's too vertical, pointing straight upstream. The hole begins to pull. He back-paddles, suddenly loses almost ten yards, but fights his way across with a huge expenditure of effort. Panting, relieved, he signals to Mandy to come across and join them. There's room in the eddy for all four. They can regroup. As she looks across to him, Mandy's face is grim and Vince guesses at once that she isn't going to make it. The woman is hunched. Her posture betrays her nerves. She is here for the group, Vince is aware, for the companionship that expeditions like this can offer a single woman in middle age, for the photographs and fun.

Mandy's first tentative stroke leaves the tail of the boat still anchored in the eddy. Before she's halfway across, she's lost at least twenty yards to the current. Barely breaking the surface, there's a stone in the middle of the river here. She could rest the bow of her kayak behind it, take a break, decide what to do next. But she hasn't seen. She isn't thinking. She drifts against the stone sideways, paddling like mad. It surprises her. With the unexpected contact, the bow is shifted the other way, back to the left bank. She fights the shift, but half-heartedly. The river has got her now. Grey and bouncy, the current swirls towards a smooth black boulder by the bank where it piles up in a tense cushion before being forced back into the centre to plunge down the next drop. All this would be easy enough to negotiate if taken face on, but Mandy is pointing upstream. She is still trying to turn the boat back across the flow when the current pushes it sideways onto the boulder. Immediately she's pinned, the underside of the kayak against the rock, the water crashing on the spray-deck.

Vince is watching all this from the safety of his eddy on the opposite bank, thirty yards upstream. He sees the woman try to brace her paddle against the oncoming water to keep her head up. He has a picture of the blue helmet, the orange paddle-blade. But it's only a fraction of a second before she's down. Now she will pull out and swim. She doesn't. Arm in a sling, Keith is scrambling down the bank. But there are thick brambles between himself and the rock. He can't get to it. Mandy is still under. Amal! Vince looks round. The boy is locked away from the stream by Vince's boat. Vince looks for Phil. Incredibly, he is fooling around in the hole. He's let his kayak be sucked in and is throwing the boat this way and that, tail up, tail down, in the spongy water. He hasn't seen anything. He can hear no screams.

Amal is trying to force a way round Vince to the stream, but now Vince breaks in himself. He will get to her first. In one stroke he's in the quick of it. The power of the current tosses the boat round. It's a matter of seconds. He is bearing straight down on Mandy's boat, still pinned upside down against the rock. The bank is to the right, the next rapid to the left. I have no idea how to do this, Vince thinks.

Keith is shouting something, but Vince can't hear, can't listen. Instead of fighting the pull of the current onto the rock, Vince speeds towards it, as if to spear Mandy's boat as he goes down. Lean into it! Keith is yelling. Vince pays no attention. Just before he hits the submerged boat, he lets go the paddle with his right hand and throws his body towards the rock to grab the bow-handle of the boat. His arm is wrenched violently, but the boat shifts. It's free. Dragged over, Vince thrusts his hand down on the bow of Mandy's boat to bounce up and prevent himself from capsizing. Now he's spun backward and dropping into the rapid. He's just got both hands back on his paddle when he hits a stopper sideways and goes down. This time he rolls up without thinking, as if rolling in white water were the easiest thing in the world. Mandy is swimming. Keith has already got a line to her. Amal is chasing the upturned boat down the river. Exhausted, mentally more than physically, Vince pulls over to the bank.

The deck just wouldn't pop, Mandy is repeating. There's a note of hysteria in her voice. She is stumbling up on the rocks. Her body is shaking. The water was so powerful, it wouldn't pop. I couldn't get out. I was drowning. Thought I might have to take a swim there, Keith laughs. Stitches or no stitches. Then the woman insists on embracing Vince. You saved my life. Nonsense! Later they worked out that the whole crisis had lasted no more than twenty seconds. Nursing the pain in his shoulder, Vince understood he had booked himself a place on tomorrow's trip.

The chair-lift begins a mile or so above Sand in Taufers. It took them up in threesomes, their feet dangling a few yards above the tall pines either side, the cables humming and clicking above them, the air cooling around their faces, the valley falling away dramatically behind. The kids giggled and took photos of each other. Amelia was quiet beside Tom. Max dangled Wally below his seat on a string amid shrieks of fake horror. Somebody had begun to sing 'Inky Pinky Parlez-Vous'.

At the top, a large timber-built hostelry, flying the vertical red and white banner of the Tyrol, sits in a wide meadow hemmed in on three sides by even steeper slopes leading up to a ridge at almost nine thousand feet. But the youngsters really don't want to walk. The sun has a sharper, brighter quality here. They could buy Cokes at the hostel, fool around and sunbathe. Since Bri can only hobble, we've all decided to keep him company, Max laughed. Keith and Mandy had stayed behind, to explore Bruneck, they said. The woman had needed a rest. So for the walk up to the glacier there were just Vince, Amal, Adam, Clive and Michela. Adam tried to persuade his son to join them. Risking nothing, the boy had survived the slalom course well enough. He doesn't want to, Vince said softly. It was clear there was something going on between him and Louise. Adam insisted. It would do everybody good to stretch their legs after being cramped in the boat. Mark didn't even reply now. He turned and ran after the others.

Then no sooner had the walkers set off up a path that zigzagged steeply through walls of flint, than Clive suddenly stopped to apologise to Adam. Michela didn't expect it. The party was brought to a halt on the narrow path. I shouldn't have hit you. A clouded look came over his handsome face. Dead right, you shouldn't, Adam agreed. Then the instructor said, Forget it, but grudgingly, Michela thought. They climbed in single file up the steep slope under bright afternoon sunshine, and as they walked and she watched Clive's strong legs in short trousers and his powerful back bending to the slope, she began to feel angry. You shouldn't be apologising, she began to speak to him in her mind. He isn't worth it. And you shouldn't be wasting time, doing stupid, touristy things, taking groups up mountainsides. The kayaking was a mistake, she told herself now. If we aren't to be happy together, what point is there in arranging these trips? She was thinking in English. What point for a man like Clive? Suddenly she understood that he must do something *serious*. That's why he has never married. He is preparing himself. Michela knew that Clive had lived with two or three other women before her. He couldn't marry because he must do something important. It's crazy for him to lead ungrateful people up a mountain, when they just want to hang around at the *rifugio* and flirt and sunbathe. He must do something that *changes the world*. Yes. Oh, but it made her so furious that he could break off their relationship, he could stop making love, just like that, before there was really any need, and that he could do it without missing her body at all, without any sense of loss. Why did I have to find a saint? she complained. I'm his last temptation. You're a saint, Clive. The voice in her head was louder now. So what are you waiting for? she demanded of him. It sounded like a scream. Whatever it is you have to do, do it!

They climbed slowly, in silence, but in her mind the noise is loud and angry. Why had he apologised? You have a cause, a goal, the voice insisted. She couldn't stop it. She doesn't want him to have doubts. Do something then! If we are not going to love again, at least let me be proud of you. Let me admire you. She stumbled. She put a hand down. How gritty and unrelenting the ground was. She felt dizzy. I haven't been sleeping enough. Above them the slope was a mass of ugly shards. Only far away did it make sense, the peaks ranged in line after line, quivering in the slow convection of the sunny afternoon. There are so many mountains, and so empty. Michela loves them for their emptiness. She loves the miniature look of distant villages in the valley bottom, the thin threads of plunging streams, this placing yourself far away in utter emptiness to look back and down on it all.

From way below came the clang of the cowbell: the beasts, the herd. Why had he humiliated himself like that? Why was he so knotted and tense and thwarted? Clive! She could have helped him. She wanted him to be free. When they stopped at a vantage point, she said out loud: I don't think I can get through the whole summer like this.

She was speaking to Clive, but quite loudly. She feels exhausted. I really can't, she said. The voice was matter-of-fact. It echoed in her head. The others didn't understand. Vince put it down to some momentary slip in English, some conversation he had missed. The climb had been long and steep. He is panting. The panorama was extraordinary. Drink? He offered her his bottle. But people were already moving again. As they walked, Vince was constantly aware of her girlish body swaying after Clive's, the man's powerful tread, her feminine lightness and flexibility. It was strange to be so attracted to a couple like this, to be so conscious of their bodies, of femininity and masculinity, their togetherness. He had seen the girl catching her man's eye. Were Gloria and I ever like that? He wanted to tell them that he approved. He imagined them twining together in love. His interest disturbs him. I approve of their loving and their politics, he thought. Two people cleaving to each other, and caring about the world too. You approve because your own life is so empty. But he did not feel unhappy this afternoon. Being near them, the taciturn man, the urgent girl, seemed to cheer him.

Then after only ten more minutes Amal asked for another stop. I'm getting a headache, he said. Pressure, Adam told him. At this point when I climbed it two years ago, we were already on the ice, Clive said. All around them, the ground was arid flint. Again Michela said out loud, I won't get through the whole summer like this.

103

Again no one responded. She said it in such a strangely detached way. Slim and tall against the sky, it was as if she wasn't quite among them. Or she is just complaining about the path. Look at this, Amal said. On a plaque nailed into the rock there was an oval photograph of a young woman's face. Vince went close to read. Katrin Hofstetter: 19.1.1979–31.8.1999. The face was bright and the woman's long blonde hair had been brushed forward to fall on her shoulder. Actually, that's about the fourth of those, Adam said. First woman though.

Eventually, they reached the snow and began to walk around the horseshoe of the ridge, so as to descend behind the hostelry. They were on top of the world here. Only far to the north, in Austria, were there taller peaks with larger glaciers. When the ice is gone, Clive explained to Vince, but he evidently wanted Adam to hear, you won't get that slow storage and release of water you get at the moment. It'll either be bone-dry, or, after it rains, you'll get great surges ripping down the slopes and flooding the valleys out. Obviously, the less snow there is, the more the temperature goes up and the more the glacier melts, so there's a built-in acceleration to it all.

Standing on the crusty grey ice, Vince turned to look in all directions at the phenomenon of the Alps. It was curious how something could be at once awesome and vulnerable. Your instinct was to shiver at the majesty, yet you were being told you had destroyed it. Amal asked if anything could actually be done. Only if the whole world changes its lifestyle, Clive remarked, and drastically. Then Adam said: A hawk, look. Apparently he has decided not to argue. Below them a large bird was slipping across the air-stream that rose from the valley. Same principle as a ferry-glide, the Indian boy said. See how he sets the angle and lets the wind squeeze him sideways. Standing right on the edge, where the ridge fell away into the valley beyond, Michela had taken Clive's hand. The couple stood together looking out over an ocean of empty air. The drop is dizzying. The hawk closed its wings and went down like a stone. Clive slipped an arm round her waist. How can I ever go back to the bank? Vince wondered.

Then Michela said: You must do something serious, Clive. She squeezed his hand hard. He turned and found her face flushed with the sun and the glare from the ice. Her eyes were melting in the bright light. Not just demonstrations, she told him. He was staring at her. They were standing on the edge. One forward step and they would be gone right out of things. Had he understood? We have to move, Clive announced. Or we'll be late. This is where the path turns down. Careful not to slip now.

Where are you taking us? someone shouted. Driving back to Sand in Taufers, the minibus had turned off the road down a dirt track. Suddenly the river was beside them, swirling through a deep gully. We're going to look at the get-out point for those of you who are on the trip tomorrow. Clive had his solemn, almost religious expression. When he speaks, Michela thought, it's as if he knew vastly more than anyone else could imagine. He hasn't told me anything.

The bank was steep but easy enough to get down. Basically, Clive pointed upstream, when you come under the bridge, there, where the road crosses, you have about two hundred yards more to paddle, and you're looking for the long flat spur on your right, here, below us. Everybody crowded round. Doddle, Phil said. As ever, he gave the impression of being let down. Yes, it's easy, Clive said. Oh, check out the marker someone's tied on the tree there. A few yards upstream, a long ribbon of orange plastic dangled from the drooping branch of a spruce. And now, Clive said, let me show you what would happen if by chance you fell asleep and drifted a few yards further down.

The dirt track turned abruptly away from the river and up the mountainside through stands of larch. Leaving it, they scrambled down a steep narrow path through brushwood and saplings. This was the gorge that made such a dramatic backdrop to the castle of Sand in Taufers as seen from the campsite. You can see why Long John Silver stuck to ocean-going craft, Brian complained. His club foot slipped. He had hurt himself. Max and Mark stayed to help. Vince grabbed a thin branch and leaned out over the water. Narrowing, the river tumbled rapidly in jumps of five, six and even ten feet, swirling between boulders and rushing against smooth walls of rock.

Clive stopped on a patch of mud and waited for the others to catch up. X-treme! Amelia breathed. They were looking down into a boil of water as the main stream went over a ledge to crash and froth around a huge dark rock just visible in a torment of backwash. This, Clive said, is grade five, verging on six. Give us the BCU definition, Amal. In his high-pitched voice, the boy sang: Only one line to follow, as with grade four – but harder to find and more technical to negotiate. Failure to follow line is seriously life-threatening. He seemed pleased with himself. Ambulance waiting at the bottom sort of thing, Louise said. Hearse more like it, Amelia added. Wicked! Phil approved. He was excited. Wally says this is nothing to Niagara, Max remarked. He was holding the bear to his ear, as if they were whispering together.

Mark stepped back. It's not do-able, though, is it? he asked. He looked worried. I mean, like, I don't see how anyone could get through that. They'd never try. Adam had been gazing with folded arms. Now he invited his son to come and stand beside him. He squatted down, pointed: Punch through the stopper to the right of the rock. There's just room, okay? You use the hole behind to brake and turn, but without falling into it. Then a determined ferry over to the far side, spin just before the bank and take the next drop where that tongue of water shoots through the debris down into the next pool.

They all considered this hair-raising manoeuvre. Vince tried to imagine the effect of gravity in the drops, the power of the water. Perhaps it was possible. Is this the hardest bit, then? Tom enquired. To look down with more safety, Amelia had put an arm round his strong waist. It was curious how she was both the gawky schoolgirl and the society snob. Louise, Vince thought, has a coarser, franker energy. Let's go and look, Michela said. She seemed to have cheered up. The sheer energy of the river was a source of pleasure.

They worked their way down a further hundred yards, scrabbling on stones and mud, occasionally pushing through the wet grass to the edge of the gully from which a soft spray drifted upward with the impact of water falling onto stone below. Immediately you looked down, the eye was captured by a kaleidoscopic shifting of dark-green and brown rock, white foam and blue transparent pools.

Fun to be had with the log there, Adam said. He was shaking his head. Life hath many exits, quoted Max. You just don't have to hit the bloody thing, do you, Phil said boldly. Hard to avoid, Amal thought. A thick tree trunk was wedged between boulders right below a pour-over. Unless you're mad enough to run river-left, that is. They were all relishing this contemplation of dangers they would never

107

undertake. The water boomed. Almost belligerently, Mark again demanded: But nobody's ever done it, have they? Sure they have, Clive replied. He had a smile on his face. There's almost nothing people haven't done. The boy wasn't satisfied. He pushed back the hair that fell on his eyes. But, like, someone you know, you've seen them?

I've done it, Clive said.

Wow! The announcement caused excited reaction. Michela looked at her man sharply. I mean Wow, wow, and triple wow! Louise said. When you went to visit your mother, Clive whispered quickly. Michela couldn't take it in. Why would he lie like this?

How many of you? Adam asked. The kids were all shaking their heads. Respect! Re-spect!

Two local guys, Clive said. From the rafting centre.

But you don't know any local guys, Michela thought.

In the Pyranha? Amal enquired. Wouldn't you need something with more volume?

And you fixed throw-lines and things? Adam asked.

No, no support on the bank, Clive said. They told me the line to follow and we went for it. River-left to avoid the log. The gap is just big enough.

You're mad, Mark declared.

I could do it, Phil said. Bet you I could do it, if someone would let me.

And you never capsized?

Everybody was looking at Clive's bearded face, the pioneer ponytail. She loves him, Vince thought again, catching Michela's gaze.

Sure I did. Three times, Clive said. See that rock there? Downstream of the pour-over, it's invisible as you approach. I came crashing over the ledge, see, and speared it. Bang on. Boat went vertical and I was down. Vince asked: How on earth did you come up? They were looking at a storming torrent of water plunging through boulders.

I've no idea, Clive told him.

The Slobs had cooked curry. Everybody had picked up a bit of colour in the afternoon sun up on the mountain. If you never eat what's on your plate, Mandy asked Phil, whence do you draw your sustenance, my boy? My what? Supply of Mars bars in his tent, Brian said. He must have about a hundred. Caroline kept setting off the hamster to general groans. It worries me to say, that I've never felt this way. Was that what you were saying to yourself, Max asked Mandy, when you were pinned underwater on the slalom course? The hamster never tired of his song. He beat his drum and waved his microphone. I was saying to myself, Mandy laughed: I think I love life, but this is what death is made of. Oh, it wasn't even a close shave, Keith protested. You could have taken a photo or two, under water. Wally had been ceremoniously handed over to Amelia, who had dropped a shoe coming down on the ski-lift. It's his fault, the girl cried, poking Tom. The young man grinned with embarrassment. She did it on purpose, Caroline scoffed, so's she'd have to lean on him, like, walking back to the car park. Slander! Amelia shrieked. She hung the red-scarfed little effigy round her neck and pushed it down inside her T-shirt between the small breasts. Let's see if anyone dares to steal it there! I consider that an invitation, Brian cried. Please, Adam said. Kids!

Keith was looking relaxed. Perhaps it was a relief not to have to paddle. Debrief, he shouted. Tomorrow's the last day. Some of you are going to run a very serious river, let's hear from the river leaders who the chosen victims will be. The others will be rerunning the stretch from the campsite down to Geiss and getting in some much-needed practice. After which we'll eat in a restaurant since it's the last night.

The last announcement caused much excitement. Shush everyone! Adam's got the list, Clive said quietly. We decided it together. Standing up by the door of the kitchen tent, Adam announced: First, I want to thank Amal, who has offered to play river leader for those who won't be going on the upper Aurino. Chicken! Phil yelled. He's scared! Shut up, idiot. So, if we can be serious a moment, folks, the participants will be – and Adam read: Clive, leader. Myself deputy. Then: Vince, Amelia, Michela, Max, Brian, Mark and Phil. Max, Brian and Phil will be assessed for their four-star paddler.

There was a surprised silence. Vince tried to catch his daughter's eye. It wasn't clear to him why she had been excluded. They were in the clearing between the tents. The girl had her head bent knotting a red scarf round her neck. What about me? Tom asked. I'm sorry, Adam said, but we can't take people who don't get their roll at least ninety per cent of the time. But I never turn over, Tom said. Keith cut in brightly. We have to accept the river leader's decisions. Mark's going and Tom isn't? Amelia protested. That's crazy. Clive said, Mark rolled up twice this morning in white water. If Tom doesn't go, then neither do I, Amelia said. Adjourn to the bar, Max was already shouting. Drinks! With Brian's foot still killing him, the lame boy had to lean on his friend as they made off between the guy-lines.

In their cabin, Michela was determined to get things straight. Why did you tell that story? Clive was cross-legged on his sleeping bag, rolling himself a cigarette. It wasn't a story. Want a smoke? You don't know anyone from the rafting centre. He admitted this was true. I went alone, he said. He tossed the tobacco to her. But I couldn't tell them that, because of all their strict rules. I mustn't seem irresponsible. Otherwise we'll have people like Phil chucking himself down there.

You're lying, she said. You just wanted to show off after making a fool of yourself in this thing with Adam. You're weird, she went on quickly. Really weird. It's not normal just to tell me we're not making love, then imagine we can go on as before. You're crazy sleeping on the floor. It's stupid. And I meant it today, you know, when I said I couldn't go on like this. I meant it.

Clive lit his cigarette. He seemed to be waiting until she had finished. The tobacco was damp and didn't draw well. I wasn't lying, Micky. He puffed. He seemed calm. Before Milan, remember when you went ahead to ask your mother if she could lend us something? That's when I did it. I ran it alone. Three times actually on three consecutive days. It's not that difficult. I did worse in New Zealand.

She stared at him. So why didn't you tell me?

He shrugged his shoulders. Why should I?

But this is even weirder. You go and do something completely suicidal and you don't even tell me. Her hands were shaking with the lighter. He used an old paraffin thing from at least twenty years ago.

It's suicidal to smoke, he said.

Yeah, I set myself alight and die. It's different, and you know it.

I didn't want you to worry about me, he said. You had worries enough with your mother. They gazed at each other across the cabin. The space was lit with a naked, 40-watt bulb. He was cross-legged, swaying slowly backward and forward, smiling softly. He seemed to have regained all the confidence, the slightly mystical impenetrability that had been threatened that evening with Adam. She was on the bed. It's clear she isn't a real smoker. She rolls cigarettes because she is with Clive. I go kayaking because I'm with Clive, she thought. She knew that. I say a thousand things Clive says. I share his opinions. Seeing the shake of her hand, she felt her closeness to her mother. It had been a disastrous visit. My hopeless, hopeless mother. I hope you understood, she finally asked, what I meant when I said you must do something serious. Did you? I think you owe it to me.

He seemed to relish the distance that had been established between them. Swaying, he pressed his lips firmly together. Yeah, I understood. He tapped the thin ash of the roll-up into his cupped hand. But I've been thinking the same thing myself, for years. Obviously, I have to do something serious.

So what are you going to do? Not just these stupid demonstrations. They do nothing. Or are you just going to start hitting idiots like Adam?

Why are you so aggressive? he asked.

If you don't understand that then you're really stupid!

The demonstrations are important, he said calmly. It's important the world is constantly reminded that there are people who care. You know that. Over the years I think they have a cumulative effect. More than people admit. But, I am thinking of something bigger.

Like what?

I'm working on it.

Like paddling down a grade-five river on your own and getting your spine smashed. You'll be a photograph on a wet rock. What good is that going to do anyone?

They stared at each other. There was a soft look in his eyes. Suddenly she feels sure that he loves her. Somehow this is worse. He loves her but it makes no difference. You said we would live together and have children. I believed you.

He held her gaze. I meant it, Micky, but this isn't the world for us. Leave be, now.

What world, then, she demanded. When will there be a world for us? This is the only one we've got.

Clive was silent.

She stood up and went to pull on her shoes by the door. You're weird, she said. I'm going to go out and fuck someone else. Okay?

He sat still, watching and smoking.

I said, okay?

Go.

She walked through the campsite. I've lost control now, she decided. Good. At least something would happen. Her mind was feverish. Everywhere there was barbecuing or the clatter of washing-up, or singing, the hum and rhythm of people at ease and pleased with themselves at the end of another day away from home. A curse on them! A young man and woman were arm in arm on the ground by a gas stove. Under her breath Michela began to mutter in Italian. *Maledizione! Siate maledetti e stramaledetti!*

The scene at the bar was the same as on all the other evenings: the second-rate band with their rhythm machine, the desultory karaoke. At a couple of tables pulled together, Adam and Vince and Mandy were sitting with Tom, Amelia, Caroline, Phil, Brian and Max. Overdoing the English accent, Michela asked, Anybody need topping up? What are you having? She stood behind them, wallet in hand. She has so little money. The kids clamoured for beers and Adam and Mandy tried to deter them. I told your parents no. Let's say you didn't see, Phil protested. You thought it was apple juice. We disobeyed you. Like, we're impossible, aren't we? Unmanageable.

The tall girl turned to the bar. Vince saw at once that she

113

was excited. Tom stood politely to help her. Michela slipped an arm around his and smiled straight into his eyes. At the bar she switched to Italian and ordered eight beers and a gin and tonic for Max. It was more than she had spent all week. Sounds lovely when you speak Italian, Tom told her. Again she smiled warmly. Want me to teach you a few words, Tommy? Hardly that much time now, he said stolidly. I'm not even going to be with you tomorrow, which is a bit of a bugger. The nights are long, she said coolly. She was purposeful. For a moment she put a hand round his waist. Tom seemed unable to respond. *Le notti*, she repeated, *sono lunghe*. Think you can repeat that? *Lunghissime*.

Back at the table the Italian girl squeezed in between Tom and Brian. Amelia was on Tom's other side. The children grabbed their beers. Adam was sending messages again. My wife, he explained. Text messages had been the bedridden woman's salvation. Is Clive not coming out this evening? Amelia enquired. The girl has smelt danger. Mandy was talking to Vince about her son's motorcycling obsession. Single parents should form a club, she said, for mutual support. Michela had downed her beer in a gulp. I don't know what Clive's up to. She looked dazed. Why? Amelia didn't reply. Phil and Caroline were sharing a cigarette. Hope it rains, the fat girl was giggling. She clearly has a problem with chapped lips. Oh not the mad bell-ringer again! Max laughed. Brian leaned across the table towards Amelia: You know you look like you've got three tits. He was referring to Wally. Except the one in the middle is the biggest! Phil shouted. He slapped a hand on the table and laughed. Shut up! Amelia was on the brink of tears. She was chewing a strand of hair. Michela now had a leg pressed against Tom's. Anyone could see.

Adam stood up and offered to go and fill Michela's glass.

As soon as he set off for the bar, Tom began to talk excitedly. Can anybody really understand why I'm not going tomorrow and Mark is? The young man has a pretty dimple in his chin, a square jaw, high cheekbones. He is handsome, virile and vulnerable. Because Adam's his dad, Phil said, puffing on his cigarette. Kids! Mandy intervened. The instructors know best on these matters. They can't take any risks. I'm not a kid, Tom protested. In his ear, Michela whispered, You can say that again. Vince saw her lips move. Her eyes are too shiny. Mark doesn't even want to go himself, Caroline remarked. He just does it for his dad. Actually, Tom, Max leaned across the table, the real reason for your exclusion is, Mandy's got the hots for you. She wants to have you all to herself tomorrow. Oh for God's sake, Max! Mandy was laughing. Then just as Adam returned with the beer, Amelia pushed back her chair. The girl was so abrupt it fell over. Without stopping to right it, she turned and hurried away across the empty dance area. What's wrong? Melly! Brian dragged himself up and began to hobble after her. Ow! He had to hop. Max got up after him. There was a vigorous flounce to Amelia's backside as she crossed the brightly lit space. Tom half stood. Michela put a hand on his arm. I'd better go and see what's going on, Mandy said.

In just a few confused moments, Vince found himself at the table with just Adam, Phil and Caroline. From the corner of an eye he was aware of Michela and Tom standing together on the far side of the dance floor where the bright light of the terrace and the dark of the field beyond seemed to fizz together. The band leader was introducing the next song with weary cheerfulness. What was all that in aid of? Adam asked. His phone beeped the arrival of another message. Vince was conscious of a desire to watch, to follow them even.

Amelia got upset, Caroline explained, because Brian said

something shitty about her being flat-chested. Adam frowned over his message. All the more beer for us! Phil cried. Theatrically surreptitious, he began to pour from Amelia's glass into his own and Caroline's. The girl had the coarse, hearty look of someone who couldn't be enjoying themselves more. I thought you were Amelia's best friend, Vince said. Speaking, he realised that these were almost the first words he had addressed to Caroline. So? the girl asked. I was just surprised to see the others rush away after her and you stay put. Her men! Caroline said archly. She doesn't need me. Brian's got a crush, Phil explained. Hopeless case.

Adam was shaking his head. Can't keep up with you youngsters, he complained. Vince asked if the message was serious. Adam began to explain that his wife tended to get a little hysterical when she knew they were going to run a difficult river. Why d'you tell her, then? Caroline demanded. Phil drained his own beer and reached for Brian's. I didn't, Mark did, Adam said. The idiot! He seemed to enjoy shaking his head at the perversity of the world. That was what was so great about Gloria, he turned suddenly, enthusiastically, to Vince. Like, nothing fazed her, you know, whatever river . . .

Now Vince pushed back his chair. Need a pee, he announced. He walked across the dance floor and around behind the bar, very conscious of the slight unsteadiness that three beers can bring on. I won't sleep well tonight, he knew. I must be on form for tomorrow. Instead of going into the loo, he crossed the track beyond the entrance to the site and walked into the pine trees beyond. This is where they must have come.

The ground sloped steeply down towards the river bank. The trees were scrawnier here, but closer together. Vince stopped. The cushion of pine needles beneath his feet created an impression of silence, though he could still hear the beat of music from the bar. It was as though the distant sound actually increased the silence in the wood. When the path became too dark to follow he stopped and listened. I am completely disorientated. He stood still. The drink made him sway. This week has rubbed out my ordinary life. It was amazing how dark it could be, black even, and so near to where he had been in bright light and company. It has rubbed out the pain, but all the things that made sense too. Gloria was never fazed, Adam said.

Vince breathed deeply. What a powerful smell there was, of freshly cut wood and dung and smoke. He took a step, caught his foot, lurched. Even staying vertical is a hard thing when the darkness is so complete. Then he heard a little cry and a giggle. Vince was electrified. They *had* come here. But why did I follow? What do these shenanigans mean to you? He was swaying on his feet. He didn't know which way to tread. A fifty-year-old widower with a big job in the City? Should I tell Clive? Now there was a sharp intake of breath, followed at once by a quiet whimper, and this time a boy's laugh. I'm so, so sorry. Get out of here! Vince began to move. He stumbled. Gloria was never fazed. Which was the way back? Twigs cracked. Shit! In a second's stillness he was aware of low voices. Then someone else was banging through the undergrowth. It's a dream. The noise was so loud. I must go the other way. Just as he turned, a bright light flashed up from very low. He was on the edge of a steep bank. The torchlight swung towards him through the trees. There was a cry. Vince ran away from it, up the slope.

Back in the tent he went through his bedtime routine with great deliberation. The branches had scratched the back of his hand, the side of his neck. Don't think anything, he kept repeating, don't think till your mind is calm. He slipped off his socks and put them in his shoes under the fly-sheet. But now there were rapid footsteps. Dad! No sooner had he stretched out on his sleeping bag than a torch shone in. Louise dived into the tent. Dad, weirdest thing happened. Just now. God! She plunged on her stomach. Turn that thing off, he complained. You're blinding me. Really frightening! Tell me. Vince began to pay attention. Are you okay? I was with Mark, you know. I guessed, Vince said. Oh, he's all right. We were just kissing a bit, in the trees behind the bar. The other side of the track where it goes down to the river. Kissing? Oh, nothing heavy, Dad, come on! When this pervert comes along trying to spy on us. Really! Like, he was only a yard or two away. I mean, he could have been a serial killer or something. It was like a horror movie. I pretty well wet myself.

Vince lay back on his sleeping bag. Did you see him? Mark did. He turned on the torch and made a dash, saw the bloke running away. Some old guy. Anorak type. Wasn't it a bit dark, Vince asked, to be fooling around in the woods? He knew what he had heard there. No, there's plenty of light when you get used to it, she said. Oh God, the phone, she announced then. The torch came on again and in the glow Vince watched his daughter's face as she rummaged in her rucksack. There was a healthy blush on her cheeks. Strands of blonde hair fell over her eyes. Where did I hide the damn thing? There. Sure enough, just a few moments after she turned it on there came the beep of a message arriving, followed by a low giggle, the sound of a thumb on the keypad. Vince said: You have a boyfriend back home, don't you? That's what all these messages are about.

None of your business, she laughed. Then she said. Course I've got a boyfriend. What do you think?

Only that you're two-timing him, obviously.

What a funny expression.

I don't know what the current word is.

And so?

Well, it's not altogether nice, is it?

Altogether?

It's not nice.

I'm enjoying it.

Louise, I'm trying to talk seriously for once! By the way, your clothes smell of cigarettes.

He'll never know, she said.

And Mark?

I told him.

And he doesn't mind?

Dad, it's a *holiday*! Everybody does this on holiday. It's what they're for. And even if you don't, everybody imagines you do.

I thought it was a community experience.

She giggled. More like an orgy sometimes. But I mean, Phil and Caroline, Amelia and Tom, it'll all be over when they're home. You can't believe Tom doesn't have a girl-friend, can you? At college. A fab-looking bloke like that.

Was it you smoking or Mark?

She said, Mark.

I'll try to believe you.

She leaned over and kissed him. You're a treasure, Dad. Then he knew she had been smoking. Do your teeth, he said.

When she came back from the bathroom, he asked:

And what if I did the same thing?

How do you mean?

Went kissing in the woods.

Dad!

Because we're on holiday.

But you wouldn't, would you?

He didn't answer this. She was right, he wouldn't. The air quickly grew warm in the tent when the two of them were together. The smoke on her sweater gave it a stale smell. They were so near each other inside here, father and daughter, and outside there was so much space and air, a tinkle of distant voices, occasional footsteps across the breezy dark in the flat of the valley beneath the mountains towering in their emptiness, trickling with the water that tomorrow would rush them down the river. Go to sleep, Vince told himself, you need sleep.

Then she began to giggle again. Who with anyway? Mandy?

What?

You kissing in the woods.

Mandy? Vince was surprised. Actually, I got the feeling that Mandy had something going with Keith. Don't they?

Oh that was yonks back, Louise objected. I remember Mum telling me. It's been over at least two years. She's been following you all over the place. She even got you to rescue her!

Oh come on. You don't get yourself nearly killed just to have me bang into your boat.

Don't underestimate a woman! Louise cried. The girl was full of confidence.

Vince thought about this. Mum came on a lot of these holidays, didn't she? he asked. And you went with her on that one in France. Right. That Ardèche thing. How was she?

What do you mean?

Vince was conscious that this was their longest conversation for months, if not years. There was a different kind of intimacy in the air. As if between equals.

I don't know. Adam was saying how Mum was never fazed. I wondered what he meant. He seems to have liked her a lot.

After a short silence, Louise sighed: Mum was like, the soul of the party. She was everywhere. On the Ardèche she organised this really nutty midnight descent of the river with candles and everything and we were supposed to be Indians. We wore headbands and feathers. But that was open canoes, she added. The water was easy.

I'm afraid, Vince said, that I don't find Mandy very attractive.

For some reason the two of them began to laugh. His daughter turned towards him and reached out. You're so predictable, Dad! Then she said, You're hand's bleeding. Just a scratch, he said. He drew back. Against a tree on that path by the rapids. And he went on: You like living at Uncle Jasper's, don't you?

It's okay, the girl said.

He didn't pursue it.

And you really don't mind not going on the big trip tomorrow?

Dad, I *asked* not to go. I get scared when it's too wild.

This surprised him. You seem so sure of yourself. Don't you want the challenge?

No. She was frank. She laughed. I don't need challenges like that. I don't want cuts and bruises. Mark's wetting himself. He doesn't really want to go either, except to show his dad. Then she added: You'll enjoy it though.

If I don't kill myself, Vince said.

In a few moments the girl was asleep. Vince couldn't. He lay on his back, trying not to wake her by moving too much. How quickly he had swung from near panic to an easy chat about difficult things. He couldn't remember a moment when he had felt less in control of his life, more subject to the flow of volatile emotions. Now there was just tomorrow's river run, then Sunday the drive home, and Monday he would be back in the bank: the busy bright foyer, the lift, the fourth floor, the coffee machine, fluorescent lighting, e-mails, meetings, phone-calls. Before the week was out, they would begin final preparation of the balance sheets. He would be anchored again, not by the breathing of someone beside him in the dark of the tent, but by the exhausting routine. The world would close in. August was the moment to finalise the foreign accounts. There would be pressure to present things other than as they were. And even if you don't, he heard his daughter's laugh, everybody imagines you do. Cheat. But actually Vince didn't. He never has. I never fudged a single figure. My career, he knew, has been based more on absolute probity and solid common sense than any genius. You'll never get rich, Gloria would tease. He can hear her voice. But we *are* rich compared with most others, he told her. She said she loved him for this. There was a condescending note. Vincent Marshall, incapable of guile, she laughed. But we *are* rich, Gloria, he insisted. The top five per cent. Isn't that enough? You don't have to stay at the hospital, you know, he always told her, if you don't want to.

Suddenly Vince was back in a particular weekend, in the rather empty comfort of their sitting room. Again, Gloria had been telling him he must take up a sport. They were speaking across the polished dinner table. It was stressful, she said – she'd just finished a week of nights in Intensive Care – to watch people dying all the time. That's why she needed to do so many physical things. You don't have to work, he told her. You could be a woman of leisure. Me? She had laughed. She put a hand on his: Come on, come down to the club tomorrow. Why don't you? You'll feel better if you get your blood moving. How can they? she asked a little later when there was some documentary on aid workers in the Third World. The television showed a boy picking maggots from his scalp. They were sitting together on the sofa, but without touching. About half our bad loans are to Third World countries, Vince remembered now. He lay in the tent listening to his daughter's breathing. How pleased with herself the girl was, to have kissed one boy while texting another. She felt alive. Then at last a real question presented itself: When was the last time Gloria and I made love together?

Vince sat up, slipped out of his sleeping bag, unzipped the tent, set off for the bathroom. I'm better integrated with the photo-electric cells of the toilet-flushing system than I was with my wife. Coming back he could see the light in their chalet was on. There are eight chalets arranged either side of a central track. Vince stopped. A blind had been pulled down but there were chinks shining through. Theirs was the last in the near row. What had happened this evening, he wondered, with Michela? With Tom? It was strange.

He checked his watch, turned left into the track between the chalets, skirted round the last building at the end. The window on the far side showed chinks of light too. None of your business, Dad, Louise said. What is my business? Vince asked. I was away week in week out doing my business, in London, then home Saturday and Sunday and Gloria obsessed by the idea I must be stressed, I must take up a sport. What was it all about? Cautiously, Vince took a step or two beyond the track towards the chalet. I am a widower with a job that makes me co-responsible, with others, for the management of billions of pounds. Gloria betrayed me, Vince decided. My daughter hardly recognises my authority. I can't tell her anything about smoking or sex. Continents away, people die like flies, as a result of our carelessness, perhaps. Or our prudent decisions, our need to balance books. It's none of your business. Vince stood in the dark on the edge of the campsite. I'm just a man, he suddenly thought. For some reason the words were reassuring.

In the safety of the shadow on the further side of the chalet he approached the window. The room is empty, he saw. Where are they? He frowned, then something moved and he realised there was a figure on the floor. Stretched out on a blue sleeping bag, wearing a pair of glasses hung round his neck on a string, Clive was studying a stack of papers in a folder. Invoices perhaps. Why wasn't he on the bed? Vince watched. Clive was underlining things, circling figures. He turned back and forth among the papers, handsome forehead frowning. It was odd.

Then the bearded face looked up, alert. The sound of footsteps set Vince's heart racing. He crouched low. Someone is coming along the track, walking quickly. The door squeaked. He didn't dare stand up yet. A pervert, Louise protested. An anorak type. Yet Vince felt sure it was his business. He heard their voices, low, flat, couldn't make out their words. He listened. They weren't arguing, but there was no warmth either. It is my business. For years I paid no attention. I let things slide. I was an excellent bank director. He waited a little longer then stood. Clive had rolled on his stomach, head sideways on a pillow of folded clothes. For just a second Michela crossed Vince's line of vision. She is naked. Her hand stretched out and the light was gone. He saw a pale blur re-cross the cabin and stretch out on the bed.

I thought they were lovers, Vince repeated to himself as he hurried back to the tent. You are a fool! You understand nothing. Gloria never walked around naked. She always put on her nightdress before removing bra and pants. I paid no attention to her. She was never fazed. Perhaps Adam honestly only meant: by river trips. She wasn't fazed by rapids and pour-overs. I saw the girl's sex, he thought. Perhaps Gloria honestly only meant, she needed her sports if she was to watch people dying every day, if she was to look after the invalid wives of canoe-club friends. Why had she stopped the Saturday outings, then, as soon as he started?

Poor Gloria! Stretching out beside his daughter again, Vince prepared himself for a night of insomnia. His muscles are aching after all these days on the water. This churn of thought, he sensed, the evening's sounds and images, they wouldn't release him. Suddenly to know you are dying like that! he remembered, to feel your body changing, you're head filling with blood. She had rushed to the phone. She had apologised. I'm so, so sorry, Vince. He listened to the words again and again. The minutes passed. Perhaps she had only meant: I'm sorry I'm dying. He let the thoughts flow on. Let them flow. I won't fight them. She hadn't meant that. I don't feel unhappy, he decided. He had seen the girl's lithe body, her dark sex. It's strange. He didn't feel depressed or guilty at all.

LIKE GODS

I know this will sound a bit weirdy-beardy, Clive said, but I want you all to close your eyes for a minute, okay? Close them Phil. Moment's sheer silence. You're all kitted up, right, you're in your boats, nice and tight, okay? You've got your hands on your paddles. Good. Now, take three or four long slow breaths, in and out. No, really slow. Fill your lungs and empty them. Mark? Slowly. And again. Okay. And while you're doing that, I want you to remember the last time you did something really cool in your kayak, something you're really proud of. Maybe it was the perfect tail squirt. Okay? You went vertical without capsizing. Or maybe you were surfing a busy wave, right on the crest, or you rolled up perfectly in a stopper. Some moment when you and the water seemed to go together like old friends. You were helping each other. The paddle was like a wand. Remember? Picture it. Keep breathing deeply, eyes closed, and picture that moment. Got it? The sheer magic, the well-being, you and the water. It was great. Right, now, on the count of three, I want every-one to say out loud, no, I want you to shout out loud: TODAY I'M GOING TO PADDLE LIKE A GOD! Okay?

Then we'll open our eyes and we're away. Ready? But I want you to really belt it out, okay? Psyche yourselves up. Even Adam who hates this mystical stuff, he's going to say it. Right Adam? Okay, on the count of three. One Two Three . . .

They were lined up on the bank. It had begun to rain, hard. The high plateau was flat here and the river seemed tame enough. I'm going to paddle like a god! they shouted. And again! Go for it! *I'm going to paddle like a god!* Great, now, everybody launch and eddy out river-right below the bend. Did I hear, like a clod? Max asked. Like a sod! Brian giggled. Your buoyancy aid's not buckled, Adam muttered to his son. Buckle it.

Michela didn't shout with the others. She hadn't eaten breakfast. Enjoy yourself, Keith had told Vince by the kitchen tent. Remember, the leader said, the key to survival is to be totally alert and totally relaxed at the same time. The Louts were cooking bacon sandwiches. The Slobs prepared the packed lunches. Food in the boat today, guys! And never fight the water, the leader confided. Which is funny, I know, coming from a guy with his arm in a sling. But the moment you're fighting it, you can guarantee you've lost.

Eat for energy everybody! Mandy shouted. The bacon smell was overpowering. Vince ate, but then felt sick. Shut that hamster up! Adam yelled. The tall chinless man went round with a cardboard box full of wine gums and jelly babies. Instant glucose, he promised. At least six packets in every boat. Believe me, you really don't have to worry, the hamster sang. Mandy came to eat her bacon next to Vince, but now he had to get up for the first of his pre-trip craps. You're going to have a great day, she told him. When they left, Tom still hadn't appeared from his tent.

The minibus led the way pulling the trailer, while Vince drove behind in his car to run the shuttle. Entering the gorge, Adam asked Clive if there weren't any places they should get out and scout on the way up, what with all the rain there'd been. The decision to include his son seemed to have settled the quarrel between the two men. They were both intent on the job. Can't from the road, Clive said. We have to scout as we paddle down. Practise for the four-stars.

In fact, almost immediately above Sand in Taufers the road left the river to climb and wind spectacularly over the valley. Jesus, Mark whispered. Clive drove surprisingly fast beside drops of hundreds of feet. Jesus Christ! It was a landscape both massive and crumbling. From the seat behind, Brian plunged his hand down Amelia's T-shirt to grab Wally. Not funny, she said. The boy couldn't get the string over her head. You're *hurting*! It had tangled in her hair. Her eyes were red. The minibus attacked another hairpin. Belts everybody! Adam shouted. Brian!

I hope I can keep my breakfast down, Vince was saying in the car behind. To his pleased surprise, just as the two vehicles were setting off, Michela had climbed out of the minibus and come over to his car. In case you get lost, she explained. Now she smiled, but without opening her eyes. She had her head back on the headrest. The nerves will go as soon as you are on the water. After a pause, she added: When you speak someone else's language, you are always repeating what someone else has said. Vince was eager to please, but couldn't understand. Her eyes still shut, the girl seemed to be elsewhere. What's repeating on me is the bacon, he said. In front, the minibus had dived down a steep track towards the river.

After the kayaks had been lifted off the trailer, and everybody had changed and put their dry clothes back in the bus, Vince and Clive had to run the shuttle: that is, to drive both vehicles back down to the get-out point, then return in the car, so that minibus and trailer would be waiting at the bottom when the group arrived, tired and perhaps cold, in the late afternoon. So forty minutes later Vince would again be fighting his nausea as he drove up the steep road a second time, now with Clive beside him. The rain had begun to fall. Large sections of the landscape grew grey and insubstantial.

Any demonstrations planned? Vince asked. Talk of the river would only make him more nervous. There was the international heads of government summit on global warming in Berlin next week, Clive said. He drummed his fingers on the dashboard. And you're going? Sure. With Michela? A bunch of people they knew, Clive explained, would be there to picket. We're in touch through the net all the time. The cheap flights make it easier.

Then Vince said that, leaving aside the clash with Adam, he admired Clive for his commitment. Why do I keep telling them this? he wondered. He was thinking of the man lying on the wooden floor of the chalet with his reading glasses and stacks of photocopies while the pretty young woman stretched naked on the bed. He wanted to understand. So often, he started to say, people can see that a cause is right, you know, but it seems impossible actually to do anything about it. They were stuck now behind a tractor pulling a trailer loaded with logs. Like, up on the glacier, you were saying how all together we've managed to destroy it, without even really trying, but individually we feel powerless to reverse the process, our lives are so set. Clive leaned forward and stared into the rain. He wore a peaked cap on his long, tawny hair. This is one hell of a river, he said quietly. Let's enjoy it. About twenty minutes later Vince got into his boat, secured the spray-deck and shouted: *Today I'm going to paddle like a god*! He didn't even notice the nerves had gone.

Four-star assessment! Clive shouted. Rescues. Time out, guys. They had run about two kilometres of hectic river. The plateau ended in a narrow race of water bouncing through stones, eroding its way into the gorge. Vince's right shoulder ached from the wrench it had taken yesterday pulling Mandy's boat off the rock. All in all, though, the old body was holding up surprisingly well. Gloria would be proud, he thought. He'd learned so much so quickly. Up front, Michela paddled mechanically in Clive's wake. The boys darted all over the place, crashing over rocks into stoppers. Wild, but manageable, Adam remarked, banging into Brian's boat when they eddied out. We need volunteers, Clive said. Three swimmers to be rescued by our three four-star candidates. All you have to do is jump into the stream from the bank. Nothing dangerous here. The rescuers will throw you a line from the bank and haul you in. Important technique, kids, because we'll probably need to do it in anger at least once today when things get trickier.

I'm on. Adam volunteered. He obviously enjoyed this registration of measurable achievement, the business of stars and certificates. Mark? he asked. Cold, the boy muttered. He was slouched in his boat. I'll do it, Vince said. He beached and pulled his deck. Michela seemed hardly to notice what was going on. She didn't offer to help. Amelia announced: Since I feel suicidal anyway, I may as bloody well. She climbed out of her boat. Clive picked up the sour catch in her voice. What's the matter? The girl exploded: Don't ask me what the fucking matter is, ask her! Without actually turning, she gestured in Michela's direction. The young woman was arching right back in her cockpit so that her helmet rested on the deck behind her. The rain fell on her smooth cheeks and closed eyes, the boat turned slowly in the eddy.

Ask your *friend*! Amelia repeated. Then she said brutally: Are you bloody blind or what? The girl was on the brink of tears. Michela appeared not to have heard. Phil was watching with a twisted grin. Vince wondered if Clive had understood. He seemed puzzled. Come on, kids, he said determinedly, sheer concentration now. Where do you want me to jump from? Adam asked. Hobbling along the bank downstream, Brian called: I'll rescue you, Melly. Count on me. Under a blue helmet, the boy's round freckled face and chapped lips made him seem no more than ten years old. Don't call me that, she snapped.

They jumped from the spur above the eddy. The rescuers had a good fifty yards to save them before anything serious could happen. It was a question of tossing a nylon throw-bag stuffed with rope, while holding the loose end of the line. Always throw just behind and beyond the swimmer, Clive explained. The rope floats faster than a body and naturally swings round to the bank you're on.

Vince leaped into the swirl. To his surprise his feet hit the bottom hard, jarring his hips – there must be a ledge – then the current took him. Even in full kit, the body felt the shock of the cold. He assumed the textbook position, on his back, feet downstream to meet any obstacles. There was a sudden acceleration as the water rushed round the spur. Now, now, now, his mind sang. He is in it. Now is always the important moment. This water, in this part of the river. Now! Max shouted. The bag fell perfectly, so that the yellow rope unravelled across the water just half a yard behind. Vince had it. Feet braced against a rock, the fifteen-year-old hauled him to the bank. Easiest fishing ever, he joked. His thin arms were strong and sure. Impressive, Vince told him.

Phil then pulled out Adam with similar ease. But Amelia wasn't concentrating. She swirled round the spur, lifted an arm for the line, floundered after it, seemed to have it, then lost it. Brian, who had sat down after throwing, the better to brace his lame foot, now stood to shout instructions. He limped and hopped over the boulders along the bank. The girl was sliding past. When she finally grabbed the rope it was with such a tug that the boy lost his balance and crashed forward into the water. Clive scrambled down the bank and got hold of him.

Who's the fucking wally now! the girl hissed as she got a foothold on the stones. Brian was nursing his ankle. He was in pain. Amelia relented. Not your fault. At the top of the bank, she turned to Michela: I hate you! she screamed. She took off her helmet and shook the water from her black hair. I fucking hate you!

Waiting quietly in her boat beside Mark, the Italian girl looked bewildered. Vince saw it. She doesn't understand. Better than a seat at the opera, Max quipped. Amelia hit the boy hard. Idiot! But now she had hurt her hand on the buckle of his buoyancy aid. Shivering and shouting, she began to cry.

Amelia! Adam said. Kids! His voice took on a pained authority. Enough. Come on now. Putting an arm round the girl's shoulders, he turned her away from the others and spoke quickly and quietly. Vince thought he heard the words, your mother. Clive was still at the water's edge, squatting beside Brian, holding the boy's bad ankle in both hands, gently flexing the joint. Back in your boats, Adam eventually called. Let's hammer on down.

Only days later would Vince have time to reflect that the following hour and a half had been one of the happiest of his life. Never had his mind thought so intensely and lucidly, never had thinking been so dissolved and extended into every part of his body – shoulders, spine, wrists, hips, feet – the way sky and mountainside, as they pushed off from the bank, were dissolving now into driving rain and all the world pouring into the river where the kayakers were no longer eight individuals picking their separate ways through a wide flow, but a closely knit team signalling each other forward along the only line possible, every paddler constantly watching two others, protected by two others watching him.

These are more serious rapids now, Clive warned. He gave orders. Sometimes they leap-frogged from eddy to eddy. Or Clive got out on the bank with Phil or Max to scout ahead, to check there was no debris, to choose a line. Then the four-stars went with him and Clive placed one boy behind a rock at some tricky point to signal the way to the others as they passed and one at the end of the rapid on the bank with a throw-bag ready for possible swimmers.

Rafted together in an eddy upstream of these perils, the others looked for a paddle blade to appear above the horizon line where the river began its plunge. There! Adam saw it. Okay, Amelia, go! Wait. Okay, Mark, go! Even Michela seems to have been drawn in to the urgency of it. She woke up. She made the signals, became part of the group. She poured a pack of candies into her mouth for energy. Now, Vince, go! And stay relaxed!

Vince's eye read the water intensely, the snags, the pull of something beneath the surface, the turbulence of a broken eddy-line, the bright rippling that marks a sudden shallow. And his muscles reacted immediately to what the eye saw and the brain interpreted, planting the paddle left and right, his whole body wired and attentive for those hazards the eye had missed: the pull of a hole, the smack of a wave, a sudden swirling round to the left against a rock wall that is dangerously undercut. Stopper! It was Clive's voice. Paddle! Pad-dle!

Phil was on the bank beyond with a line. A great curve of water arched down before him into the boil. Vince crashed through. How different, his mind was singing as he waited

133

in the calmer water for the others, how different from the knowledge of the financial institution, from discrete units of measure to be added and subtracted, the mind racing but the body only a burden in its frustrated inertia. To everyone's delight, it was Adam who was first to swim. He pulled out, trapped in a hole. Max tossed him a line. The man didn't seem upset. Wipe that grin off your face, he laughed to his son. Shit happens.

Should they stop for lunch? This was the place Clive had chosen, a small clearing on the left bank where a stream plunged in. But Adam was worried that the river had started to rise. And with this rain still teeming down it's getting muddier every minute, he pointed out. Clive reflected. The kids needed a break, he decided. We're tired. Also, there was a waterfall to see here. Something they really shouldn't miss. Stretch our legs. Afterwards they would still have a couple of hours jammed in the boats.

Everybody had replaced one of the two buoyancy bags behind the kayak's seat with a dry-bag full of food and drink. Clive had no buoyancy at all, only every conceivable item of tackle crammed into the stern of the boat. Time for the Kiss You! he announced. I beg your pardon, sir. The what? Unpacking a bag no bigger than a stuffed coat pocket, the instructor produced a large cylinder of some thin nylon fabric perhaps four yards long by two in diameter. K-I-S-U, Adam explained. Don't build up your hopes, kids. Karimore Instructor Survival Unit. As the cylinder flapped open, the wind snatched at the edges and the rain streamed on its waxy surface. Bundle in, Clive ordered. He spread it on the flattest patch he could find. The ground was coarse sand, shale and pine cones. Everybody in!

As soon as you were out of your boat, the body began to chill. Their wetsuits steamed. Mark's teeth are chattering.

My feet are numb, Amelia wailed. But inside this nylon cylinder, they immediately began to warm up. Clive arranged them sitting down in two lines of three, facing each other. At the ends, he and Adam pulled the material closed round their shoulders. Now they were in a strange blue space, breathy and damp, with the fabric held up only by their bent heads as they ate their sandwiches. First to fart gets lynched, Phil threatened. Where's me air-freshener, Max quipped. The neoprene of their kit was rank. Don't you think they could sell wetsuits with more attractive fragrances? But Vince was startled by the sudden intimacy of it. Six faces were less than a foot from each other as they chewed, eyes constantly meeting, knees pressed against and between each other.

A steady breeze nagged at the fabric where it was loose, and where it was tight the rain pattered sharply. Michela had ended up opposite Amelia. All morning her face had been blank. Now, forced into contact, she leaned forward a little so that their foreheads were almost touching. I didn't think, Michela said. Honestly. She spoke softly. I'm so sorry.

Amelia looked down. Sitting beside her, Vince heard and held his breath. I'm so sorry, his mind echoed. Amelia rummaged in her dry-bag, found another sandwich. Guys, she announced suddenly, Wally says someone here has got really foul breath. She shook her hair. Isn't that right Wally? The protecting bear was tied on a loop in her cag. She kissed it on the nose. And he hopes it isn't Adam, since that's who's going to be looking after him tomorrow. Dead right! Mark crowed. Instructor level two fails to roll up in simple hole. What a wally! Max was shaking his head: When boys are men, the men will be boys. All in a day's chaos, Adam smiled. Actually I was just testing the rescuers. There were loud

135

groans. Everyone's doing brilliantly, Clive told them. Sheer genius. Like gods.

Vince chewed his food. Michela had said those same words, but instead of plunging him into misery and isolation, it was as if the phrase had been exorcised on her earnest young lips, dissolved into the warm steamy atmosphere of a new family. So sorry. Amelia hadn't acknowledged or rejected the apology. Vince turned to see if Adam had noticed, but the man was laughing with his son at his own misadventure. They were all curiously one, in the damp, blue air, in the suffocating intimacy of the KISU. Then there was a rude shout, right beside his ear. From outside. A hand grasped the fabric and shook it. A drunken voice.

Adam released the edges he was holding, rolled backwards. Excuse me? In a moment they were all fighting their way out of the flapping cloth. Vince recognised the man he had seen that first day at his shack by the river. He held an old fishing rod, a battered bag, a bottle. He was shouting, shaking his head, turning to point theatrically down the river. He bent down and spread out his arms and moved them outwards as if touching something low and long.

Leave us alone, you're drunk. Adam was abrupt and sharp. Hang on, Clive said. Listen, he asked, speaking slowly to the man. Want some food? Eat? He had his lunchbox in his hand. The man stank of spirits. He started shouting again. His eyes were mad. Max understands German, Vince said. Everybody is shivering. The bloke's drunk, Adam insisted. Come on, then, Max. But the man's voice was slurred, he was shouting and yelling in dialect. The only thing I can get is *gefährlich*; the blonde boy shook his head. Ge-what? Phil asked. We know it's *gefährlich*, Clive said patiently. The man knocked the sandwich out of his hand. He seemed angry. He stared at them all, gesticulating at the sky, along the river.

His movements were jerky and unnatural. He says the river's dangerous today, Michela said. But the visitor had already turned and was picking his way along the bank downstream, his body bowed, jerky but oddly agile.

Clive watched him go. We've got about fifteen minutes to visit the waterfall, then we'd better get moving. You could see from the mud in the water, he said, that the river was coming up fast. Are you sure there's time? Adam worried. This is an important experience, Clive repeated. Quite a find. You'll need your helmets, Michela warned. Brian said he couldn't walk. His foot was hurting. I'll stay with him, Amelia offered. Oh Kiss You! Max shouted as the two pulled the makeshift tent around them. Hope the old pervert doesn't come back, or you're dead meat.

The little group climbed steeply for about two hundred yards among tall trunks, their knuckly roots fastened into the rock. Everything was twisted, crushed, flaking, leaning, broken, sharp. Everything dripped and drizzled. Phil began to throw pine cones. What did that word mean, ge-what-sit? It means absolutely-fucking-terrifying, Max lied in his poshest voice. I wish, Phil sighed. Don't worry, he said the same to me, first day, Vince remembered. I think he has trouble imagining there are people who can't speak his language. Or people mad enough to kayak, Mark muttered. A cone bounced on his helmet. Then they met the stream tumbling down and saw the waterfall about fifty yards ahead where the slope ended abruptly against a wall of rock. I've seen bigger, Adam remarked. The water poured down steadily in a broad sheet. Wait, Clive said.

They had to scramble up in the stream itself now. The rocks are slippery, but they have their wetsuits on and rubber shoes. Use your hands, folks! Clive had to shout over the noise. Can't afford any injuries now. Sometimes a leg sank in up to the thigh. It was definitely colder than the river. Oh my poor bollocks! Phil sang. Look at this! Max had found something jammed between two stones: a sheep's skull. Attractive fellow, Adam said. Friend of Wally's no doubt, Max declared. Pioneer of canyoning! He threw the thing at Phil, who dodged to let it rush off in the stream. Vince offered Michela his hand as she jumped from one boulder to another. She refused it.

At the top, at the foot of the rock wall, the falling water had hollowed out a pool about fifteen feet across. Clive waded round and climbed out on a narrow ledge just to the left of the fall. Instead of the rain, a fierce icy spray blew into their faces here. A strong breeze was rushing down with the water. The roar was so loud they had to put their heads together to talk. Adam — Clive challenged the man — why don't you walk across and see what's behind. Walk under the water? That's what I said. You're joking, Adam told him.

It was difficult to say from close up, with the spray stinging their eyes and the trees dripping gloomily all around, how high the waterfall might be. Forty feet perhaps. That's why I said to bring helmets, Clive explained. There was a deep chill in the air. I thought it was for the pine cones, Max laughed. But how do I know the water's not too deep? Trust me, Clive told him. Glistening with bright drops, his bearded face suggested both prophet and explorer. There was a glint in his eye. He looks older than he is, Vince thought. Mark was watching his father. Go on, Clive yelled. I'll give it a whirl, Phil offered.

Adam immediately stepped into the water. His leg sank to the knee, then the thigh. The water crashed on his helmet. Leaning forward, his hands supported on the rock behind the fall, he edged along with nervous slowness. There was no regulation way of doing things now. The waterfall is perhaps twelve feet across. The man had reached the middle when suddenly he stumbled forward through the curtain of white spray and disappeared. Jesus! Mark breathed. For about thirty seconds there was no sign of him – Don't worry, Clive laughed – then Adam reappeared further along and began to climb out from the water. From the opposite bank he turned and shouted something, held up a thumb. Now you, Clive told Phil, and try to enjoy it more than he did.

One by one the group inched along the ledge, then, with nowhere to stand on the far side, people began scrambling back down the slope to the boats. Vince was second to last with only Michela behind. As he stepped into the falling water, he was astonished by the force of its downward thrust beating on his helmet. His neck tensed to resist. Nobody said I wouldn't be able to breathe. The air was all water. His eyes are blind, ears full of sound, cheeks stinging with cold. His hands advanced, pressing numbly on the slippery rock behind the fall. Then, as he imagined, the resistance suddenly disappeared. There was no wall. He stumbled forward through the heavy water and stood, thigh-deep, in a space that might have been the size of a tall wardrobe. So little light filtered through, it was impossible to make out what was above him. Vince stood there breathing deeply.

Why didn't he just hurry on then, as the others had? Was it guile? Suddenly, it seemed essential that he should have come here, that he should know this cold, roaring place, at the heart of everything, he thought, but dark and hidden. It's important that there are places like this. He couldn't think why. But he knew the Italian girl would be coming. Any moment. He waited, breathing the saturated air. Sure enough, she suddenly blundered forward through the water and against him. He could just make out her pale face as she yelled something inches away. What was it? He couldn't hear. He started to edge out, but she is holding an arm. He turned to her. She pulled him against her. Her hands had fastened tight on his jacket. Their cold wet faces are together now. Still she was yelling something. The water thundered. He shouted: I'm crazy about you. Absolutely crazy! He was shouting at the top of his voice knowing she couldn't hear. I do nothing but watch you. She shook her head. Their eyes had caught each other, gathering a faint brightness from the shadow. Something was quivering there. She put her hands behind his head. Their helmets banged. And for perhaps three or four seconds she pressed her cold lips to his. Then she let go. She pushed him. He turned. Stepping outwards, the weight of the water was again so unexpected he lost his footing on the ledge and fell outwards. The pool was up to his neck and he had to swim. By the time he reached the shallow water, Michela was already ahead, hurrying down after the others.

Mystical experience? Clive asked Adam as they got into their boats again.

Claustrophobic, Adam replied. He had his sardonic smile. Place could use some good garden lighting.

Bit of a toilet, if you ask me, Phil sneered.

Vince?

Can't describe it. He shook his head. What could he say? A great wind was blowing through him. Like a place, he hazarded, I kind of always knew existed but had never been to. Does that make sense? He didn't look at Michela as he spoke, but saw Clive lift an eyebrow in her direction. There was a squint of anxiety in his expression. The Italian girl's voice came very flat and clear: Last place on earth, she said. Terminal.

Did we really miss anything? Amelia was demanding of Max. And has anybody got any lipsalve?

Rapid poke in Mother Earth's old womb, Max said. Core of the universe kind of thing.

Earth's what?

For Christ's sake, Phil, where have you been, where did you come from? The womb!

Cunt to you, Brian explained, checking his spraydeck.

Kids, Adam began.

Not exactly, Amelia protested. She pressed a stick of Vaseline against her lips.

Thereabouts, Brian said. And just as wet by the sounds.

You should be so lucky, Max told him.

Cunt is warm, Phil objected.

Unless you're into necrophilia.

Kids, I said enough!

Then they were on the water again. It was distinctly dirtier now as the rising streams brought down earth from the mountain sides. There were the first bits of debris. A broken branch, a dead bird. Yuck, Amelia said. Bugger off, foul fowl. The creature rolled over softly in the eddy-line, limp feathers outspread. How quiet the valley seemed, Vince thought. The dull roar of rain and river made a strange ferocious hush.

Just before the first rapid, Clive told Phil and Max to go ahead together and scout. First sign of anything really tricky, out of your boats and check it from the bank. This is the definitive four-star test, okay?

The boys paddled off and disappeared over the horizon line. The others chattered. Adam acknowledged that the little cave behind the fall was worth a visit, but didn't see why Clive wanted to insist on the word mystical. Michela stared glassily into the water: because it was where she and Clive had kissed so passionately three weeks before, she thought. Amelia was asking Brian if they would let him have his four-star even if, with his bad foot, he couldn't do this scouting business. Then Mark shouted, Listen up!

It was Max's voice. He was hoarse. Shrieking. Unable to get along the rocky bank, the boy had climbed five or six yards up in thick bushes. Quick! He's drowning. Quick. Oh God! Hurry. Help!

Clive thrust his boat out into the stream. Adam! With me. Everybody else, stay. The two men were out of sight in a matter of seconds. Max was crashing away again through the trees. About halfway through the rapid, the instructors found Phil trapped under a tree that had fallen, uprooted, across the water, its trunk just clear of the flood, the branches beneath forming an impassable sieve. This was a place to die in. But a man was already out there. Straddled on the trunk in a mass of broken twigs, he had got a hand under the boy's shoulder, keeping his face just half out of the water. That crazy bloke was waiting there shouting, Max explained later. The boys had gone down over the pour-over, heard him yelling, seen the obstacle and tried to eddy out. But Phil must have planted his paddle exactly between two rocks as he turned. When he lifted it, the blade had gone. He hadn't even felt it snap. The river had him. The boat was dragged beneath the tree. The water pulled him down into the tangled branches.

With a coolness that was the opposite of his reaction to the violence in Milan, Clive found two half-submerged stones to wedge his boat between, got out and tossed his tackle to Max who had arrived on the bank. In a moment he had brought Adam alongside of him. But for all their competence, with the strength of the current sweeping into the matted branches and the difficulty moving along the bank and then out onto the trunk, it took the men almost fifteen minutes to get the boy free. Meantime, the old tramp held onto his shoulder in the freezing water, shouting incomprehensibly, while the instructors secured ropes to the belt of his buoyancy aid.

Pulled clear, Phil retched and vomited. Never again. He would never get back on the water again. His gormless face was white, lips bloodless, and his whole body shaking. Never, never, never! He shook his head violently. It's my fault, Clive told Adam. He studied the narrow gorge with its steep banks, the fallen tree. We'll have to portage.

The kayaks were dragged out with ropes. They must find a way round. At this point it was clear that the person who really ought to have been excluded from the trip was Brian. Safest in the water, the crippled boy couldn't carry his boat and couldn't even walk unaided except on a fairly flat surface. Ask the guy if there's a path, Clive told Max. *Wie heissen Sie?* Max asked. The man was squatting on a rock with his shoulder bag and rod, filthy khaki trousers soaking below the knees, a sodden raincoat. He had shaved perhaps a week ago. The stubble was white. Roland, he answered. There was a smell to him. He wore boots with no socks. Roland. He grinned now. I'm Max, Max said.

The man began an expansive monologue, gesturing constantly towards the tree. He seemed to be scolding them. *Gibt es ein Weg?* Max asked. *Ein Wanderweg?* The man pointed up. Tell him how grateful we are and ask him if he can help us with the portage, Clive instructed. We have someone who can't walk. Tell him we'll buy him a meal. Anything.

Max interpreted, but Roland didn't seem to understand. Max repeated the offer. The man picked up his rod and opened his bag. It stank of fish. I think he's saying he has to stay by the river. *Cius*, Roland stood up abruptly and without moving began to wave as though to people already in the distance. *Auf wiedersehen, au revoir*. It was clownish. We should have scouted ourselves, Adam said. But if his paddle hadn't snapped . . . Max objected. We'll debrief later, Clive said. We've been lucky.

The slope above the river bank was slippery with rain-water trickling down through roots and pine needles and patches of exposed rock. Having got back to the main group and then found a way up to the path far above, they arranged a pulley with the throw-ropes and hauled the eight boats more than a hundred steep yards through undergrowth and thickets. Clive lifted Brian on his shoulders and staggered zigzagging among the trees. Keep your helmet on, he told him. Good view, the boy said, ducking his head. Then they regrouped along the path. It was narrow but clearly marked, following the contour of the gorge through slim pines a couple of hundred feet above the river.

The rain still fell heavily. They hoisted the kayaks onto their shoulders. How far do we walk? Back to the minibus, Phil said. I'm not getting in the water again. The others were silent. Each boat weighed twelve kilos plus whatever kit they had. Emergency candy supply, Adam announced cheerfully. He still had a dozen packs of wine gums. Clive carried two boats, one on each shoulder. Brian used paddles for crutches. He seems undaunted. How far? Mark repeated. There's a sort of chute here, Clive explained. He had run it twice. Too fast and steep to get back in on. Especially in the state we're in now. About quarter of a mile. Maybe half.

Suddenly they were exhausted, what with the waiting around, the cold, the dragging the boats one by one up the slope. Everyone had a blister, a rash, scratches. Only Vince was still in a strange state of elation. Why had he behaved like that? He hadn't even told himself he was crazy about her. So why had he shouted it? And why had she kissed him, then hurried off? But he wasn't really thinking of

Michela. He wasn't sure at all that she mattered to him. His main thought is: When I wake up tomorrow, will I really have changed? Is it over, the paralysis of these awful months? The canoe bit into his shoulder. He didn't notice. He wanted to speak to Louise, though he couldn't tell her of course. Phil almost died, he chided himself. It didn't seem important. Okay, here, Clive eventually decided. He put down the boats. We'll try here.

Clive and Adam slithered down the slope to scout. They have found an understanding, Michela noticed. She sat apart from the others, her body numb, her mind fixed. I am not going back to the campsite, she decided, not to the chalet. Clutching her knees, she rocked back and forth in the damp pine needles. It was like the moment on the train between Brescia and Milan when she had told herself that she would never see her mother again. That's it. I will never speak to you again. This clarity is a relief. She didn't question the moment with Vince beneath that thunder of water. She didn't see the wooded slope in the rain. Her head is leaden. But she knows: I'm not going back.

Do-able, Clive announced, but only if everyone's feeling positive. While the instructors were away, Phil had been going over and over the accident with the others. When I started to go under the tree, I thought I was dead. There was like, this roar of noise. I was grabbing at the branches, shitting myself. I must have swallowed a bathtub full. From time to time, as he spoke, the boy had fits of shivers. Jesus, Jesus, Jesus, he shook his head fiercely from side to side.

They were sitting on their upturned boats on the path in their uncomfortable waterproof clothes. Now Clive appeared from the woods with his solemn smile, weighing them up. Time for a morale massage, kids, he said. You've got to tell yourselves that essentially nothing has happened and that you're going to go on paddling just the same way you did this morning. Like gods. When no one replied, he said slowly: In the end, it's all here folks, he touched his forehead just above the nose. It's just a question of believing you can do it. It's in your head. Phil, he went on briskly, you take my paddle and I'll use the splits. It was a BCU rule that a trip leader carried a collapsible paddle. But Phil said no. He was shaking his head wildly. No way he was going back on the water. No fucking way. I've got a flask of tea, Adam told him. Warm you up. Come on. Then Mark said: Don't chicken out, Phil. Suddenly Max was on his feet. Shut up! he shrieked. You fucking stupid wimp! How can you talk about chickening out? Phil nearly fucking died. He was choking. It's a miracle that bloke was there. And you, you . . . Max seemed about to explode with frustration. You're useless! You're shitting in your pants the whole time.

Two years older, Mark muttered, I didn't mean anything. I . . . Just stay out of it, Adam told his son quietly. He said nothing to Max. If you really can't, Clive told Phil quietly, then I suppose you can climb up to the road and just wait for as long as it takes for us to come and pick you up. We'll get someone else to volunteer to stay with you. But it can't be me or Adam. There have to be two instructors with the group. Then Amelia said, actually, if she wasn't mistaken, the road must be on the other side of the gorge. And she was right.

The pressure of the group now was to get the boy back on the water. There was some discussion. The leaders couldn't decide how much of an emergency this was. The day hung in the balance. What's the water like, Phil eventually asked. Adam said coolly: More or less the way you've always wanted it, Phil. Worst comes to worst, Clive said, you can ferry over to the other side and climb to the road there. But everybody remembered that the road had been dizzyingly high, right at the top of the gorge. As they set up a rope and sling to lower the boats down, Michela got to her feet and walked over to Vince. At once he was tense with expectation. She put her mouth to his ear: He wants to save the whole world and now someone in his own little kayak group is going to die. Vince was shocked. The girl's face was pale with anger and scorn. Her dark eyes were gleaming. As he was trying to think what to reply, she turned away.

We should abort, Adam announced. Half an hour later they had got the boats lined up in a thicket of young saplings precariously rooted over a drop of perhaps four feet into a roar of muddy water. The river has come up two or three inches, Adam insisted, in the time it's taken us to bring the boats down. I've got my mobile in the dry-bag, he said. We can call Keith and sort something out.

Michela said, Really, it's fine. There's nothing specially difficult from here on. Vince stared at the swollen water. A couple of small planks came tumbling down, part of a broken pallet perhaps. We should abort, Adam said firmly. Your dad's scared you won't be able to make it, Max taunted Mark. Max! Clive said. Shut it! Okay? Enough! Now listen, come round — they were huddled on the mud among the thin trees — listen, if we played it strictly by the rule book, I think Adam would be right. We can rig up a pulley across the river, do a rope-assisted ferry-glide, climb about a thousand feet and spend till midnight and gone getting the boats out.

He paused. The others were watching. Amelia was trying to press the water out of her hair. But I'm for running it, kids. The higher water will make it faster. A lot of the usual obstacles will have gone under, so it's going to be less technical, just a bit wilder if you have to swim. He spoke calmly, but very intensely, turning his bright eyes from one to the other. All the afternoon's poor light seemed to be drawn into his face. Obviously, one or two of us are at the limits of our ability here, but that's when an experience helps you grow, doesn't it? Now who's for it?

Me, Michela said in a flat voice.

Me, Amelia echoed.

There was a powerful charisma emanating from the bearded man. I don't want to put any pressure on anyone, he added. It was a lie.

Well, I'm not for walking, Brian grinned.

That made three, four with Clive. Adam cut in: The rule is, we don't do anything beyond the ability of the weakest member of the group. Especially if there's real risk of serious injury. And that's undeniable. The weakest member of the group was clearly Mark, but Adam didn't say this.

Okay, I'll get back in, Phil said, I'll try it. He grinned, but it still wasn't his old voice. If you think I'm up for it, like.

Vince wavered. The water was frightening. It was only Clive's will that was pulling them round. I'll give it a go, he eventually said.

But Adam seemed extremely agitated. Had he promised something to his wife? I'll stay behind with you, he suddenly announced to Mark. The boy hesitated. The launch looked daunting to a degree. There was no eddy here to hide in. They must push the boats through the bushes, climb in right on the edge, then plunge four or five feet straight into the brown flood with a rock to get pinned on only ten yards downstream.

You can't stay if we go, Clive said calmly: the rules demand two instructors.

So you can't go if we stay, Adam said.

The antagonism had surfaced again. But Clive seemed

more relaxed and authoritative now than when the problem was politics. His face radiated that manly reassurance that had made Michela fall in love with him. I'm the river leader, he said quietly.

It doesn't make sense to go, Adam said, if we think there's a real danger.

There's always a real danger, Michela said quietly. Just being alive.

Vince felt the anxiety of not understanding what was going on. The girl had been silent all day. What was at stake? Why did she insist now? Then, pushing his fringe from his eyes, raising his thin nose in a sort of defiance, Mark said, I wanna do it. He hesitated. Let's hammer on down, he said. Let's do it.

On one condition, Clive cut in quickly. We forget all arguments, okay? Max? Mark? Amelia? All individual niggles. Forgotten. Is that clear?

Alles klar, Max said. He turned and offered a hand to Mark. The boy took it. His narrow eyes were full of anxiety.

Community experience, Amelia said solemnly. She lifted two fingers in a V-sign.

We look out for each other all the time, Clive insisted. With no distinctions, no likes, no dislikes. We're a team.

Right, Vince said. This was the delirium of the real thing, he thought, the highly levered gamble. Adam said nothing. One by one then, Clive ordered. His voice had the assurance of military command. Myself, Max, Brian, Phil, Amelia, Michela, Mark, Vince, Adam. Same procedure as this morning. I scout with Max. Otherwise, we're three boat-lengths apart. And nobody ever out of sight. Okay? Sorted, Phil said. We're going to paddle like gods; at the bottom you'll feel like you've never felt before. You'll have adrenaline coming out of every pore of your body. And tonight we'll go out and get blind drunk, promise. The beers are on me. All of them. What a hero! Max applauded. May Wally protect us, Amelia announced. Adam said calmly: Okay kids, if we're going, let's go.

Somehow Vince's boat got tipped the wrong way as it shot down the bank. At once he was over. The paddle was dragged violently down. His knuckles banged on something hard. They banged again and scraped. Keep calm. He has the experience now. There's time. As the boat reached the speed of the current, the pressure on the paddle eased off. Vince crouched forward into position, swung his arm over his head. Coming up, he found Adam right beside him. All right? Just fine, Vince said. He even smiled.

Ten minutes later, Vince was only a couple of boat-lengths behind Mark when the boy tipped over in a swirl of water piling against a rock wall on the outside of a bend. It seemed the kid made no attempt at all to roll up, because his head was already bobbing in the water as Vince passed. Max had been placed on the bank at the first safe pool and tossed his throw-bag. Amelia and Brian were chasing the runaway boat, while Vince followed the swimmer into the bank. Okay? Max asked. Bash on the knee, Mark grumbled. Then he started to grin: Just one more thing to tell Mum. He's lost his fear, Vince saw. He felt moved.

Half an hour later they had to portage again around a rapid that Clive felt was too much. There are risks and risks, he said. Adam carried Brian this time. From a well-trampled path they were able to see three six-foot drops in quick succession, twisting from left to right and back. Ex-treme, Phil breathed. His confidence is coming back. There was a general feeling that they had cracked it now. Fucking fantastic, Mark kept repeating as he carried his boat. Bet I could do that too, he crowed looking into the boiling water. Fucking fantastic, Dad! Language, Adam said mildly. And don't start celebrating till you're home and dry.

Amelia went down in the next rapid, it was her first swim of the holiday, but again Max was on the bank to pull her out. Am I a safe pair of hands or what? he demanded. As she scrambled ashore a long dark box floated by, banging on the rocks as it passed. Brian shot out into the stream to inspect the thing. Some kind of cupboard, he reported, shaking his head. You wonder how this stuff gets in the river. Clive told them to watch out. A knock from a log coming over a rapid can be fatal. This is the last stretch now, kids, he shouted. Remember, we go under the road bridge and it's two hundred yards on your right. I'll be there ahead of you. There's that orange plastic strip on a tree too. On your right, just before the spur. You can't miss it.

As soon as they launched again, Vince appreciated that the danger was over. The river was wider. The gorge had broadened and flattened before its next plunge into Sand in Taufers. He felt exhilarated, but also slightly disappointed. The tension that had seized the mind entirely was dissolving. Clive no longer went ahead to scout with Max. The line of boats grew more ragged as people chose their own routes through easy rapids. And the rain had eased too. The cloud was lifting, the late afternoon brightening. With the sudden change of temperature, a mist began to steam off the water.

Yee-ha! Phil ran straight up against a smooth flat rock, forcing his boat vertical. Adam shook his head, exchanged knowing glances with Vince. Clive has won, Vince thought. Michela was wrong, thank God. The Italian girl had dropped back a little and was paddling slowly down on her own. They glided under the road bridge. The water was barely turbulent here. I must thank the man, Vince told himself. Clive got it right. He is a man you can follow. Even Adam was radiant. Here was the orange ribbon fluttering from the spruce tree. The rock shielding the eddy was just beyond. Easy! Ahoy, canoeists! Max was already out. He had scrambled up to the vantage point where they had been yesterday. He waved his paddle. Paddlers, ahoy! Vince was just turning to pull out of the current when he saw that Michela was not stopping. She paddled straight by.

His responsibilities over, Clive was kneeling on the bank helping Brian to get out of his boat. The swelling on the boy's ankle had reached the point where he could barely stand. The others were in the eddy or already beaching. A watery sun was brightening the patches of mist. Bringing up the rear, Adam was turning into the slack water right beside the big rock. With almost cartoon merriment he was whistling the hamster song. It was the biggest smile he had smiled all week. He banged his paddle on the water so that it spun up in the air over his head, caught it and held it there, using only his hips to control the turn and deceleration as the kayak crossed the eddy-line. Someone applauded. Epic! he laughed.

Hey! Micky! *Micky!* Apart from Vince, only Max had seen. What are you doing? This is the get-out. It's here! Micky! Come back!

Everyone looked. The girl was still well within striking distance. She could still regain the slack water. And in fact she had swung her boat round to face them now, about ten yards down, but drifting rather than paddling. For Christ's sake, Clive called, get to the bank! Sitting erect, the girl lifted her paddle and tossed it away into the stream.

Vince has never thought of himself as courageous. He is

not a man of action. But with no caution now, he veered away from the eddy and set off straight for the girl's boat. A clamour of voices rose behind him. Vince had no idea what warnings were being shouted. He knew what was waiting if he crossed the water's horizon line, shimmering in the mist up ahead. But it seemed to him that since she had no paddle he must catch up with the girl before the drop, he would drag her to the side, somehow. Reach forward, was all the voice in his head was shouting. Reach forward! The kayak surged.

Using her hands in the cold water, Michela was keeping her boat turned upstream towards the others. Now she raised her arms, pulled off her helmet and dropped it in the water. She shook the water from her short hair. Vince was almost there. The girl's drifting kayak began to spin. Grab the sling, he shouted. He released the thing from round his waist. Clip it on! He would tow her. But the girl had put her arms straight down by her sides. Her eyes are closed, Vince saw. It was the concentration of the diver on the high board. She leaned her head away from the approaching rescuer and capsized.

They were only a few yards away from the rapid now. The boom of the rushing water had drowned out any cries behind. Yet to the very brink the river was flat and calm, sliding mud-brown under a bright strip of surface mist. Two ducks flapped up as the red boat tipped over. They raced for the trees. Vince leaned to grab at the upturned hull. There was nothing to hold. He rocked it. She hadn't pulled out. Now the stream was accelerating. There is no time. Leaning on the hull, he reached right under the water, found an arm and tugged. She wasn't helping. Her hands were stiffly at her sides.

Quick! He pushed the boat away. For a few moments he

back-paddled furiously, but only to get his bearings. He knew he was beyond the point of no return. The capsized hull went over. Turning his head a split second before taking the plunge Vince saw another paddler approaching rapidly. It would be Clive. Then he was on the brink looking down into a chaos of spray and stone. There was no time to choose a line. Relax, a voice sang in his brain. Don't fight the water.

He fought. What else can you do? For two or three seconds he held his own. He had come over at a good spot. He planted the paddle way out to the left to drag the kayak away from a rock, tried to force it into an eddy as the water crashed between two boulders, failed, then leaned right out again to brace as the boat was dragged down in a deep hole of foam. Suddenly upside down, he rolled up at once. He was careering backwards now. The sight of the flood of water rushing towards him shook what confidence he might still have had. He thrashed the paddle. He was over again. A rock slammed against his helmet.

It was all frenzy now. His knuckles and wrists are scraping on the bottom. A desperate swinging of arms and hips unexpectedly tossed him upright. The boat was thrown against a wall and he was down again, pinned, head under water, the river piling onto his deck. I've lost it. Blindly, his fingers felt for the tab. Mustn't panic. The spraydeck popped but the sheer pressure of the water had him trapped in the boat. He panicked. Yaaaah! Vince screamed away his last breath and every last ounce of energy to force himself out of the boat. Air. I need air. In the flood his knee took a tremendous knock. Boulders and branches rushed by. There was the log they'd seen. He was falling, then abruptly trapped against another rock, arms and legs outspread, stomach crushed on stone. But he had his head above the water. He could think. He found a hand hold. Clinging and slithering and fighting, he pulled himself up onto the round, rugged top of a boulder.

Vince was in the very midst of the torrent. Had anything been broken? Chunks of flesh were gone from his knuckles. Every muscle was trembling. I'm alive, I'm alive. His wetsuit was in shreds at the knee, the leg completely numb. His teeth chattered. His boat was gone. There's something wrong with my neck. Can I move it. Yes, yes. Just stiff. Then Clive appeared. His yellow kayak shot down the rush from above. The man's big torso and hands were moving rapidly, the shoulders swaying, the paddle flashing left to right, back and forth. But it was perfectly deliberate, even graceful. Vince saw the bearded face beneath the helmet. Clive! he shouted. Clive! Their eyes met. But there was no acknowledgement from the canoeist. The face was in a trance of concentration and as he slewed the boat around the rock Vince was on, leaning hard on his paddle, Vince saw that a sort of grim smile was playing on Clive's lips. He plunged down the rush and was gone. Only then did Vince remember the girl. Clive was going after Michela. She must be dead, he thought.

Vince crouched on all fours. It didn't seem safe to sit. He would have to put his legs in the water. He was afraid it would snatch him away. He was afraid if he stood he might faint and fall. I must wait for the others. How cold it was! He felt sick. How long would they be? I might pass out. They would have to throw him a rope. How will I hold it? Try to stop your body shaking, he ordered himself. Relax. Breathe. Breathe deeply.

The water thundered above and below. Even the foam was brown with mud. What is taking them so long! Then Vince realised that he was happy. He was euphoric. Something has shifted. He smiled. He couldn't worry about the Italian girl. In a strange flood of emotion, he felt grateful to her. He was weeping. Grateful to his wife too. Gloria gave you this, he whispered. She died and I took her place on this trip.

Still crouching, shaking, he looked at his hands. They were bluish-white. The cold had stopped the bleeding. All the skin on the knuckles of the left hand was gone. He could see a bone. It was uncanny. Vince took hold of the ring on his fourth finger. It hardly pained him now to pull it off. The pale gold lay on the dead white palm and in a gesture he couldn't understand, he let it fall into the fast brown water.

Oy! Vince! Wake up. Hey, Vince! It turned out they had been shouting at him for ages. Adam was in the brushwood on the bank, about ten feet above the water. Max was beside him. They had secured a line to a tree and were tying themselves to it in case someone should get pulled in. At the third attempt they managed to land a throw-bag directly in Vince's hands. But his fingers wouldn't move. He couldn't tie it. Yelling over the sound of the water, Adam repeated his instructions. Pass an arm through a loop. Now, hold on tight and jump. Vince hesitated. Wrists and knees and feet and neck were all so stiff and numb. Trust me, Adam shouted. Vince looked across at the man. Trust me, do it.

Vince jumped. His head plunged into the dark water, but already strong arms were dragging him across. His face came up. He felt a surge of energy and when his feet banged into the rocks at the edge he was able to use the rope to climb out and up. Michela? he asked. He went down on his knees. Adam was looking at him curiously. I called the ambulance, he said. On the mobile. Max was opening a space blanket. He draped it over the kneeling figure. Wrap it round you. Come on. And he laughed. You don't know how long I've been waiting to use this. I thought I'd never get my money's worth.

'EL CONDOR PASA'

People had to eat and so they were in a restaurant ordering pizza. Nobody really knew Michela. Had anyone spoken to her, really spoken? Tom had made love to her the night before, but they hadn't talked. He had talked all week to Amelia. Made love is the wrong expression. She had forced it on him. She had been brash and abrupt, acting a part that wasn't hers. He knew he was too young to understand. You thought that was what you wanted, then it wasn't. Now Amelia and Louise both seemed far too young for him. He was eager to confess, but didn't know whom to speak to. He sat silent and shocked. He felt old.

On the other side of the table, it was hard for Mark not to shout his excitement with the day's achievement. He has run a wild river. With his father present. He has overcome fear. In other circumstances there would have been a buzz of euphoria. Now high spirits were forbidden. She was definitely alive when they put her in the ambulance, Mandy insisted. The adults took refuge in the technicalities: that Clive had dragged her out of the boat so quickly was the crucial thing, even if it meant swimming the last part of the rapid himself. He had done everything possible. And her being unconscious would actually have helped, Keith thought. The buoyancy aid is designed to keep your mouth out of the water. The guys at the rafting centre had given her mouth-to-mouth as soon as they pulled her ashore. Impossible to know how long she had been without oxygen. But why did she do it? Amelia demanded guiltily. I hate you, she remembered screaming. She hadn't acknowledged Michela's apology. She's so pretty, she protested. So intelligent. They all had the impression that the Italian girl was very intelligent. Never heard a foreigner that spoke English so well, Caroline gave her opinion. I thought she was a happy person, Amal muttered.

Then Adam and Vince arrived from the hospital. The Waterworld group were sitting round one long table in the Meierhof in Sand in Taufers. They had booked of course. The space was large and noisy. It was Saturday night. On the level beneath them, a burly boy with a ponytail was at work beside the pizza oven, while across the restaurant beneath tall pink curtains an improbably old musician, stiff in suit and tie, stood behind a keyboard cranking out the predictable favourites: 'Santa Lucia', 'Lily Marlene', 'Spanish Eyes'. She's in coma, Adam announced solemnly, but stable. Nobody understood whether this was good news or bad. Clive says we'd better leave tomorrow as planned, he added. Vince had his left hand bandaged. There was a dull pain in his hip. Get your orders in, folks, Keith told the new arrivals, or we'll be here all night. It was ten already. Tomorrow they must drive eight hundred miles.

Vince found a place between Amal and Tom. Can I ask you a question? Adam had asked, driving him back from the hospital. They had taken Vince's car. Adam had waited two hours and more while Vince was X-rayed and medicated.

He had gone back and forth between Casualty and Intensive Care where Clive sat with a sort of furious patience in a busy corridor. As long as it's not about money supply, Vince laughed. He was exhausted and aching. When we came running along the bank and saw you there, on that rock, and started calling you . . . Adam hesitated. And you didn't reply . . . Yes? Maybe I'm wrong, I don't know, I had the impression, well, I thought I saw you doing something with your hands. He stopped. I threw my wedding ring in the river, Vince told him. He stared out of the windscreen. After the day's rain it was a softly transparent evening of deep shadow and brightly lit road signs. Steering the long bends up the valley towards Sand in Taufers, their headlights swept this way and that across the hill to the left, the trees that screened the river to the right. Vince sighed. Anyway, the answer to your question is: I don't know why I did that. Oh. Adam waited. Then he said: I thought perhaps it had caught in a wound or something. Vince didn't reply.

At the table, he ordered a ham and mushroom pizza. Then Mandy appeared at his shoulder. She had left her place beside Keith and walked round the table. She bent to speak in his ear. You risked your life, Vince! she said. Amal was talking across the table to Phil about a stunt kayaker who had shattered his pelvis trying to run a huge waterfall in Kenya, a hundred-foot drop. Vince was obliged to look up at the woman's kindly face. It was criminal of her to put you in danger like that. I'm okay, he told her. An odd feverish quiet had fallen on him. He was impatient for the parenthesis of this holiday to be over, so he could know how he really felt. If Adam hadn't insisted he eat, he would just have gone to lie in his tent and wait for tomorrow.

Now Mandy was bending to push a kiss on his cheek. I'm so glad you're okay, she said. It was disturbing to see the brightness in her small brown eyes, the smile on her weathered cheeks. She was wearing lipstick. A toast to Vince! She stood up and raised her glass. Most improved paddler! Louise shouted: You're a hero, Dad. The whole table yelled, To Vince! Adam's cheers were particularly loud. The admirable Vince! Then Keith was explaining that a coma was normal in these circumstances: a sort of defence mechanism, actually: It only gets dangerous if it lasts more than about forty-eight hours. Vince's pizza appeared. I'll cut it for you, Amal offered. Mandy was taking a photo. The amazing thing is that there were no fractures. Once again Vince met his daughter's warm eyes across the table. Her hand and Mark's were touching. Thank you everybody, he said vaguely.

The others had already finished their first course, and were ordering sweets. As Vince bowed his head to his plate, the noise level rose around him. Under the influence of a couple of beers, the long table was breaking up into a series of conversations shouted across each other. Subdued concern about what had happened to Michela dissolved into a last-evening excitement. When all was said and done, the Italian girl was not one of their group. Nobody was missing her. Yeah, she just chucked away her helmet! Mark was repeating to Louise. And, like, we're all staring, thinking, Wait a minute . . .

Clive always had a negative effect on his women, Mandy was telling Adam. She spoke harshly, almost angrily. Both Adam and Keith seemed uncomfortable. Remember Deborah, she demanded, who used to teach two-star preparation? The group leader muttered something about not being one to throw the first stone. Then in response to a question from Amal, he announced: Ten sharp tomorrow morning, everybody. That means tents and gear all packed and the trailer hooked up and ready to roll. Otherwise we won't make our ferry. So much for Wally protecting us, Caroline was complaining. It's hardly his fault, poor little thing – Amelia pulled the creature from out of her T-shirt – if people go trying to get themselves killed. Is it? The pretty girl was beside Brian, but darting occasional glances at Tom. I feel a bit guilty, she confided.

Slowly chewing his pizza, Vince's mind drifted. He began to notice the restaurant. It was a large room with space for a hundred and more. The walls were a light varnished pine, the upholstery pink and flowery, the tablecloths red with white flowers in white vases, white candles, and everywhere there were ornaments and trophies dangling from the ceiling, hanging on the walls, perched on ledges and along the backs of the long sofa-benches that divided the tables.

How bright the room is! Vince was suddenly aware. On different lengths of wire, scores of plastic lampshades were designed to look like pieces of old-fashioned parchment stitched together. To the right of their group, suspended on three taut pieces of twine, were a dozen carved wooden hearts. There were aluminium tubes in the form of elongated bells, wooden cats and dogs and squirrels and fish, all hanging from the varnished cross-beams and swinging very slowly in the smoky draughts of opening and closing doors. A stuffed owl raised its grey wings on the wall behind Brian's head. An eel was pinned in a coil beside the red and white banner of the Tyrol.

Meanwhile, the ancient musician, dressed, Vince now understood, like an undertaker, was picking out 'El Condor Pasa'. His moustached face, that so much resembled the photos of the old men on the tombs in the little churchyard on the hill, was completely impassive. The computerised keyboard added the accompaniment. I'd rather be a hamma sandwich, Max had begun humming, than an escargot!

Spearing two bread rolls, he made his knife and fork dance together on a dirty plate. A deer with shabby antlers gazed across the bright glassware. The Chicken Song, Caroline cried, let's ask the bloke to play the Chicken Song! The fat girl burst into uncontrollable giggles. A stuffed fox bared his teeth. It is too much, Vince whispered.

Rather be a banana than a . . . a . . . Phil was tone deaf. Oh shut up! Tom told him. Than a what, may I ask? Max wanted to know. A dildo? Brian suggested. Oh do leave off. Tom seemed livid. He turned to Vince and asked in a low voice: Have you any idea why she did it? There was an explosion of laughter from a group of men drinking schnapps. Obviously locals, they sat with their dark-red cheeks and heavy moustaches mirrored in the shiny black slabs of the windows. The curtains hadn't been drawn. Never had Vince been so struck by life's coloured density.

You see, the young man confided, something strange happened last night. He looked around to check that none of the others were listening. Without a flicker of expression, the keyboard player switched to 'Sweet Little Sixteen'. He was seventy if he was a day. A condom than a bog roll, Phil howled. Kids! Adam said sharply. It was really weird, Tom insisted. Vince tried to pay attention. You mean you and Michela, I suppose? he asked. The young man's soft eyes were full of anxiety. Did everybody see? Pretty much, Vince said. I feel bad, came Mandy's voice over the buzz, us going away without even saying goodbye to her! At moments it seemed to Vince he might just fade into all the bright surroundings. Perhaps this is the effect of shock. The earnest Tom was looking hard at him: I mean, it's so strange her doing that with me and then the next day, well . . . You see? He's pleased with himself, Vince realised. He's dying to tell someone. Trying to close the conversation, he said: She must have been going through a crisis, you know, and whatever happened with you was just part of it. But Tom became more intimate and agitated. You don't think it's in any way, I mean, at all, my fault?

Vince drained his beer. A sense of irritation helped him to focus: You certainly ruined Amelia's holiday, he said abruptly, though actually the girl had her head down beside Brian's now over a plate of profiteroles they were sharing. The really strange thing, you see, Tom lowered his voice even further, is that she didn't say a word. You know. Nothing! I felt so stupid. This wasn't in fact quite true. Over and over Michela had kept repeating something in Italian, fierce words that meant nothing to Tom, as if he wasn't really there. I mean, if she'd said she was depressed or something . . .

Kids! Kayakers!

It was Keith's voice. Standing up, the group leader banged a spoon on the table, then lowered the volume a little when other people in the restaurant looked round. A tampon than a loo-brush, someone whispered. Kids! Keith sighed. Bright with emotion, his eager, glassy eyes looked round the table. Tonight was supposed to be a big celebration, of course. And normally, as you know, I'd have asked everyone to sum up what you thought of the holiday and we could have voted the Wally of the Day and so on. Adam! muttered a voice. Keith half smiled. But that doesn't really seem appropriate, does it? With what has happened. Now he got silence. In fact − the speaker bit a lip − the truth is we *all* deserve the Wally award today. Yes. He scratched his beard. The whole point about Wally, when we invented him, was that he goes to someone who's been careless. They have to protect Wally for the day, and that, that protecting, I mean, that not being careless, is what protects us all. We remember we have to look out for each other. I'm sure those of you who did the upper Aurino today will have seen how important that is. Instead, the fact is that we've all been incredibly careless, because nobody realised that one person among us, okay, not really part of our group, but still certainly with us, one person was feeling bad, very bad. To the point that she tried to kill herself, and, doing that, like it or not, she selfishly put the lives of two other members of the group in danger. Clive and above all Vince.

Following the old musician's arbitrary repertoire, the keyboards had launched into 'A Whiter Shade of Pale'. The schnapps drinkers were roaring. Yet it seemed to Vince, as at certain moments on the river, that there was a deafening silence around the table as Keith delivered this layman's sermon, at once inescapably true, but embarrassing too, and somehow pointless.

And when you go home now, Keith continued, and inevitably you talk about this, to your mums or dads, or whoever, obviously I want you to make sure they understand that this wasn't, strictly speaking, a kayaking accident. That's important. In nearly twenty years of activities, Waterworld have never lost anyone in a kayaking accident. We've never even been close. You all know how many precautions we take.

Looking up from an inspection of his bandage, Vince found Adam staring at him diagonally along the table. And his eyes were saying: Today anything could have happened. He has his mobile, Vince saw, lying on the table before him. He's in touch with his crippled wife. But getting it right on the water, Keith finished lamely, doesn't let us off looking out for each other in other areas of life. Dead right, Mandy said. She too looked at Vince. Which is the lesson I'd like you all to take away from this trip. Mark, Vince realised now, had his hand on Louise's leg beneath the table. The boy's face was radiant.

To close on a more cheerful note, though, Keith's voice suddenly reverted to its ordinary authoritative jollity, I want to extend my warmest congratulations to Max, Phil and Brian who've all earned their four-star awards with flying colours. And special congratulations to Max, who, from what I've been told, scored top marks for group awareness and river rescues. Well done, Max! Mandy started to clap. He's a he-man! Brian shouted into the general applause. A jolly good fellow! To everyone's surprise, young Max, with lemon shirt and green cravat, had tears in his eyes.

I'll drive you, Mandy told Vince at the door. You can't hold a steering wheel with your hand like that. In the restaurant's small car park the others were piling into the minibus. Two or three couples had decided on a last romantic walk. In the car, the small woman adjusted the driving seat, ran her hands quickly and practically over the controls, found the headlights. Actually, I was just thinking, you're going to need someone to drive you tomorrow too. It's over eight hundred miles. When Vince began to object, she said. After all, we live so near each other, don't we? At the end, I can drop my stuff off at my place, drive you home and just walk back. Again Vince protested that he thought he would be okay by tomorrow. Most of the journey would be motorway with just one hand on the wheel. Mandy didn't appear to have heard. Louise'll be wanting to travel in the bus with Mark, I bet, she chuck-led. We can have some adult conversation at last. You get fed up with all of this group and kiddie stuff after a week.

The car was creeping along the few hundred yards to the campsite. Mandy braked for a rabbit and almost came to a standstill. When Vince said nothing, she asked: Was it really terrifying? I imagine you're still jittery. I keep seeing myself in that pin yesterday, you know, trapped down there and the deck not wanting to pop. Yes, Vince said vaguely, then he asked: You know when I started at Waterworld, what was it, two years ago? Yes? Mandy turned into the dirt track of the campsite. Well, a couple of months later, I mean just after I'd started lessons, you probably won't remember, Gloria stopped. She'd been canoeing about ten years, then she stopped right after persuading me to start. I mean, she really made an effort to persuade me. The exercise would do me good, etc. But then she gave it up. So then it was just me, and Louise too. We were in a beginners' course. Saturday afternoon. So? Mandy asked. So, I just wondered, Vince sighed, I wondered if you knew why she did that. I mean why she stopped right then?

They had turned off the track to park on their pitch behind the kitchen tent. Even towards midnight there were still some small children playing in the fluorescent light by the bathrooms. Is this my starter for a thousand pounds? Mandy asked. They sat a moment in the stillness of the car. In the distance someone was playing an accordion. Oh, it doesn't matter, he said and he made to get out. Mandy put a hand on his arm. Why did she *say* she stopped? To concentrate on her tennis, Vince said. She went to the tennis club. Well, that sounds fair enough. But then, Vince insisted, then she booked herself on this trip, didn't she? And on the Ardêche trip last year. She only stopped as far as the Saturday afternoons in the estuary were concerned. When I went.

Mandy ran a hand through her hair. She turned to him and smiled. The shadowy space was quiet and intimate. Why are you asking me this, Vince? You were on that trip too, weren't you, he said, in France? I always go on the Ardêche trip, she told him. It's my job. And? The woman breathed deeply. Her lips had puckered into a shrewd smile. She leaned across the car, put her hand round his neck and drew the widower towards her. When he neither resisted nor responded, she shifted her mouth to his ear and whispered warmly: Saturday afternoon is just training time, but trips are trips. She pulled back from him, leaving just a hand on his shoulder. *N'est-ce pas?* Her eyes were smiling.

In his tent, Vince let the flood carry on over him. I don't know where they are, he told Adam when the man came to enquire after his son. It was almost one o'clock and the river was still flowing over and over him. Is it really carrying me back to London, he wondered, back to the City, the service flat, the empty fridge? Where else? A man gets tied up to the ground. Was that how the song went? Lying in the dark, he was intensely aware of waiting. He could feel a strange momentum. The thoughts flow by and I am waiting, he told himself. Why should I live in a service flat and keep a house that is empty? I'm not waiting for Louise. There are so many decisions to be taken. Louise wouldn't live with him again. Gloria would be furious, he thought, to know that their daughter was out late at night with a boy, and him, Vince, doing nothing about it. No, it was a different kind of vigil, lying quite still in the fresh evening as the river rushed over him. I tossed away her ring, he muttered. It's just a holiday flirtation, he assured Adam when the man again came to enquire. The more worried the other father was, the more Vince would show he was relaxed. It's the kind of thing people do on a trip, Adam, you know, he said lightly. It's two o'clock, the chinless man grumbled. They're too young for this kind of thing. Apparently not, Vince laughed, and he asked, any sign of Clive getting back? But how amusing, he reflected, that Adam shared this anxious trait with Gloria. I didn't toss it away in anger, he told himself when he was alone again. He tried to hold on to some image of her: of Gloria at breakfast, Gloria humming 'El Condor Pasa', one of her old favourites, Gloria back from tennis, her face flushed. The flood carried him on. Away, I'd rather go away! He remembered her humming that. I was too self conscious, he suddenly thought, the day I scattered the ashes. Too conscious of the ceremony of it, eager for feelings I didn't really have. The grit had clung to his damp fingers and blown in his eyes in the estuary wind. Whereas the ring thing was just the opposite. I did it *naturally*. And now someone in his own little kayak group is going to die! First the Italian girl said, I'm so sorry, almost as if she had *known*, and then she comes to me to announce her death. Why to me? Because Tom wasn't at hand perhaps? Tom hadn't been chosen for the trip. Or because I waited for her under the waterfall. She knew I was waiting. *I* was the care-less one who should have understood that message. But I had to concentrate on my paddling. I was terrified. Now he saw Michaela's strange expression again as she sat, beauti-fully straight-backed, in her boat, arms by her side, eyes shut – she leans that pretty head, the long neck, to the left and begins to keel over into the muddy water.

Vince sat up. What is this vigil for? He must sleep. I have eight hundred miles to drive tomorrow. He must find some way of not being alone in the car with Mandy. And Monday, the City, the fray. Mandy wants a ménage, he thought: the service flat during the week and her house with my kid and her two at the weekend. A man gets tied up to the ground. Stupid song! He shook his head, listened in the dark. There are always people chattering in campsites, distant pleasures and dramas. Quite possibly my daughter is having first sex this evening, Vince thought. She seems so adult. I *asked* not to go, she had said. She didn't need the thrill of fear. She was quite happy with herself without going on a dangerous river expedition. Am I waiting to hear if Michela is okay? he wondered, a young woman I hardly know, with naive political views and a cripplingly dysfunctional background. She had been quite rude two days ago in the hospital waiting room. But this afternoon she put her lips against mine under the waterfall. What long eyelashes she has! And dark eyes. A man, Vince thought, whose invalid wife was always in and out of hospital, could surely be forgiven a little love affair with the diligent nurse who played tennis so well. *El condor pasa.* A bird of prey. Perhaps they never made it to the tennis courts. Mum was the soul of the party, Louise wept. I wouldn't throw the first stone, Keith said. It was as if, all of a sudden, outside the tent, the mountain air was full of whispered conversations. How many photographs there were on all these paths of people who had died in falls and accidents! It would have been Gloria made the move, Vince thought. She was the hawk. It seemed he was overhearing snatches, debris of old conversations carried on the flood. Perhaps one day I will feel I was mad to imagine this. Mandy, he told himself soberly, most likely had an affair with Keith, but then wasn't able to stop him going back to his wife. Keith wasn't a widower. Somebody laughed low in the distance. It sounded like mockery. Monday I'll be at my desk, Vince told himself for the thousandth time. Would his secretary notice the absence of the ring? Will people say, Ay, ay? What is this vigil for then, if I know what the future is; my office, my desk; if my daughter is beyond me, if I missed the moment when I could have been helpful to Michela. Again he saw the elegant neck bend towards the water. A swan. She was a swan. She gave herself to the water. Here and gone. She had turned the boat so she was facing back to Clive, to her man. She was punishing him. Then there was the downward rush of the stream. With extraordinary vividness, Vince was in it again. He was shooting down into the rapid. He felt the acceleration of the plunge. I want to do it again, he realised. If I could. That rapid, those impossible manoeuvres. The speed and wrenching when he dug in his paddle, the icy foam and the slam of the rock on his helmet and the wild slewing and turning to the limit of control and beyond. I want to do that again, Gloria. Gloria. Oh Gloria, I want to do it again!

Vince? This was more than a whisper. A voice called him softly. He was sitting bolt upright, knees drawn towards him. The zip squeaked. Vince, can I talk a bit?

Clive! How is she? What's the news? In the dark light Clive's bearded face showed surprise: I thought you were talking to someone. Waiting for Louise, Vince said. She must be out with Mark. All these youngsters, in love! Clive managed a faint smile. I need to talk a moment. I've got a favour to ask. I'll get up, Vince said. There's no room in here. Come to the chalet, Clive told him. He would put on a coffee.

The fly-sheet was soaked in dew. Vince headed for the bathroom first. The fluorescent light greeted him like an old friend. He wanted to burst out laughing. What a volatile state! If I only could. He was thinking of the rapid. Then, heading for the chalet, it was with a sense of wonder that he remembered taking the same path only yesterday, to spy on their erotic happiness. Perhaps my own marriage wasn't so bad, he thought. He and Gloria had always shared the same bed.

Clive was making coffee on a gas ring. It's a pretty big favour, he warned. He busied himself with the flame and the percolator, then began moving rapidly around the room gathering various bits and pieces. Leaning against the bed was an open backpack.

Vince sat on a stool by a counter along the wall. It was odd, he thought, how cluttered and at the same time impersonal the room was. There are no pictures or ornaments. It was all kit and tackle and clothes and papers. Ask away, he said. Clive went back to the coffee, shook out the dregs from two cups, brought a mug to Vince, then stood facing him. I want you to hold the fort here for a few days, while I'm away.

At once Vince felt alert; some animal intuition told him he was in danger. Standing before him, feet squarely planted, steaming mug held in both hands, Clive was searching for his eyes. His own were intense and persuasive, brightly blue. The thick beard and the strong tanned forearms thrusting from rolled-up denim sleeves made such a man of him. He didn't seem tired at all. I have to leave in a couple of hours, he explained. For Berlin. I should be back on Thursday. Meantime, someone will have to stay here to be near Michela and visit her and so on. I thought, with you having your own car, you'd be best placed to do that. I've got to drive down to Bolzano, to the airport.

Immediately Vince said: Really, I'm afraid I must be back at work Monday. I've already been away too long.

Clive ran his tongue over his lips, half smiling, still looking directly into the older man's eyes. He drank from his mug, then set it down on the counter, turned abruptly, crouched beside a small chest of drawers and began pulling out underwear. Vince's mind is racing. How is she? he asked.

Clive pushed the clothing into his backpack. She's going to be okay, I think. The scans suggest she'll be out of the coma any moment. It isn't deep. So they say. He spoke without emotion, then got down on the floor to straighten out the sleeping bag and roll it up. You can stay here in the chalet. It's rented for the whole summer. I'll show you where everything is.

Vince watched the man, his efficiency and hurry. He gave the impression of someone who has heard an urgent flood warning and is moving fast to get out, someone used to flood warnings. Or again of a soldier preparing his kit before action. There was a lithe quality to the man's rapidity, a sureness and presumption that was seductive; and Vince was reminded how, during the walk to the glacier, he had looked up and seen Clive climbing quickly through the stones and the girl doggedly following. Exactly the man I'm not, Vince thought. The man who attracts women. He was half aware now that he had been thinking this all week, since the moment Clive had stood and leaned across the table to slap Adam's face. Clive completely dominated Adam today on the river, he thought. In the end he won him over. Or at least wore him out. He won over the whole group. Only his will brought us safely down. Don't you think, Vince said at last, that you should be beside her when she wakes up.

No. Clive didn't turn to Vince, but had started collecting things and laying them on the table now: keys, a torch, a map. Actually, I'm the last person who should be there.

But . . .

She can tell you about it, Clive said. I'm not going to explain. I said at the hospital that her uncle would be arriving in the morning.

Her uncle?

Clive finally turned and grinned. That's you. Look: these are the essentials for living here. The long key is for the door, the small one for the padlock on the gas cylinder under the window outside.

I imagine you've told her mother.

No.

But that's the first . . .

Next to myself, her mother is the other worst person for Michela at the moment.

Vince tried to be judicious. In so far, he said, as an attempted suicide is always a cry for help, don't you think the person, or people cried to should be the ones to respond? Again he saw the girl turn her boat to look back across the water, to her lover.

Clive pulled the cord tight to close his backpack. In that case people would only have to threaten to kill themselves to get exactly what they want, wouldn't they? There's still some food in the fridge, by the way, milk and cheese and stuff.

Vince drained his coffee. I'll tell Mandy, he said. She can use my car. I'll go back with the minibus.

Clive stopped. As if making a considerable concession, he interrupted his packing and came to sit at the counter on the other stool. He was very close now. He pulled a tin of rolling tobacco from his pocket. Again Vince was aware of the shape and power of the forearms lying on the counter as they rolled the cigarette. The fingers were thick but nimble.

Mandy won't do it, Clive said, nor will Keith, because they are *in loco parentis* as far as the younger kids are concerned. And Adam is the wrong person.

We'll see, Vince replied. I don't know the terms of their contract, but I can't see why one of them couldn't stay. Like I said, I can leave my car. Actually, Adam seems perfectly suitable to me, if he can get the time off work.

Clive lit his cigarette, narrowed his eyes. Listen, I've been thinking about this all evening. Again he was searching for eye contact. I'd rather it was you, Vince.

Vince laughed. Clive, he said softly. He adopted the voice of the older wiser man addressing an over-enthusiastic employee. Clive, listen, I'm a bank director. I have just taken my longest holiday in ten years. I am expected back in the hot seat on Monday morning. There will be hundreds, literally hundreds, of e-mails to answer, reports to consider, a team of accountants awaiting my instructions. I have responsibilities, Clive. The person who has to stay here, with his girlfriend, is you.

Clive smoked. It is towards three in the morning. Around them the camp is quite silent, so that they can almost feel its silence and darkness tugging at them. I pulled her out of the water, he said. And now I'm going to do what she expects me to do. I have my responsibilities too.

Like shouting at a demonstration? I can't imagine in her present state Michela cares too much about that.

I've got something important to do, Clive said evenly. She will tell you. Otherwise I wouldn't be going. They both sat on their stools by the counter with the room's one dim light reflecting in the thin glass of the window beside them. Vince could hear the other man's breathing, then the whine of a mosquito. Both smiled. Vince waved his hand.

That was quite a river today, Clive said after a moment. You enjoyed it.

Vince nodded. But he was not a man people could just push around. All my old professional self is coming out, he realised. Getting to my position in life is not just a question of a way with figures.

Clive was studying him. At the beginning of the week, you'd never have been able to do it.

No, Vince admitted. No, it felt good today.

You've learned a lot.

Vince waited.

And it's not just a question of the proper BCU strokes, is it? In a certain sense, it's not even to do with paddling.

No, Vince agreed. It's not just a question of paddling.

It has to do with the spirit, Clive said, breathing smoke. He hurried on. There's no point in denying that, is there? So why be afraid of the word?

It's to do with the personality, Vince said carefully. That's for sure.

Clive told him: So, you keep an eye on Michela, then you can go out on the river again if you like. Go and ask at the rafting club; they'll give you a guide. There's always someone.

Vince laughed with exasperation. But I told you, I have a job.

Clive again blew out a ring of smoke. I chose you, he said, because the sheer fact is, that you want to stay. Don't you?

No, I don't. I'd be letting people down.

Crap. Clive checked his watch. He stroked his beard. Isn't it a bit ironic, he began again, that a guy who supposedly has so much power and influence and money, a guy at the top of his career, isn't even free to take an extra few days off when he wants? He's in such a straitjacket, serving multinationals and the like.

Vince sighed. Clive, listen, to do anything, or become anyone, you have to get involved with a group, don't you? You have to accept a yoke, something that allows you to gear into the world. Otherwise you're just a loose cannon. Even in the kind of politics that you are in, you have to be part of a group. You can't go and demonstrate on your own. You wouldn't achieve anything. I chose the bank ages ago and I'm committed. Then he added: It's like a marriage.

Clive immediately took a deep breath and raised his eyebrows. Vince himself wondered why he had said this. The other man sensed his confusion. It's only four days, he said. At most you lose a week. If you're really so important, they'll wait. If you're not, who cares anyway?

Now Vince thought: that's actually true. Suddenly he wondered why he was resisting so much.

I should be back Thursday, Clive said softly. Towards evening.

What do you mean, should be?

The return flight is Thursday. The next group arrives on the Saturday. He added, If it's really like a marriage, your job, a wife waits, doesn't she? You're not betraying anyone, are you?

Vince stared.

You're not that kind of person, Clive said. Nor am I for that matter. The cigarette was down to a soggy butt drenched in tar. Clive dropped it in his mug and wiped his hands on his jeans. It really is important that I go.

If I'm going to stay, Vince said, you could at least tell me what's going on between you and Michela, why you think she did it, how I'm supposed to behave.

Smiling broadly, Clive jumped to his feet. Thanks, he said. For just a moment, he took Vince's arm and squeezed it. The grip was powerful, but somehow furtive too, an end, not a deepening of intimacy. I was forgetting. I must give you her health card. Any expenses – sometimes they have a charge for scans and things – keep track and I'll pay when I get back.

Clive!

She can tell you, he said. His voice was petulant now.

You're scared, Vince said quietly. If I am going to stay, you can do me the favour of telling me why you think she did it.

I'm not scared. Clive spoke abruptly. And I'm not going to tell you anything.

Why wouldn't you tell me, if you weren't scared?

Because it's none of your business! And believe me if I

was scared I'd tell you right away. Anything I'm scared of I do at once.

If I stay, it becomes my business, Vince said.

All at once, Clive seemed quite beside himself. He turned. Vince was still sitting, quiet and curved, on the stool by the counter. Are you going to hit me now? he asked.

Clive must have seen himself in the window behind Vince's head. He stepped back. Sorry, it's been a hell of a day, he said. I took a few knocks myself. Listen, Vince – he seemed to be thinking quickly, shrewdly – it's been a big shock for me, Micky doing that. You know? It's painful to think about. He pursed his lips, ran his tongue behind them. In the end, what can I say, it's just a banal break-up, men and women, you know, different thoughts about the future. The sheer fact is, we were more together for the politics than anything else. Just a regular break-up.

That's not true, Vince said. Anyone can see you two are in love. Both of you. The way you look at each other, the way you keep touching.

Clive had his lips set. A glazed look has come over his eyes. Think what you like, but I have to go.

Vince sighed. Show me the keys and things, he said.

Outside, the night had finally grown chill. He used the bathroom again, then walked back to his tent. Louise still hasn't returned. Lying down, without even bothering to take jeans and sweater off, Vince tried to decide if he was pleased with this turn of events. Louise would be happy to sit beside Mark in the minibus. I have escaped Mandy, he thought. In the end, he had been lying awake waiting for something to happen, for some improbable transformation. The sparrow rather than the snail. Stupid words. You *want* to stay, Clive said. Do I? As before an exam in the distant past, or the night before his wedding for that matter, he had been keeping himself awake to avoid entering the gorge, the moment when all choice was gone. I'm a chubby chicken waiting for the chop! So now you've delayed it a few days, he told himself, a week. Big deal. I haven't thought about Michela at all, he realised. I certainly didn't jump at staying because of Michela. Unless Clive had guessed something about that moment when he and she had been together under the waterfall. How long was it? Thirty seconds. A minute? Why did I shout those things? You're not betraying anyone, Clive said. He asked me because he senses I like her, perhaps. It was odd how strong and fragile the bearded man was. I chose you! As if he was Jesus after disciples. No, it was hardly, Vince thought, because of that kiss, that brushing of lips, that I threw away my wedding ring. Last place on earth, she had said of the waterfall. Now Vince remembered the photo of the girl who'd died up on the glacier. What was her name? Suddenly the obvious occurred to him. He jumped to his feet, crawled out of the tent, slipped on his sandals. His car was parked beyond the kitchen tent, beneath a tree. Sure enough, there they were. He peeped through a steamy back window. Only for a second. The seats were down and he could just make out their heads poking from beneath the old blanket he kept in the boot. It was pointless to wake them now. They're not in love, he thought. They had wound down a window an inch to breathe. Should he wake Adam? The sound of a Jeep starting over by the chalets was star-tlingly loud. Headlights moved up the track, turning the tents to blue and orange transparencies. Clive escaping. No, I'll pretend I don't know. He waited until the noise had faded and the hushed flow of the river rushed back into the silence from beyond the trees. It was all a pleasure, he decided, going back to his tent. Gloria would have been furious.

TOD

No, I'm not her uncle, Vince said. He wanted that clear at once. It was a scandal, a complete scandal, Mandy had raged when he explained the situation. The mad morning bell-ringer was at work. The valley was full of sound. Vince smiled and kissed her cheek. Seven a.m. You're a disgrace, Adam told his son. Your mother will kill me. You don't tell her everything you do, the boy said. His nose was blocked from the swimming he had done yesterday. Everybody's nose is blocked. Vince packed up the tent to clear their pitch, then set off to the hospital while the others were still having breakfast. Thanks Dad! Almost at once his daughter texted him. He had said nothing to her about her night out. Despite not having used it all week, his phone was down to its last bar. And almost at once she sent a second message. Can't believe you're not hurrying back to the office!

He hurried to the hospital. It had occurred to him Michela would need clothes, pyjamas, toiletries and so on. He unlocked the chalet and searched. Clive hadn't tried to tidy or left any notes. How different from their own home where everything had always been ironed and ordered, where Gloria always left explanatory yellow Post-its on cupboard and fridge. Vince wasn't even sure if the things he found had been washed. The intimacy excited him. There were toiletry products with Italian and German names. A complete scandal, Mandy repeated, running over to say goodbye again. I wish I'd been there to give him a piece of my mind. She was angry. She took both Vince's hands. She is jealous of the girl, Vince knew. It was silly. Of a girl who had tried to kill herself. Our families are indissolubly linked, Adam said wryly. The man offered his hand. Steady on, Vince smiled. He wouldn't open to him. Don't worry, I won't fight the water, he told Keith. The paunchy man had a twinkle in his eye. Wish I was staying, mate. He was enjoying Mandy's rage. Please, Tom whispered, give her my love. This — he handed over a beer-mat with a scribble — is my e-mail address.

And now Vince was repeating to some sort of ward sister that he was not Michela's uncle. He spoke very slowly and clearly. It was important to have that farce out of the way. I-am-not-her-uncle. No. The truth was he had only just learned her surname: Donati. But I would like to see a doctor about her. Yes. She hasn't woken up, the nurse warned. The woman was grim. She shook her head under a green cap. Not voken, she repeated. And not all the staff were here on Sundays. Vince waited more than an hour in a corridor before a doctor took him into a small office to insist that they must inform the girl's next of kin. They couldn't discuss the matter with a stranger. As always, Vince explained the situation truthfully. He had put on the most serious clothes he had with him. Cotton trousers, a battered linen jacket. The doctor didn't agree: On the contrary, I think it is very probable that she really wants her mother to know most. He too spoke with a strong accent. She wants to say, look,

Mutti, I can kill myself too. For some children, this is a way of showing they have become adult.

Vince was polite. I can only tell you the very little I know, he said. His whole career had been built on a habit of complete candour. He didn't trust himself to lie. From the one personal conversation I had with her, he said, I would say that seeing her mother might be counterproductive. She might react very badly. She was very angry with her family. The doctor pursed his lips, played with his pen. He was a small earnest man in his mid thirties. No doubt he knows the regulations. Her boyfriend, Vince repeated, the man she lives with, will be back on Thursday. He had to go to Berlin. The doctor shook his head. I don't think so, Mr, er, Marshall, yes? I don't think the partner of a pretty woman goes away at a time like this. What could be more important?

Vince offered no comment. They looked at each other across a metal table-top. You have hurt yourself too, I see? Just a couple of stitches, Vince admitted. Aren't you a bit old for falling in rivers? This was irritating. I don't think age has much to do with it, doctor. The doctor played with a pen. You have only known her a week, then? Five days, Vince said. And why are you the one to stay now? Her boyfriend asked me to; I was the only person with my own car. So you have no special relationship with her? Vince sighed. A friend, nothing else, a member of the same group. Then he added: People have a strong sense of solidarity, you know, doctor, when they do these things together. I'm sure that is true, Mr Marshall. Now, you will please inform the mother of this accident, or you will find the telephone number so we can inform, okay? Okay, Vince said. He hesitated. Can I see her, though? Should I leave my own phone number? I have a mobile.

To his surprise, he was allowed to sit by the bed. There

was a cabinet to put her clothes and things in, but Vince decided first he would find a laundry. Michela lay as if deeply asleep. Her breathing seemed normal enough; the face, with its high cheeks and tanned skin, was transformed by a huge bruise beneath the eye. She's sweating, he noticed. He wondered if perhaps they had covered her up too much. Gloria always had stories about the incompetence of nurses. I'm on Gloria's territory, he thought. He picked up a hand and said, Michela. Michela? He wouldn't call her Micky. Funny, her hands were quite unscathed. She hadn't grabbed at anything. She hadn't tried to save herself. The skin was cool and soft. Not the heavy cold Gloria's had been.

After twenty minutes he left her and walked into Bruneck, but everything was closed. Church bells were clanging. He couldn't buy a phone charger and he couldn't find a launderette. He bought a coffee, a pastry, and sat out in the same square where he had been with Keith and Michela three days ago. I am waiting again, he thought, waiting to be someone new. But it had been a pleasure to use his old persona on the doctor, the quiet authority he knew he transmitted. When he returned to the campsite the others had gone. How hot it is, Vince realised, when you're not spending the day on the river. The air in the chalet was stifling. He suddenly felt tired, uncomfortable. In Sand in Taufers he bought a *Herald Tribune* and discovered it was the warmest summer ever recorded. In France old people were dying like flies. Clive was vindicated, then. What could be more important at a moment like this than a summit on global warming? The markets seem stable enough, though. Vince didn't study the figures. He glanced, but his mind wouldn't focus. I'm still on holiday, he decided.

He drove to the river where it tumbled into the gorge above the town. This was where Clive had parked the minibus after their walk on the glacier. I can't keep away, he realised. He stepped carefully down the steep path that followed the rapid, trying to remember not to grab at anything with his bad hand. Pushing through tangled branches, he found a place that allowed him to see the fifty yards of wild water he had traversed. There was the rock that had pinned him. Was it? He wasn't sure. It was strange to think he had been upside down in that tumult. Tons of water crashed constantly against a black solid mass. I didn't really take it in. But this was certainly the rock he had climbed out on. Yes. He recognised the dome-like shape, the way the stream swirled round and by. What happens to a ring under water? How far would it travel? Is this, perhaps, it crossed his mind, how the old tramp first started hanging about the river, after some accident? A death even. His wife had drowned. Or a child. Probably not, Vince thought. Probably he had fished on the river as a boy. It's the natural place for him to be. And yesterday he had saved Phil's life. How casual that seemed! The boy had forgotten almost at once. Then Vince realised his phone was ringing. He liked to keep the tones discreet and the water was thundering. Mr Marshall, could you come to the hospital?

It was after three now. I can't believe it! Michela was muttering. Her lips were pale. She was attached to a drip but nothing else. In the only other bed, beneath the window, an older woman was unconscious. Michela! Vince said. Again he was surprised they had left him alone. You're awake! He felt an intense, nervous pleasure, an apprehension. Where's Clive? she asked in a low voice. I thought they meant Clive was coming.

With no air-conditioning the room was stifling. The window was closed. The girl is confused, he realised, and sweating. She tried to sit up but fell back, as though oppressed by some invisible weight. Shouldn't she be sedated, he wondered? Perhaps you're not supposed to sedate coma patients. Why are you here? she whispered. Where's Clive? Vince tried to be natural. He wiped a sleeve on his forehead. I don't really know why, he admitted. Clive said he had to go to Berlin. He asked me to stay.

Vince wondered how much he should say to the girl, what allusions might upset her. The doctors hadn't given him any instructions. I've brought your clothes and bathroom stuff. She stared at him. Actually, I'm not sure if they've been washed. I couldn't find a launderette. Staring, she seemed to find everything he said incomprehensible. Again she tried and failed to sit up. She was pinned to the bed, panting. When's he coming back? she asked. When can I see him?

He said he should be back Thursday.

A look of puzzlement clouded her eyes.

When Thursday, what day is it today?

The flight is due Thursday, that's all I know. In Bolzano. Today is Sunday. He saw her fists clench on the bed. Until then, I mean, if there's anything you need . . . Do you have a mobile, by the way. That might . . .

And that's all he said? Is that all he said?

Vince was unprepared for this. It occurred to him that he had been spared any hospital scenes with Gloria. Only the morgue. Casting about, he told her: Actually he did say something about going because you would have wanted him to.

She managed to turn a little in the bed and pushed the sheets aside. Everything oppressed her. Me? And you believed him?

Vince said, I don't know anything about you two, do I? I'm sure he believed it, though.

Making a huge effort, she dragged her head higher up the pillow. The drip bottle swung on its pole. Crumpled and damp, the white hospital smock they had given her clung to her body. Vince can see her breasts. Apart from the facial bruise, her body appears to have flushed through the rapid without a scratch. You really believed him! Her voice was harsh and dazed. Are you stupid?

It's hardly up to me to believe or disbelieve. Vince kept his voice quiet, adult. I told him I thought it would be much better if he stayed with you, not me. He said he had something very important to do and you would understand. You would want him to go.

Ah, important. Again she grimaced. It was as if she were looking for the energy to express her anger. What could Clive ever do that was important?

Vince watched her. He was annoyed with himself for not having prepared the meeting at all, not having scouted ahead. He doesn't want her to suffer some kind of relapse. Clive saved you, he told her in a matter-of-fact voice. He pulled you out. Without him, you'd have drowned. She thought about this for a moment. I wish I had drowned, and him too, she muttered. I wish we'd both drowned! Now leave me alone! she finished. Leave me alone and don't come back! I don't want to see you.

Vince stood up. You should have thought more before coming, he told himself. He sighed. You rest, he said, I'll come back tomorrow. Don't, she said. I don't want to see you. Go back to your bank and your calculations.

He was at the door when she must have noticed the bandage on his hand. Oh, did you hurt yourself? For the first time, her voice registered curiosity. She was propped on one elbow. I went down after you. I couldn't avoid it. She began shaking her head rather strangely. I didn't ask you to, did I? I didn't say you did, Vince replied. He paused a moment by the door. I'm not complaining. It was quite an experience. As he turned to leave, he heard her repeat. Don't come back. Please.

Vince spent the late afternoon cleaning the chalet. He could have got in his car and driven right back to London if he had wanted to. She's awake now, he thought. She's out of danger. She can give the doctors the phone number of family and friends. She has her clothes, her health card. I forgot to leave any money, he remembers, washing a pile of dishes. But he knows it's a detail. Someone would drive her back here. It was only a few miles. And it's only about sixteen hours to London, he thought. If I drive through the night. I needn't even be late for work. She made it perfectly clear she doesn't want to see me.

He settled down to clean the chalet. To do it seriously. There was this urge in him to get in the car and go. He felt his body straining towards it: the air-conditioning, the long hours at the wheel through the continental night, the autobahns, the tunnel beneath the sea, the early morning on the M2, old friends at the bank, authority. For years now Vince has wielded authority. But the resistance is steady and strong. That was not the way forward.

Sweating and sticky, he heaped a hundred odds and ends onto the big bed and found a broom to sweep the floor. It was one of the witches' variety with yellow bristles that caught between planks of bare wood. He scraped in corners. There are nail parings, the tar-drenched ends of rolled cigarettes, a couple of cotton buds, crumpled receipts, a piece of chewing gum, even a dried-out teabag. They don't keep a clean house, he thought. When was the last time I used a broom? He didn't feel critical, but dogged, trying to establish a geometry, a system. Both Clive and Michela are powerfully present to him. He can hear their voices. Sweep from the walls in, he decided. There was a cleaning firm for the service flat in Vauxhall. Everything is always clean when Vince gets back after a long day, everything in the right place. Then he found a rag, put it under the tap, wrung it out and wiped the floor twice. In this heat, with window and door wide open, it dried at once. At six-thirty the sun dropped behind the glacier. The valley began to cool. It was a relief. Some kids had started kicking a ball where Waterworld's kitchen tent had been.

He tried to sort out the clean clothes from the dirty and put the latter in a bin-bag. Why am I doing this? he wondered. The girl's underclothes in one drawer, sweaters in another. These two people are in grave trouble, he thought. He gathered stray books together on a shelf – *Strategies of Subversion, Carbon War, Stupid White Men*. Why will people never give up anything? someone had scrawled inside a cover. We must give up things! Clive, he thought. He stacked papers, invoices, brochures, printouts of e-mails. Some were signed 'Red Wolves', with an indication of a website. There was an IBM Thinkpad, but he didn't turn it on. Did Michela have a mobile phone? he wondered. If so, where? He opened and closed various drawers. They are asking too little for these holidays, he reflected, considering a paper quoting the price of the canoes. It would take for ever to recover the outlay.

Suddenly, Vince realised he was crying. The tears are flowing as he shifts the bed and sweeps the big dust-balls from under it. He doesn't stop. There are two old Durex foils. I should have done this before wiping the floor, he realises. Nobody has swept here for a month and more. I'm doing what Gloria always did, he mutters: tidying up. He shifted the bed back into position, turned up a photocopied pamphlet: 'The Bomb in the Garage: How To!' He shook his head. It used to infuriate him, having got home late Friday night, that Gloria would then spend Saturday morning cleaning. I never protested. He crouched down with the dustpan, collected up the dust and the foils and tobacco shreds and sweet wrappers. Should I wipe again? These are tears of shame, he decided. He didn't stop. He tipped the mess into a Despar plastic bag, wrung out the cloth again. Could that have been what she meant? He got on his knees. That she was sorry for the Saturday morning cleaning sessions. The wet wood had a musty smell. We could have loved each other better, Vince thought.

He had nearly finished now. Adam was a detail, he decided. He wiped the table and counter and moved the chairs back. In six months, nothing has brought him so close to his dead wife. So close to the edge. He sat on the stool by the counter. There was still the sink to sort out. Deep trouble, he muttered, thinking of Clive and Michela again, their books, their bad investments, their aggressive concern about the world. Was there any bleach about? he wondered. They need an accountant. Then a vibration in his pocket told him a text had arrived. Let us know your news. How is M? Mandy. M awake, he replied. All well. Safe journey.

Vince stood at the open door of the chalet. The campsite was busy with new arrivals organising their gear. The evening was moist and warm and beyond Sand in Taufers the profile of the mountains rose quiet and clear into a pale sky. Did that girl commit suicide? he wondered. Katrin Hofstetter. The name came to him. It hadn't seemed an obvious place to fall from. The path was easy. He gazed up above the castle to the glacier. They hadn't visited the castle. The landscape is patient, he thought, staring at the high slopes. It waits patiently. But perhaps memorials aren't always put

188

exactly in the place where an accident happens. That might be dangerous. Perhaps she had died a hundred yards away, on some tricky bit. I left no memorial for Gloria, he thought. They're not the fashion these days. He imagined a plaque on some boulder up in the mountains, his wife's photograph and a date. Perhaps that way you could restrict remembering to a place, a routine, an anniversary visit. Jingling the car keys in his pocket, Vince walked through the campsite towards the village. Even after shedding the ring, she won't let me go. Unless it was just a question, he thought, dropping the Despar bag in a bin, of not being used to having nothing to do. I arranged a holiday, Vince realised, that would be all action. I did that on purpose so as not to think. I am always so busy. And how strange that through all those years, in the office, in the flat, at home, these mountains had been waiting here. They always will. Even after the glaciers have melted. The world waits for you to be tired of your life. To save himself having to choose, he went to the same restaurant they had eaten in yesterday evening.

As soon as he sat down, Vince knew he was touching bottom. The place was not the same without the group. This is it, he realised. They hurried him to a corner, a small table for two. The waitress spoke no English. She was in a hurry with all the other clients, the holidaymakers. Trying to get a grip, Vince looked around. The room assailed him. Without the others, he has no resistance. This schlock is horrible, he realised, these dangling hearts that aren't hearts, these fake trophies, these dead animals, this awful international music with its sugary electronic rhythms. How could I have loved it so much yesterday? Why did I find it so wonderful?

The same ageing musician presented the same impassive face above his keyboards. A mahogany face. The tune was 'Smoke Gets In Your Eyes'. He must have grown up with the accordion and folk dances, Vince thought, or with the organ in church, with festivities and solemnities. How can he play this stuff? The music suddenly seemed very loud. It's a betrayal, Vince thought. The man was not incompetent. He's betraying his past. And the voices were swelling too. There was a huge buzz of voices. The international clients aren't listening to the entertainment that has been laid on for them. They bring their money, Vince thought, but not their attention. The musician's eyes stared across the heads of the holidaymakers. Into nothingness. He pays attention to nothing. Like a photo on a grave. And knows no one is paying attention to him.

Suddenly, Vince was covering his face with his hands. I miss them. His head was shaking. I miss Brian and Max and Amelia and Tom. People I've only known a few days. Gloria is dead, a voice said. Oh then please, *be dead*! Vince wailed. *Die!* He had spoken aloud. Don't come back please, Michela said. Don't come back.

Entschuldigung? The waitress is at his side. She wants to take his order. I am about to make a scene, Vince thought. He forced back his chair. I'm sorry. The waitress had seen his tears. Her face didn't soften. I'll have to go. He turned and made quickly for the door.

There is no question of thinking now. He walked swiftly along the lamp-lit street. This is a complete impasse. I don't want to see you. What had he expected? How lightly he had scorned Mandy's sensible interest. Abruptly he turned into a bar. Whisky, he said. They would understand that. He pulled out his wallet at once. Behind the counter a young man was moving quickly between the beer-taps and now Vince noticed kids playing at screens around the walls and others sitting at keyboards typing out e-mails. This must be where Louise and the others had come most evenings. It was smoky. I still haven't said anything to the bank, Vince remembered. Where Phil had downloaded pornography. The barman was showing him an ice-bucket, eyebrows raised enquiringly. Vince shook his head. Louise scorned Phil and his dirty pictures, but in the space of a couple of days she had slept with a boy she hardly knew. Why did I let her do that? She's far too young. Vince sipped the whisky. He doesn't like whisky. Then downed it. I should have said something, about relationships, about commitment. I'm nervous about calling the office, he realised, like an adolescent afraid of parental reproach. Yet he only has to inform them of an emergency, a forced absence. For God's sake, I'm one of the most important people in the bank.

The whisky burned outward from his stomach. It was satisfying to do something out of character, something destructive. He feels nauseous. He feels better. I constantly feared Gloria's reproach, he thought. He put the glass down. Why? He had shed her ring, but not the sharp reproachful voice that runs in his head. You never take a holiday. You've given your whole life to that bank. If we moved to London, though, he told her, we'd have more time together. That was always how the conversation went. But she wouldn't give up her job. Gloria was secretly happy I didn't take holidays, he realised now. Without modulating his normal voice at all, he asked: Is there a bottle I can have. *Was?* A bottle. Can I buy a bottle of whisky? To take away. The young man smiles. He can see I'm in trouble. *Haben wir eine Flasche Whisky?* he calls to a sour-looking girl making up sandwiches. That's his wife, Vince thought. He stepped out into the street with a bottle of something called Highland Dew.

Where was he going? He hadn't crossed the bridge that led back to the campsite. He was walking along the road down the valley to Geiss and Bruneck. As soon as he was beyond the village lamps, the pavement disappeared. To the left was a thin strip of woodland between road and river; all around, the quiet mass of the mountains. He was exposed to oncoming headlights, swerving as they saw him. Three, four, five together. The glare is blinding. He had to stop. Then there was a break and the darkness and silence flooded back. He could walk again, until the next car arrived, speeding, glaring. Two worlds that alternated. The landscape, the traffic. We ignored each other, Vince thought. That was the simple truth. That's why it is impossible to be alone now. For years you ignored each other and now she won't leave you alone, now you must pay attention. I am talking to myself, Vince stumbled. I am lost.

But at that very moment he found the path. The bushes opened to the left, down towards the river. He trod slowly in the dark. The old man will have a lamp, he thought. Sure enough, he met the river at exactly the point where they had tackled the wave the first day. Got it right! He stopped a moment at the river bank. The black water was fast but unhurried. The foam of the stopper glowed a little, as though phosphorescent. He looked across. I know the call of it now, he told himself, the water's invitation. He could understand the gesture of the limp arms, the girl's neck bent like a swan's towards the current.

Through the bushes a few yards on, the tramp's shack was in complete darkness. For some reason, Vince moved very quietly, stealthily even. He trod on tip-toe with his whisky bottle in one hand. The dwelling is made of old plywood panels anchored with nylon cord, draped with tarpaulin and corrugated iron. Vince bent to move aside a blanket. *Ist jemand da*? He had prepared the words. He didn't know if they were right. He poked his head in, but saw only three or four small grey chinks where light leaked from outside.

The smell was powerful. *Ist jemand da?* Vince repeated softly.
Suddenly the whisky bottle was wrenched from his fingers.
Ow! As he turned, a torch shone in his face. He had a vague
impression of an arm raised, of the whisky bottle attached
to it. No, he yelled. *Für Sie!* He tried to protect his head.
Trinken. Geschenk. Don't you understand? Roland! Finally he
remembered the man's name.

There was an old mattress laid across two loading pallets
and an assortment of filthy cushions and blankets, fruit boxes
with plates, tools, fishing gear. Roland lit a gas lamp that
hung from the sagging roof. He must have some money,
then, Vince thought. Some relationship with the world. It
was hard to get accustomed to the smell. *Rauchst du?* Unlike
Clive, Roland smoked regular cigarettes. I've accepted a cigarette! Vince hates smoking. Roland was talking excitedly all
the time. They sat at each end of the mattress. The cigarette
trembled in his fingers. Roland drank straight from the bottle
and handed it to him. Occasionally the flow of words was
interrupted at what seemed to be a question. But this was
not the German Vince had learned for O level. *Ja,* he filled
a gap at random. He knew it wasn't necessary. *Ja, ja.*

He handed the bottle back. Roland cocked his head to
one side. The face was gaunt and in the white light of the
gas it was as if the skull were somehow outside the skin, had
risen through the broken veins and blemishes, the loose lips,
long sparse hair. He's younger than me, Vince realised.
Roland's eyes were young and glassily blue in bloodshot rings.
The Adam's apple jerked sharply when he drank. *Nein,* Vince
said into the next pause. The bottle came back. Then he said.
Ich bin allein. It wasn't clear whether Roland had understood
this. Talking fast in a German that was strangely liquid, sing-
song almost, he fumbled in a pile of paper bags, brought out
a roll of bread, made to break it. It wouldn't break. He started

smiling, then laughing, making a comedy of his failure to break the bread, then at last handed half to Vince.

Meine Frau, Vince said, *ist* . . . He couldn't remember the word. My wife is dead, he said. Roland began to speak again. Drinking from the bottle, Vince was vaguely aware of hot ash falling on his trousers. *Tod*, he remembered. Gloria *ist tod*. Roland shouted something quite raucously, then lowered his voice to a muttered monotone. Vince watched. The man was fumbling in the pile of paper at the head of the mattress again, but this time found nothing. He shook his head theatrically. The air was heavy with smoke. At some point Vince heard the shout, *Draussen! Draussen!* Roland was yelling. His voice was suddenly clear and he was making a throwing gesture towards the blanket across the door. *Ja, Sie ist tod*, Vince repeated. He felt a sharp pain burn into his fingertips.

When he woke it was broad daylight. His bladder was aching. He had been in a board-meeting, pissing under the big polished table. Almost at once the shame was swamped by a pounding head. His hand went between his legs. He hadn't. Hadn't heard the bells either. Roland must have stretched him out on the mattress. Vince stumbled out of the shack and had to lean both hands on a tree while he relieved himself. What time is it? I'm late. Ten-thirty. The phone was still in his pocket. He had slept in all his clothes. He felt suddenly for his wallet, then was ashamed of doubting the man. Why wouldn't the phone turn on? Why was it taking so long? Vince realised he had never turned it off. It was dead. It's Monday. *Tod*, he thought. He shook his head and began to shamble back to Sand in Taufers under a blistering sun. Amazingly, it was getting hotter.

Hello, is that Colin? There was no electricity in the chalet. He had bought a car charger, but there was no shade in the campsite to park in while he phoned. All the places under the trees were taken. When he opened the car doors, the air swirled with heat. The seats and steering wheel were too hot for bare skin.

Vince, old chap! Welcome back. Not before time. Are you coming up for coffee?

No, actually, I'm still here, Col, I'm still in Italy. There's been a bit of an emergency I'm afraid. Accident.

Colin Dyers began the inevitable mix of concern and cautious questioning. Not Louise?

Vince hasn't had a hangover for more than a decade. Explaining the situation, he was aware that he didn't sound his normal self. Thank God for that, Dyers said. Though actually we were rather counting on your being here. The older man's voice was rich with catarrh. He was conventional and astute. That was very kind of you to, er, stay on for the young woman. I was the only one with my own car, Vince said. There was a slight, significant pause. Paul has been collating the figures from the States, Dyers said. There are a couple of urgent questions to be addressed.

Then Vince was aware of how absolutely unlike himself this behaviour must seem from the point of view of his colleague. Not so much the staying behind, but he could easily have phoned Dyers or one of the other directors on Sunday. He had their numbers. He could have warned them at once. He could have presented himself as extremely concerned about this delayed return, about all the many problems one had to deal with at this time of year. I should be asking who is handling what, sounding worried that I'm not personally in charge. Listen, Col, I can make it to an internet point, he said, if you want to send me some stuff to look at. And I'll have the phone on twenty-four hours a day now. I had trouble finding a car charger.

When do you think you'll actually be back, Dyers asked. There were strict rules of course about what could be committed to e-mail and phone conversations. Vince hesitated. He had stretched his sleeping bag on the car seat so as not to have to sit on the scorching material. The charger was plugged in. The heat trembled round his head. A fly was buzzing against the windscreen. Next Monday, he said. At the latest. You are well yourself, though, aren't you? Dyers asked. I've had a wonderful holiday, Colin. Wonderful. Just the break I needed. That's great, Dyers said. He would be sitting at a desk stacked with tasks and reports. At least one other person would be in the room awaiting his attention, one other phone-line is on hold and as he speaks the man's eye will be ranging constantly over the constantly incoming e-mail. Vince said: Listen, Colin, just give me this week. Trust me, okay. I won't let you down. Dyers immediately responded. We'll expect you next Monday, Vince. Back with us.

In the chalet, Vince opened the two windows and lay on the bed. His head aches. There was no way to shade out the light. He had left the phone to charge in the car. Closing his eyes, it suddenly occurred to him that there was an obvious purpose to this empty week. I must think about Gloria. I must give time to it. Real time. Not the few confused minutes before falling asleep. I must go at it as a task, a job.

For seven silent hours then, Vince lay on the bed in the chalet and told himself the story of his marriage. He remembered first meetings, holidays. He tried to list presents, to recall decisions, the cars they had owned, her father's death, the miscarriage after Louise. He remembered Gloria's sporting achievements, her body, her brusque but loving ways. She was loving, he thought, despite the austere, hurried meals, despite the Saturday morning cleaning. He remembered a way she had of dressing too lightly, of insisting they sleep with the window open, he remembered her fortitude when the first company he worked for had failed and there were mortgage payments and her father was ill. She had been solid then. She was never frightened of life. He remembered her laugh, her loud raucous laugh. She was taken from me, he said to himself at last, before there was time to understand, before I could prepare. I didn't sit by her bed. Perhaps it was a love story, he decided. In its own way. He tried to remember Christmases and dinners and discussions about Louise, about schools. He felt better. He stood up and switched on the radio. There was a small digital set on the counter. He brought it back to the bed and lay down again. The problem is not the past, he decided, but what to do next. He was surprised by this sudden clarity. What a strange night last night! He pressed the search button looking for a station in English. Reception wasn't good. The mountains no doubt. I haven't eaten for twenty-four hours, he thought. He remembered Roland trying to break his piece of stale bread. At last a woman's stern voice was talking about Iraq, about an election, an international disagreement, a plot to kill someone. Gloria would listen to two or three news bulletins one right after the other. Vince had always thought there was something disturbing about this attachment to chronicle. To return to the Berlin summit, the woman was saying – her accent was American – the three men who have chained themselves to the railing outside the Reichstag, now claim to have a bomb that they will explode if the police try to remove them. Vince got up, went out to the car, turned on the phone and texted a message to his daughter. Thinking of you, he wrote. It was lovely to be on holiday together.

SELF-RESCUE

Was it possible though? In the same internet café where he had bought the whisky, Vince studied a photo on the Guardian website. He has written to all his closest colleagues apologising for his absence, giving generic instructions, promising that he will be in the office on Saturday morning and will work through the weekend. The three men are wearing masks. Willing to Die to Wake Up the World, is the headline. Their spokesman speaks three languages fluently. No one knows who they are. The police have cleared the area. How can they sleep? Vince wonders. Or piss or shit? The masks are bags of white linen with holes for eyes and mouth. A strategy to prevent the police putting pressure on them through relatives, the article surmises. The temperature is in the mid-thirties. They are in full sunlight. Vince recognises the Reichstag with its pompous monu-mentality. He has visited the city more than once. But what he is looking at very closely is the exposed wrist of one of the men where it is handcuffed to the railing. This man seems to have a familiar build. Or perhaps not. He presses the 'back' button to return to the Waterworld site where

Mandy has already posted four sets of twenty pictures. The quality is good. Here you are folks! she has written. Our mythical Community Experience! Vince searches for one of Clive and clicks to enlarge. The instructor is photographed face-on in his yellow boat, paddle held across his blue buoyancy aid. It's a fine face, lit up somehow, the eyes glinting, the beard giving an impression of vigour, a secretive smile playing round the lips. Vince tries to find some distinguishing mark on the exposed wrist and forearm, but it's hopeless. A tattoo or a scar would do it. The red boat just poking into the background must be Michela's, he thinks. Or my own perhaps. He glances at one or two of the other pictures. Although there is loud music in the café, it's strange the silence that gathers around these images. Max doffing his straw hat. Caroline balancing the singing hamster on her head. Vince returns to the *Guardian*. He checks all related articles. They have the latest figures on global warming, speed of temperature rise, glacier retreat. There is a map predicting flooding, shaded in different colours to suggest possible dates. Holland gone mid-century. The Po valley gone. World in state of denial, a psychologist writes, like a party on a riverboat drifting towards Niagara. Odd he used that metaphor. Can it really be Clive? Vince goes back to the photo. The three men have small coloured backpacks. Ready to blow themselves up, is the caption.

Vince checks his mail again, then spends the day repeating last Thursday's walk up on the glacier. He takes the chairlift above Sand in Taufers, finds the path, bends his back to it. He has put on his walking shoes. Making the trip alone, he gradually becomes aware, all around him, of the same silence that emanated from those photographs, the silence of voices that are no longer there. All my life has a kind of silence to it, he reflects, these days. He remembers Clive's uncomfortable apology to Adam. It's a noisy silence. I don't think I can get through the whole summer like this, Michela had said. Vince stops to straighten his shoulders and look around. He had imagined she was referring to the heat. I didn't pay attention. Same with Gloria. And it's hot again now on the steep slope. The views are awesome. The peaks rise up one after another, quivering, immense and blue, but mainly bereft of snow. Perhaps we can feel a new tenderness for the landscape, now that we know we are killing it. Further down the valley there are cowbells clanging. Every time an animal moves, tiny, far below, a bell clangs in Vince's mind. It must drive them mad. And across the wide air that separates him from a further slope comes the tinkle of children laughing. Some party or other. Vince listens, he picks out the distant figures. This is the silence of the mountains. Does Michela know what is happening? he wonders. How will she react? There were a hundred thousand, the *Guardian* said, at Sunday's demonstration. It won't be Clive.

Long before he reached the top, Vince was aware of speeding up, of marching more purposefully. He wants to get to Katrin Hofstetter's death marker. On the way, he has seen three or four other memorials. Why didn't I see them last time? Now he comes across a small iron cross driven into a boulder and the name of a young man, Karl Länger. There's no photo, but a plastic rose has been fixed to the cross with a piece of wire. It's the girl's photo that draws me. Vince is aware that he has become hypersensitive to everything, and aware that it won't last. I should enjoy it, this intensity.

The high ridge where the glacier begins is a strange mix of heat and cold. The sun is burning his forehead and the grainy ice freezing his feet. Then he can't find the photo where he thought it must be. It's irritating. He stands aside to let a group of German hikers pass in the opposite direction.

Only four days and I've forgotten. *Grüss Gott*, a stout woman says. *Grüss Gott*. Eventually he finds the memorial twenty yards further on, facing west from a low wall of rock. 1999 she died. The thirty-first of August. How strange. And what a little miracle of technology to seal a photo so well it can survive the winter blizzards, the summer sun! The face is not quite as he remembered it. She's prettier, happier, the hair wavier, brushed forward on one shoulder. Katrin Hofstetter: 19.1.1979–31.8.1999.Vince imagines her eyes staring west into the sunset when the world around is all desert, when hikers no longer pass by, the planet is quite dead, and for the first time it occurs to him that those men chained to the railing in Berlin are not, perhaps, completely mad. Dyers and Hilson and the others will be in some committee meeting now. Much of the money the bank deals with is oil money. Inevitably. Glancing round to check that the path is quiet, Vince takes out his wallet, removes an ID photo of his wife and, without looking at it, lets it drop into the glassy crack between glacial ice and rock wall beneath the little memorial. In company, the dead may visit him less often.

Driving back, below the gorge at the entry to Sand in Taufers, he stopped the car at the sign 'Rafting Center' to the left of the road. In a small closed yard stood rack after rack of wetsuits and life-jackets. A tall, blonde man was loading gear into the back of a van. Do you know of any kayak guides I could contact? Vince spoke clearly and slowly in English. Not for myself, he explained. There was a group who already had their own instructors, but they might need a guide to show them round the local rivers. An expression of caution and recognition crossed the young face. You are with the English people, right? The girl who is nearly . . . He made a comic, choking expression. Right, Vince said. My name is Gerhard. The young man reached out a damp hand. She is okay? I helped to pull her out of the water. Very pretty girl. Vince gave his name. How much would a guide cost? he asked. It occurred to him now that there might be some local resentment of the English canoe group moving in like this on their pitch. We could have to talk about that, Gerhard said. I could have to see who is . . . who can help. Okay. Vince explained that he would only know on Thursday if their own guide could come or not. Then the work would be from Sunday onwards. I'll call you Friday morning. Gerhard gave him the Rafting Center's pamphlet, with a phone number.

The protestors have set a deadline of Wednesday evening at six o'clock, the radio said. Tomorrow. Vince listened stretched on the bed. It was early evening. There is one demand: a commitment to reduce greenhouse-gas emissions in line with Kyoto. Outside the open door of the chalet, the campsite sounds reminded him of the previous week: the singing, the shouts of children playing, radios, the occasional drumming. A diplomat who spoke in some unrecognisable tongue was translated as saying that his country would never be seen to reward terrorism. They were calling it terrorism. You have to keep a clear head, said an American. Vince was struck by the idea that the men at the railing might have very clear heads. As they saw it. Certainly they were keeping their nerve, despite the heat. How clearly I saw everything as the boat tipped down into the rapid. The image is sharper in his mind than any photo. What does clarity mean exactly? All those years doing the accounts, how clear-headed I was! How blind. Police spokesmen said they were taking the bomb threat very seriously. Vince looked at his watch. I could go and have a drink with Roland again, he thought, and get thoroughly muddled. Instead he fell asleep easily and early and woke in the night to hear the radio crackling voicelessly and feel the cool air drifting in through the open door. I didn't even close the door. Returning from the bathrooms, he was aware that his mind felt peculiarly healthy and purposeful, but without quite knowing what the purpose was. Caught yourself smiling, he muttered.

On the Wednesday morning he drove down to Bruneck, stopping at Geiss to check the bus timetable. He had put a change of dry clothes in the car. If someone like himself, he thought, could paddle the easy section of the lower Aurino on his own, then, in the event, there would be no guide required until the Monday.

Arriving at the hospital, he found the ward sister and asked her if she could tell Fräulein Donati he was here and would she be willing to see him. About five minutes later Michela appeared in the corridor, belting up the towelled robe he had brought her three days before. What are you doing here? she asked. I thought you'd gone. The bruise on her cheek has drained to yellow. She is standing very straight. Vince only shrugged. We can talk in the garden, she said brusquely.

Turning, she walked away so quickly he had to hurry to catch up. Her sandals slapped down two flights of stairs, along a corridor and out into a courtyard with five or six benches. I told you not to bother, she repeated over her shoulder. That's why I sent the nurse to ask if you were willing to see me, Vince answered. Michela went to a bench in the shade and curled herself up right in the corner, arms folded, knees drawn in under them. But Vince could sense she was better now. Her body had a quick feminine lightness as she moved. You look well, he said. Not because I want to, she told him.

He waited. The so-called garden was just a few square yards of lawn and shrubs with a near life-size Madonna, carved in wood, on a pedestal in the middle. Has Clive been in touch? she asked. No. He sat uncomfortably with his hands on his knees. Again it was fearfully hot. He was sweating. Actually, I was wondering if either you or he had mobiles, you know, it might be useful. He hates them, the girl said. What do you need to call us for anyway? Vince let it pass. Also, I thought you might need some money, but I couldn't find a wallet or anything, in the chalet. I don't have one, she told him. Clive left some money for me with the doctor.

Vince was surprised at this level of dependence. Again he waited. He wasn't going to tell her anything, if she didn't know. Eventually she said: They're letting me out tomorrow morning.

So you'll be there when Clive gets back.

Right.

Casually, he asked: You don't know if he had any special plans for while he was in Berlin?

No. At once she was more alert. Why?

Oh, I just wondered what on earth these demonstrators could actually get up to for four whole days.

She relaxed. If it's like other things I've been to, there'll be a kind of alternative conference in some abandoned warehouse or other.

Catching a smile in her voice, Vince turned to look at her. A soft irony was playing round her lips. He raised his eyebrows. Quite unexpectedly, she reached across the bench and took his bandaged hand. Is it bad? Vince couldn't hide from himself a sudden flutter of excitement. Just a couple of stitches. He didn't say he was planning to take out a boat this afternoon. So why haven't you gone back? she repeated. I wasn't very nice when you came last time, was I? Vince bit his lip, cast about. I promised Clive I would stay. Then I thought, you know, I might as well take advantage of the chalet for a couple of days. He wasn't so much lying as speaking at random. You're sad, aren't you? she told him. He hesitated. Not especially. Yes you are. One night I was sitting outside, behind the kitchen tent, and I saw you walking to the bathrooms. Really late. You had your shoulders bent – she sat forward and mimicked, cruelly, her face comically gloomy – like you were carrying something that wasn't there. Something pretty heavy. Oh, that's just old age, Vince said. He had expected to talk about her problems, not his. She laughed. Not true, you're sad. Why not admit it? Your wife died, didn't she? That's right, he acknowledged. The girl was looking at him. Did you love her?

Vince was unprepared for such a direct question. Yes. I did, he said. Of course I loved her. Poor fingers, she muttered. She was still holding his hand. And did she love you?

Yes. Listen . . .

You do know there was a nasty story going round?

Vince turned and looked straight at her. He pulled his hand away. She shrugged her shoulders, pursed her lips. She had done it deliberately. Her eyes are glinting. But he won't rise to it. Speaking very quietly, he asks: So what have you been up to these last couple of days?

Nothing. Lots of neural tests and scans and things.

Results?

Apparently I could be an athlete.

Great.

She didn't reply. She still has a mocking smile in her eyes. I suppose, Vince tried after a moment or two, the hospital must get pretty boring when you're not really ill. I mean, people must end up watching the TV and listening to the news the whole time.

There is a TV room, but I haven't been, she said. I can't bear TV voices. I can't stand the way the world talks. I . . .

but she stopped. She was repeating things Clive said. Oh, and a counsellor came to see me, of course.

Any good? Vince felt more relaxed now; she doesn't know. He told me I'd chosen a dangerous way to cry for help. Is that all?

Michela sighed. I didn't really talk to him. I've seen counsellors before. They work for money. My mother's seen millions of counsellors.

Did they get in touch with your mother?

I wouldn't give them her number. Michela lifted her face in a wry smile. Can you imagine? Another hysterical loser is the last thing we need.

You're not a loser.

Oh please, the girl said abruptly.

Vince breathed deeply. So what are you going to do when they discharge you?

I'll have to see through this summer. There are the canoes to be paid for. We owe the bank.

Vince said: I've been thinking about that.

What?

I've been thinking about your business. Frankly, you need to do a few sums again.

In what sense?

You're not charging enough for what you're giving, for the investment you've made. I picked up a couple of papers off the floor, in the chalet, and couldn't help but see some of the figures. I hope you don't mind. If you want, I could work out the right price to ask.

Clive did all of that, she said. Talk to him when he gets back.

I will. The fact that she was so convinced that Clive was coming back made his melodramatic suspicions about Berlin seem ridiculous. Again they fell silent. The heat in the little courtyard was oppressive, yet neither of them mentioned it. Finally Vince took a piece of card from his pocket. Tom asked me to give you his e-mail.

Who?

Tom. Tom.

Right! Oh God, she put her face in her hands, shaking her head. He watched her. Was she laughing or crying? I am drawn to this unpredictability. Without looking up, Michela reached out an open hand for him to put the card in, took it and shredded it into little pieces. They sifted down onto the gravel. Tom, she sighed. She was still shaking her head.

Vince said, So why don't you tell me about you and Clive?

After a moment she threw her head back rather dramatically. Took you a while to ask, didn't it?

Vince held steady. She is wishing I would go. She doesn't want me here. Yet for some reason, even if it was only the merest social inertia, Michela began to talk. They had met in London, she said, at a peace rally. She began to tell Vince the story of herself and Clive, how she had liked him at once, how enthusiastic he had been, how full of projects. They went for long walks across the city, talking about everything they saw, kissing, hugging. They liked to walk in the rain, roll cigarettes under bus shelters. Clive really cared about things, about mountains and rivers, got so upset at the state of the world. He looked after me in every possible way, she said. When she glanced up at Vince there were tears in her eyes. They had made love so much. They started living together only a couple of days after they met. Nottingham. Carlisle. I'd never lived with a man before. Clive had been teaching an outdoor survival course. He taught me how to paddle. He's a great teacher. When he wants to be. But sometimes he sort of loses interest. He hates bullshit and hypocrisy

207

so much. He's sort of obsessed by the way people just go on and on consuming. Then we went to the French Alps. He was teaching courses on the Durance. I worked in a restaurant to build up some money. It was wonderful.

So you should be happy, Vince said.

Don't pretend to be stupid! She glared. I hate that!

What I meant—

What you want to ask is why I kissed you under that waterfall, why I went after Tom like that.

Again he felt that flutter of excitement. Actually I was thinking more of your tossing away your paddle at the top of the rapid.

The kiss meant nothing, she said. It was a joke.

Vince watched her. She smiled now. As always there was a sardonic twist to the lips. The fact is I'm not good enough for Clive. That's the truth of the matter.

Rubbish.

Perhaps I know things you don't. She was biting the inside of her lip now.

Tell me.

You wouldn't understand.

Vince waited. Michela had put her feet on the ground and was sitting forward now, her hands on her chin. She turned her face to him rather brashly.

A couple of weeks ago he said he wouldn't fuck me anymore because I was no good in bed.

I don't believe you.

Oh well then, if he doesn't believe me! If the banker doesn't believe me!

Clive doesn't seem to me the kind of man who would talk like that.

She had begun to breathe very deeply. She pushed her head down, between her legs almost, breathing hard. For a moment he thought she might be sick. Instead of leaving be, he asked. Why don't you just tell me the truth? It can't be that bad.

Sounds like you didn't believe your wife was the kind of person who did the stuff she did.

Vince let it pass. I'm sorry, she said. She spoke softly, half laughed. I just can't believe you haven't gone and left me alone. You should have gone. I can be really awful.

Still Vince said nothing. He has ceased to ask himself why he is bothering. Two griefs are calling to each other. Tell me, he says.

What's the point, he'll be back tomorrow.

There was a clatter and a young woman appeared, stepping backwards between the swing doors, pulling a wheelchair. She forced down the handles to turn it on its back wheels and pushed its occupant into the shade against the wall. It was a young man, his head lolling on one side, his tongue pushed out between his teeth at the corner of the mouth. Michela watched. The nurse squatted down and began to do something with the young man's hands. Almost before Vince was aware of it, Michela began speaking very slowly and softly. He told me this world was such shit that it was pointless our being together. Okay? He said it isn't a place for love. This isn't the right world, this isn't the right world. He must have said it a million times. This isn't the right world for love, Michela. For us. She was crying now, Vince saw. Not sobbing, just letting tears run. Her voice was still steady. That's why I can't watch the news, the atrocities, the wars, the elections you know? I can't read the papers, I can't listen to the radio. I'll just hear his voice telling me I can't love him. I mustn't love him. I see a fire, smoke, and it's Clive telling me it's not the right world. I see a truck with filthy exhaust, the same. I see a cripple on a wheelchair and it's Clive saying we mustn't have sex, we mustn't have children in an ugly world. Oh God! She put her face in her hands and sobbed. Vince sat still. He made no move to touch her. Deliberately coarse, she sucked up hard through her nose, then wiped her face on her sleeve. Her lips quivered. The eyes were miserable and defiant. Satisfied?

I believe you now, Vince said.

Oh, well, thank God for that. What a relief!

He hesitated. What I don't understand, though . . . I mean, he didn't leave you. You were still together. And now he's coming back and you'll be together again. I don't understand that.

You don't understand! I wish he had left me. I wish he had done something cruel and left me. He could have kicked me out when I went off with Tom. Everybody must have seen. He should have told me to get lost.

You could always leave him.

She tried to smile. I thought that was what I was doing on the river the other day.

There must be easier ways.

Not that I can think of! Then she was laughing and snuffling. No, don't worry. Don't worry, Mr Banker, I haven't the energy to try again. She shook her head. You can't imagine the energy it took. Actually, come to think of it, I can't believe my mother's tried so often. That must be why she's so wiped out all the time.

Unthinking, he asked. What did it feel like?

What do you mean?

When you did it. When you turned the boat over.

The question has surprised her. She sat back, closed her eyes, smiled. Actually, you know, it felt great. When I finally decided, like, when I said, I'm going to do it, I'm really going to do it, it was great. I didn't feel anything going down. I mean any pain or anything. I just let myself go in a sort of trance. It was the waking up that was shit. She looked up. And you? What?

Well, you came down after me. How was it?

Absolutely terrifying! From nervousness, Vince burst out laughing. You know how Keith kept saying not to fight the water? Well, I started fighting the moment I dropped into the rush and the water won in about one second flat. The only weird thing is, he hesitated, wondering how to put it, the strange thing is that although it was frightening, I mean I knew I could die, I had the sense I was sort of detached, my mind was clear. And now I keep waking up wishing I could do it again.

I suppose, she said, that Clive came down with no trouble at all? She looked away.

That's right. She's still in love, he thought, watching her face. He made it look easy. As he spoke, Vince remembered the man's bearded face as he passed the rock that he, Vince, was stranded on. Yes, Clive had been smiling! But he didn't want to say this now. Instead he suddenly offered: Look, if you tell me what time they're letting you out, I'll come and get you tomorrow.

Why don't you just leave now? she asked. Aren't you supposed to have a terribly important job? Not to mention a lovely daughter. Why don't you go? You can see I'm all right.

Do you want the lift or not? I'll go home Friday. After Clive is back. As promised.

She looked up and smiled. He was struck by a certain mischief about her fine features, sly eyes, a wayward shrewdness. Okay, she said, taxi-driver.

Vince parked the car at Geiss and had a beer and a sandwich in the Brückehof while waiting for the bus. He feels good. He is almost pleased now to be so lost. Disorientation need not be a problem, he thinks. The bus came on time, full of housewives returning from their morning's shopping in Bruneck. An older man fanned himself with a newspaper. A couple of young hikers were consulting maps. Nobody spoke to Vince. He got off at the stop before Sand in Taufers and crossed the bridge to the campsite. The canoes were stacked on the trailer beside the chalet. Clive had told him where the keys were hidden. The boat he had been using was the third from the top. He dragged the others off, put them back, locked the chain again. My hand feels okay, he decides. It was two o'clock. Four hours to the deadline in Berlin. He has stopped imagining that it could be Clive now, yet feels attracted to those men. Suddenly all kinds of behaviour seem explicable. They are gambling their lives.

It felt strange putting his kit on alone. He took the bandage off his hand, clenched his fist, thrust it carefully through the tight rubber cuffs of his cag. Then the spraydeck, the buoyancy aid. Again he was struck by the noisy silence of doing things without others. He heard Louise's voice now: Dad, where are my thermals, I've lost my thermals. There was always something she couldn't find. And Brian's. I'm Brian, the boy had said, Max is the fairy. Vince smiled. Car keys, he thought. Where? He threaded the leather loop into the ties that held the boat's backrest. Perhaps I should have been a scout leader.

With the kayak perched on the bank where Keith and Clive had deliberately capsized them all the first day, he checked and double-checked the spraydeck, running his fingers round the rim of the cockpit. The tab was out. I won't drown. His buoyancy aid is tight, his helmet tight. I'm afraid, he thought. Just being nearer the water made the world cooler, even shivery. Now, paddle like a god. Vince tipped forward and the boat slid in.

At once, he was surprised by the pull of the current, even where the water was calm. He had barely thought of this when he was with the others. Perhaps because they always moved along together. He was already twenty yards downstream. He broke in and out of a couple of eddies to build up confidence. It was worrying how awkward he felt, how loud and inhibiting his mind seemed to be. I should be back in the City with my figures and phones and papers. Then he remembered the beep of a reversing truck coming through the trees, remembered the mist on the water, the ducks flying low. It was the quiet stretch before the first rapid.

There is no mist now. Midges rise off the shallows in small clouds. Where had they entered the rush? I was following Mark. But where? He back-paddled, ferrying a little this way and that. This is why people need guides. To choose the line. River-left, he decided. He put in three or four strong, determined strokes and met the chute perfectly. This was the place. He steered through the rush, saw the terminal stopper racing to meet him and began to paddle hard. But the river seemed to be higher today, the stopper more powerful. As he ploughed through the soft foam, the tail of the boat began to sink. The canoe was pulled down. Vince stayed absolutely calm. The icy water gripped his face. The noise was furious and muffled. Wait, wait till it flushes you out. Five seconds later he rolled up in calm water. Everything is in order. Hand okay? More or less. He is laughing. Paddle hard now to warm up again.

Two hours later, just moments from the get-out point, the bridge at Geiss where his car is parked, Vince made the inexplicable error. Moving out of an eddy into the stream, he tried that clever flick of the hips the boys made that sunk the stern into the oncoming stream and lifted the bow vertical. He was feeling that confident. It worked perfectly. The front of the boat reared up. Vince experienced an entirely

childish thrill. He was on his back on the swift water looking up at the sky beyond the nose of his kayak. The boat
came down on top of him. No problem. Under water, he
was happy. He set up the roll carefully and swung the paddle.
Basic self-rescue. Been here before. He didn't come up. Or
rather, he came half up and sunk back. Still, no problem.
He had got a gulp of air. He set up again. He repeated the
roll stroke confidently.

The same thing happened. The boat hung a moment on
its side, then sank back. Now his mind began to cloud. He
can't remember how far it is to the next hazard. There are
rocks in the water. There is a small drop, the rush beneath
the bridge. Any second now something will crash into my
helmet. Try once more. But his knee was slipping from its
brace position now. His body was cooling fast. This time he
didn't even come half up. He didn't get a breath. Now he
is afraid. His right hand felt for the tab on the spraydeck
and pulled. Exactly as he broke surface, his back slammed
into the central pillar of the bridge.

The river split in two for a few yards here, rushing under
dark arches. Vince had had the wind knocked out of him.
The boat had gone the other side. He was sucked under a
moment. The paddle caught on something. Then he was up
again the other side of the bridge. All okay. But the boat
was yards away. Vince swam for the bank. There were stones
and roots. He stumbled, floundered, sat in the shallow water.
Get your breath back. The car keys, he remembered then.
The car keys were tied into the boat.

Recovering his energy, he was struck by the inexplicable
nature of this reversal. Losing the boat, the keys, if he did
eventually lose them, was not the kind of disaster that changed
your life. An irritation, an expenditure. But why had it
happened? I must get going, Vince decided. I must get them

back. He was on his feet. I didn't try anything beyond my capabilities. The path, he saw now, was not on the road side, where he had climbed out, but the other. I did five miles of river with no real trouble. He hurried back to the bridge and crossed. The kayak was already out of sight. Five miles! He tried to trot, but his breath was short, the wetsuit rubbed behind his knees. Then less than a hundred yards from the end, I fail to do something I can do perfectly well.

There was no sign of the boat. He would have to scramble through a thicket now. Already he was seriously overheated in this powerful sunshine. For a moment he thought of taking off the heavy rubber cag, the helmet. But what if I need them to retrieve the boat? He pushed through the trees. The path has gone. I felt so confident, so sure, so close to taking a decision that would have changed everything. Then the river had rejected him, reminded him he was the merest novice. Or I screwed up myself, on unconscious purpose as it were.

The thicket ended, but there was still no sign of a path. A meadow of deep grass sloped down towards the river. On the opposite bank was a timber business of some kind. He had trotted almost half a mile through long dry grass before he saw it. The river took a sharp bend to the left, and immediately after that he noticed something odd, something red in the water. The canoe was almost completely submerged, pinned against a boulder in the middle of the flood.

Vince gazed. The boulder was the first of a small rapid. Nothing dangerous, a fall of only a yard or so spread over five or six little steps, but the pressure of the water that was holding the boat must be huge. The glassy surface curled upward to pour into and over the red hull. It was about twenty feet from the bank, and Vince has no rope with him. Or rather, he has a rope, in a throw-bag, but it is attached inside the boat. The cockpit is facing upstream, the river pouring into it. So he might be able to get at the rope. Or even the keys, though they were hidden away behind the seat. On the other hand, the water might have carried the throw-bag away.

Vince squatted on the bank and stared, lips pursed. Then, amid the anxiety, he began to feel the pleasure of it. The water swirled round the bend, piling on the further bank. There is a scattering of stones, some breaking the surface, some below; trees on the far side, meadow on this; the boat right in the middle, the water piling and nagging against it. High above, the mountains shimmer gently in the heat rising from the valley. Against the dark green of the forests, a hang-glider is spiralling with rainbow wings. Nearer at hand, a dragonfly darts over the muddy bank. Without the boat, no car keys. No ride back to the chalet. The river is challenging me. I accept.

Vince tried to measure the force of the stream. What if I allow my future to be decided by whether I retrieve the boat or not? He felt excited. He walked about thirty yards up from the boat to the apex of the bend. The water was sweeping round and away from the near bank across the river. You won't even have to swim hard. He plunged in. In his overheated state, the cold was even more of a shock. But it was too easy. The current was taking him exactly there. He steered himself round a rock. He mustn't be swept past. You're going too quickly! He grabbed at the submerged cockpit, missed, just got a hand on the handle at the bow. It was his bad hand. He saw the black stitches sunk in inflamed knuckles as he pulled himself along the top of the boat. The stream was holding him against the hull now. He grabbed the rim of the cockpit and felt inside. The rope was there, in place under a stretch of elastic cord.

With some difficulty, Vince had tied the leading end of the rope to the bow-handle and was planning to toss the rest, in its bag, to the bank, when the folly of this occurred to him. Without anyone to catch it, the stream would pull at the rope floating in the water and carry it away. I need someone on the bank. Pressed against the kayak, his shoulders just above water, he untied the rope with fingers that had already lost their sensibility. Can I throw it unattached? It must reach the bank with the trees. No. Feeling under water, he loosened the waist of his cag, thrust the rope between the two rubber layers and tightened the waist again. Then he pushed off sideways into the rapid.

It wasn't so much a question of swimming, but holding his body in such a way as to reduce the blows to a minimum. This isn't serious stuff, he thought, letting the water flush him through. As he was swept round the end of the bend into calmer water, he remembered the boys' four-star test. Clive prepared us well. It isn't him in Berlin. As soon as he had passed the rapid he began to swim to the shallows.

On the wooded bank, he scrambled back upstream through thick undergrowth till he was opposite the boat. He unravelled all the yellow rope from its bag, tied one end around a slim tree-trunk and the other to the belt of his buoyancy aid. Just before plunging in again, he suddenly thought: Stop, think. Nothing more dangerous than momentum.

He sat on the edge of a four-foot drop into the water. He was on the other side of the river now. The bank was undercut by the current swirling against it. Instead of taking him towards the boat, it will pull him back in to the bank. Vince stared. If I swim diagonally into the current, as if ferrying, how far will I get? He had no idea. I must psyche myself up, he decided. I'm tired. Fleetingly, he was thinking of the memorials on the mountain. People who no doubt thought they could overcome some obstacle, or didn't even realise they were in danger. We know catastrophe is await-ing us, wrote the psychologist on the *Guardian*'s web-pages, yet we choose not to see it. The hell with that, Vince grinned. He started to walk upstream. Twenty yards from the tree where the rope was tied, he chose his spot. For perhaps a minute he took long deep breaths, filling his lungs. Now, plunge and swim.

Keith called it power swimming. Head well out of the water in case of rocks, arms crawling like crazy, feet paddling hard. I'm being swept away. Pointing upstream and across, fighting like mad, he can't see the boat. Something banged his left knee. Then his helmet. I've overshot. No, it was the boat's stern. He grabbed it. Suddenly, his body is dragged under. The rope has snagged on something on the river bed. It's tight. The current is pulling him below the stern of the boat. Calm. Vince tugged. It won't come loose. Don't wait to be short of breath. He released the buckle of the life-jacket, let the rope go and was swirling through the rapid again. This time, before he could get into position, feet first on his back, he took a fierce knock on his shoulder. For a second his mind clouded. Then he was through to the calmer water, swimming for the shore.

He needed more time to rest now. Sitting against a tree-trunk, eyes closed, his thoughts have lost any structure. The river, the boat, Gloria, the men chained to the railings in Berlin, the girl's lips approaching his, the torch coming through the undergrowth, his daughter's perfume bottle, Dyer's voice: We were expecting you back . . . everything is present to his mind. Everything is muddled, as if dissolved in the blood flooding his head. Slowly, he began to focus again. There's no real danger, he thought. I'm just tired.

He fought his way along through the undergrowth, found the rope, pulled it in. One tug in this direction and it came easily. This time he packed the rope back in its bag and clipped the bag itself to the life-jacket belt. It would unravel as he swam, rather than being loose from the beginning. That way it shouldn't snag. He walked back to where he had dived in. A fish flipped up from the water. A trout presumably. This must be the last attempt, though, he told himself. He feared for the moment when his strength would just go. Adam had warned them of that moment. The cold finally gets to you. Now dive.

Vince tried to keep the strokes fast and determined. Suddenly he had a sense that he was both fighting the water and not fighting it. Perhaps this was what Keith meant. He was fighting, but not *against* the water. Use the thrust to force your way across. Then he was sweeping past the boat on the far side. Almost a yard further than last time. The rope wrapped around the boat, under it probably, and held. At once, he grabbed the rope tight and pulled himself, like a climber, into the small boiling eddy behind the boulder. He could stand here.

Now he was behind the rock with the boat on the other side. Without the pressure of the water against him, he could move. He had time. He tied the rope to the bow-handle. Now all he had to do was dislodge the canoe. He kicked and pushed and shoved. It won't budge. It needs to be pulled away sideways, he realised, slipped between the opposing pressures of current and rock. Whereas I am behind it.

Vince is almost screaming with frustration now. Then he understood. Once again, he launched into the flood, let himself be flushed through the rapid, swam to the bank, climbed back, very slowly, to the tree, the rope. He sat on the bank a while, just gazing at the yellow rope sinking into the white water, attached to the red hull. Then he began to pull. The rope came taut. At the third tug he felt the boat shift, it definitely shifted, and with a couple more yanks it was free. It went tumbling away through the rapid. Vince lifted the rope as high as he could to keep it clear of the rocks. Good. Inevitably rope and boat were swinging in to the near bank. Vince scrambled back downstream. When he arrived, the canoe was already there, banging against the bank, the yellow rope taut.

He pulled the canoe ashore, felt inside with shaking hands, found and released the buckle, retrieved the keys. Then leaving canoe and kit in the trees, he began the long walk back. There was no way along the bank this side. He had to strike away from the river till he reached the road. Then it was a good half mile. He kept stopping to sit. Have I ever been so tired? But his mind was full of pride. I did it! I screwed up, then I put things right. This is infantile, he thought. He felt wonderful. Towards Geiss he was aware that the sun had fallen behind the peaks. Already! The wetsuit was chafing him, under the arms, behind the knees. How late is it? he wondered. The boat will have to wait till tomorrow.

When he reached the car, he didn't even have the energy to undress and change clothes. Seven o'clock. He turned on the radio. I should have put some food in here. I need sugar. Checking his mobile for messages, he was vaguely aware that the German newscaster he was listening to had used the word *Mord* in the headlines. *Selbstmord*. When are you coming back, Dad? Louise had written. Miss you. Things to talk about. An hour later, in bed in the chalet, he thought again, it won't be Clive. The American Forces radio station said that the protestors were as yet nameless. They had blown themselves up before the deadline when an armoured car had approached them.

PASSWORDS

Vince already had the boat loaded in the back of the car when he reached the hospital. His left shoulder and right knee were aching. When Clive returns, he can tell her about it, he thought. But if Clive didn't return? Surely if Clive were one of the three, the police would know, they would already have come to the chalet. Vince had thought of hiding the laptop; but then someone might imagine I was stealing. Michela was already waiting for him on the steps at the main entrance, wearing dark glasses. Suddenly she looks like some kind of celebrity. She has a bright blue mini-dress. They let me go into town yesterday afternoon, she smiled. She seemed cheerful. I spent Clive's money. Then she added: I've decided to live, by the way. Her tone was deliberately casual. Glad to hear it, Vince told her. He was awed by her easy elegance, a sort of natural disdain she has.

Throwing her bag in the back, Michela asked, how come the canoe? He had had to lower the back seats. I went out on my own. This morning? She raised her eyebrows. The bruise on her cheek was almost gone. He explained. He had had to drag the thing through brambles. You're mad, she told him. You could have drowned. Against all his plans, this prompted Vince to say: Did you hear what happened in Germany? She was opening the passenger door. They were in the hospital car park. The pause she left was so long, settling herself now in the seat, wriggling a little to be out of the way of the nose of the kayak propped between the headrests, that he wondered if she had heard. This afternoon, she said firmly, I must check through all the kit. There's some administrative stuff to do as well. And tomorrow morning I'll have to shop, because the deal is that we have to provide the food for the first meal. They're supposed to arrive after lunch. She turned and looked straight at him, smiling falsely. I'm not to mention it, he understood. She knows. As soon as Clive gets back, he said, I'll hit the road.

When she opened the chalet door, she hardly seemed to notice the transformation that had taken place, the clean floor, clean sink, tidy table. She put her bag down. To work! Vince drove her to the post office, the bank, the internet café. She and Clive had a business e-mail. She made notes of one or two messages. At the post office there were brochures from equipment manufacturers. Invoices and cheques. Heads turned as she stepped out into the street. The blue of the dress was dazzling in the sunshine. She is conscious of those looks, Vince saw. She is enjoying them. But there is still something brittle about her. She is tensed for Clive's return. Take me to lunch, taxi-man, she told him. She is warm and mocking. The Schloss Café is good, she said.

This was at the end of a dirt road two or three hairpins above the castle that dominates the village. An ample terrace was packed with tables. What time did he say he'd be back? she asked. To Vince's surprise she has ordered steak and wine. They are sitting under a red and white sunshade looking down over pine trees into the warm green hum of the valley. Yesterday's river is a harmless brown ribbon flecked with white. Early evening, I think, Vince said. He didn't give a specific time. Vince has never bothered with sunglasses, but feels the need for them now. The slopes and mountains are pulsing with light. The very air is too bright. I should be back Thursday. He remembered Clive's voice. The man hadn't said when.

Good! She was rubbing her hands. Just a few hours, then.

He is struck by her cheerfulness. Her hair is glossy from a morning wash. Perhaps she's had it trimmed. She's eating and ordering without any concern for the price, as though this were some special celebration.

I was wondering . . . he began.

Ye-e-e-es? she laughed, raised her sunglasses for a moment. Her eyes are playful.

Wouldn't it be better, maybe, to come to some agreement with Clive, about the, er, money side of things, then for you to go and live elsewhere, perhaps, with friends. I mean, with the situation as it is, you risk getting upset. Or getting more attached, without solving anything.

She put down her knife and fork, patted her breast. I was wondering, she mimicked, head cocked on one side, voice pompous. Wouldn't it be better if Mr Banker minded his own business? She burst out laughing.

Please call me Vince, he said.

Anyhow, I don't have any friends, she said.

Vince found this hard to believe.

Not in Italy. And anyway I don't want to speak Italian. But we've been through that. I don't even want to think it.

Go to England.

Are you inviting me? she asked.

Vince was taken aback. Actually, I wasn't.

She smiled brilliantly. Please, Mr Ba— No, sorry, Vince, please, stop worrying about me. Okay? Come to think of it, after lunch, you might want to get going right away. If Clive is late you risk falling asleep at the wheel.

Vince told her he enjoyed starting a long drive in the evening, then stopping at a hotel as soon as he felt drowsy. She refilled her glass. She is drinking steadily. Behind her sunglasses he senses the eyes are searching him. She said: You think he might not come back, am I right?

Vince was caught out. Not at all, I just promised I'd stay till he did.

The waitress arrived, hovered, went off.

Why wouldn't he come back?

Oh I'm sure he will, Vince said. His voice sounded wrong. And then, I'll get moving, obviously.

They ate. The fare was standard but good. The day was too hot again, though they were pleasantly shaded, lightly dressed. Vince's body ached in various places from yester-day's adventure, but when sitting down to meat and wine these are not unpleasant aches, more reminders of being alive. Perhaps Michela feels the same way about the bruise fading from her cheek. There comes a point when a wound makes you more aware of the healing process than the damage. Even the tension between them is something to savour.

Tell me what you will do when you get back home, she asked. He explained that strictly speaking he wouldn't be going home. He must drive straight to the office. There would be at least ten days, non-stop, of sixteen-hour work stints, sandwiches grabbed in the canteen, a few hours' sleep in his service flat.

What's so important?

It was a question, he says, of deadlines for filing accounts, mainly for the bank's American operations. Things can often be accounted for in various ways.

You mean you have to look for loopholes, to avoid taxes.

Vince shook his head. Not at all. He smiled. Everybody thinks that. Actually, it's a question of choosing the form of accounting for every transaction that most nearly and clearly represents reality, so that everybody is in a position to understand what's going on, the directors, the institutional investors, the shareholders. If they don't understand the situation, it's hard for them to know how to behave.

So, at least with money, you know how to behave. She was smiling. She enjoys making fun of me, he thought. My job is more to do with defining what has happened, he said, not making the investment decisions.

And after those two weeks, you can go back to your house and daughter?

He explained that Louise lived with her uncle's family.

Why?

I spend the week in the city and her school is a hundred miles away.

You put your work before her, Michela said.

Vince has understood that these provocations do not necessarily indicate hostility. When Gloria died, I didn't know what to do. I was thrown. I thought the best thing was to keep working as before.

Giving your whole life to money.

Vince poured himself more wine. You let me off the hook with that kind of crude attack, he told her. Mouth full, she raised an eyebrow. Money, he spoke quickly, is that invention which makes all resources measurable in common terms and hence transferable, so that people don't have to swap a cow for a field. Yes? Or a goat for a kayak. The bank is that place where the units of wealth can be stored so that resources can be exchanged when and where it is most convenient. Or alternatively they can be used by someone else while the real owner is deciding what to do with them, so that wealth is not just left lying around in heaps of gold. A banker is not serving money, he's at the centre of a complicated network of exchanges that makes life possible.

Yes, Professor. Of course. But the way it actually works stinks, doesn't it? No one is thinking where the resources should go. Only where money is most likely to multiply. There's no morality in it, let alone compassion.

In my case, Vince said, the morality is in the honesty of representation.

She had finished. She wiped her mouth with a paper napkin, pushed her chair back, crossed her long legs. What do you do in the evening, then?

Vince shrugged. Nothing. I get back to the flat late. Bit of TV. Bed.

And at the weekend?

Maybe I take the canoe out on the estuary. Which is going to seem pretty dull after last week.

Or you could visit Mandy.

I could, yes.

You must have lots of friends, she said.

Not really.

Oh, I find that hard to believe. Again she is mimicking. She is almost too good at it. He smiles. Acquaintances, I suppose. Business friends. Gloria's friends.

You don't really want to go back to your job, do you, Mr Banker?

Vince remembers that Clive had suggested the same thing. Perhaps they had talked together about him. He decided to be honest. You know, I don't quite understand what I want. Actually, I don't know how I can understand.

It would mean knowing the future, knowing myself. I've changed.

You see, Michela said, I was right, you don't want to go back. The young woman seemed very pleased with herself. She lifted her glass to her lips again.

Vince looked down the valley. Clouds were gathering over the peaks now. Perhaps there was the first smell of a storm in the air. There seemed to be a lot of birds on the move. I feel I would like to take a risk, he said. That's all.

Like you did yesterday on the river.

I suppose so. I had a good time. I mean, even when it was bad.

You know what Clive says?

What?

A fragile candour crept into her voice. You know he liked to run rivers that he really shouldn't? Like on the last day of the trip. We should really have got off the river at lunchtime, you know.

Looking back on it, yes.

Well, Clive always says, the trouble is, after the high of getting away with it on the river, nothing has really changed. It isn't a real risk. That's what he said. Not a real risk.

Vince watched her. Behind the enigma of the sunglasses there was a sudden vibrancy. So, he asked, what would a real risk be, as far as Clive is concerned?

She was shaking her head slowly. He waited. You don't want him to come back, she said, do you?

Vince hesitated.

Tell the truth! She was trying to laugh, but her voice faltered. Give an honest account.

I've been worried he might not, Vince admitted now. Actually, well, I contacted a possible alternative guide, you know. Just in case. So you wouldn't be in trouble with this group that's coming, I mean contractually, if he doesn't turn up.

You did what?

Vince feels ridiculous. He explained his conversation with the people at the rafting centre.

But why should you care? It's nothing to do with you.

I . . . it seemed a way to help. Vince began to search in his wallet for the card he had been given. Shuffling through three or four, he heard her say:

So, you think Clive blew himself up.

Vince shut his wallet. He looked up. Her face wore a strange expression of triumph, pained and exulting. He shook his head. He didn't know what to say.

If he doesn't come back, you want to stay and have sex with me, right?

God! Vince was appalled. No. For heaven's sake, Michela!

Why else say you're staying till he comes back when you don't think he is coming back. I don't mind if you want to have sex with me. Most men do.

It's not what I want, and certainly not something I've been planning.

Don't be so upset! She leaned forward across the small table and put her hand gently on his. Vince can see the tops of her breasts. There's a sort of . . . she smiled, but slyly. Yearning is the word, isn't it. There's a yearning in you.

Vince said firmly. I'm sure Clive wasn't one of the people who blew themselves up. He's not that crazy. And I assure you that I'm not trying to get into your bed.

She withdrew her hand abruptly. Let's get the bill and go. She stood up, pulled the dress down a little on her thighs. But climbing into the front of his car, she asked, When was the last time you made love?

I beg your pardon.

Come on, Mr Proper, don't pretend you didn't understand.

But why do you ask me a question like that? She has him riled now.

Why not? I just wonder if you're, er, giving the best possible representation of all your various transactions. Laying it on, she said: I'm concerned for you of course. It was crazy of you to stay here when you should be back in London accounting for all that money. Oh, and by the way, I don't think those men who blew themselves up were crazy at all.

Despite his age, Vince has no experience of conversations like this. Perhaps this is why he can't leave be. Michela has a strange glow on her face.

Let's talk about Clive, Vince says. You didn't seriously imagine I thought he might be one of the three. Watching the road as they began to drive, Michela told him: The last time Clive and I made love was four days before your group arrived, and one day before two people were killed in a demonstration in Milan. I don't know if you heard. The police charged some demonstrators and two protestors fell under the wheels of a tram. We were right close by. That night Clive was mad. He smoked a lot of dope. Then the day you arrived, that night, he told me that we weren't going to make love anymore. He was obsessed that he should be doing more about everything that was wrong.

Maybe, Vince said, negotiating the unsurfaced road, to go back, that is, to what we were saying before – maybe the real risk, for Clive, would have been to settle down with you.

Don't be sentimental, she snapped.

Vince was remembering Clive's peculiar charisma. It had to do with a sort of sovereign aloneness. He turned the car onto the main road through Sand in Taufers. After a moment's silence, Michela picked up: Anyway, I told him, if he really couldn't live because of how things are in the world, he should do something important, not just go chucking himself down dangerous rivers. Again an odd ring to her voice made Vince glance sideways. Michela was sitting on her hands, back straight, lips pressed tightly together. He wondered then if she had bought her new dress and sunglasses before or after hearing that news from Germany. Seat-belt, he said. You haven't done up your seat-belt.

They spent the afternoon checking out the equipment. Michela changed into some old denim shorts. Vince pulled all the boats off the trailer and Michela got into them and checked what size of person they were padded out for, more or less, and put a sticker on the boat – small, medium, large. There were twenty people in this group, she said. From Birmingham. I hope I can understand their accents. But at least five would have their own kayaks. There was no one under seventeen. It should be a question of removing padding rather than adding, she said. Towards four, the first thunder rumbled far away up the valley. Clive will have to drive in the rain, she said. It would take him an hour from Bolzano.

They had all the boats out on the baked ground between the chalet and the pitches and Vince moved quickly to stack all of them on the trailer again and cover the top with a sheet of heavy plastic. Shit, we're two paddles down, Michela discovered then. The one Phil had broken. The one she had lost. If necessary somebody could use the splits, but that still left one short. I'll go to ask at the rafting centre, Vince offered. They'll have paddles. The first big raindrops were falling. A wind rose. All around people were hurrying to zip up their tents and tighten the guys. Stay here, she said. We can ask tomorrow. If necessary there's a place in Brixen we can buy from.

They hurried to the chalet. The rain began to fall in slapping waves. The wind gusted violently. Hang on, Michela said. Let's freshen up. She stopped just outside the porch, on the steps, and let herself be soaked. Vince was already in. The doors and windows were banging. He turned and saw her shoulders shiver as the yellow T-shirt darkened. Then she came in, drenched, laughing. But the moment everything was shut, it was hot again. How tense we are, Vince realised. He had thought they were relaxing, sorting out the boats. Instead it seemed they were more on edge than before.

It was past five o'clock. Her T-shirt was clinging to her body. Vince looked away. Bending forward, Michela peeled the shirt off, towelled herself quickly, put on another. Then took off her shorts. Her pants are white. He couldn't understand if she was doing this on purpose. She seems so natural, opening and closing a couple of cupboard doors. Where did you put my jeans? she asked. I can't believe you sorted our stuff out like this. Second drawer from the top, he said, I think. You're weird, she told him. He gazed determinedly out of the window where somebody was trying to ride a bicycle under an umbrella across a field of mud. There! She was dressed. Let's be English and make tea.

The rain beat on the wooden roof. They sat quietly over their tea. There was too much at stake to say anything now. Outside, plastic bags, bits of polystyrene, a sheet of newspaper, are being chased about in the wind. Michela's face is crossed by sudden spasms. Vince watches. A moment of misery is transformed into elation. She gets up and walks back and forth between sink and table. She throws herself on the bed. Oh shit! Suddenly Vince is aware she is smiling at him. A warm smile. Then she is gathering up an armful of clothes, kicking the wall. She wants it to have been Clive who killed himself, Vince thinks. And she is terrified he has done it for her. The news, the girl suddenly said. Where's the radio. Damn! It was a couple of minutes past six.

She found an Italian station. Vince can't understand. Her face is concentrated. She's sitting on the bed, chin on hand. Then, with a grimace, she turns it off. So? Oh various groups have claimed responsibility. Police think they may have identified the one who spoke to them, matching the recordings they made of his voice. They didn't say who though. Then she was furious. Can you believe they had some prick expert comparing them with the Islamic suicide bombers. I can't believe it. They're not terrorists. They didn't hurt anyone else. Then not a single word about what the conference decided! Vince watched her. Nothing, most probably! The girl was full of pent-up energy. Their world is burning up and all they can do is criminalise the people who care. She stretched forward and grabbed her ankles. For a moment her arms seemed to be straining to pull her legs towards her, while her knees thrust down against them. Ow! She sat up. In a hundred years from now, those men will be heroes, saints.

Vince's phone was ringing. He saw from the display it was his colleague, Dyers. Vince? Listen, I won't be in the office tomorrow when you get back. His wife's father, the director said, had just passed away. He was going to Edinburgh for the funeral. I just wanted to tell you what you'll find on your desk when you get back.

Vince listened and asked pertinent questions. At the same time his gaze met Michela's. Their eyes held each other's as they never did when they were talking. It was close in the room with the rain outside and the accumulated heat of the morning in the wood. Vince was sweating. I'll give precedence to the stuff from V.A. then, he said. I presume we can rely on their assessment. As he spoke, her bright eyes were intent and enquiring. There was just a hint of a smile on her lips. Vince imagined her passing judgement on the work he did every day. She wants to see into my world and dismiss it. Is everything okay there now? Dyers was asking. Ready for the drive back? I should be leaving in a hour or so, Vince said. Michela raised a mocking eyebrow. When he closed the call she was still watching him. Should be? she asked. Then she said, Look, call the airport. We can find out what time he landed.

Vince gave her his phone and she called directory enquiries. The rain still clattered on the roof. He said it was a charter flight, Vince remembered. Michela spoke in Italian. Her voice seemed sharper, more nasal. They were sitting together now on the stools by the counter beneath the window. The earth outside was black and splashing with puddles. The trees screening the river were waving darkly, but above the peaks, to the right, Vince could see a break in the clouds. It is easing off. Michela suddenly smiled. Waiting to be connected, she ran a fingertip round the wound on his left hand. Then she saw the white mark on his ring finger. She looked at him, lips pursed, head cocked.

Pronto? Sì. Volevo sapere . . . Vince didn't understand. The conversation went on longer than seemed necessary. Apparently Michela was objecting, insisting. He understood the words *Germania, Berlino, Dusseldorf*. She closed the call. There is no charter flight, she said. She shook her head. It's a small airport. There was a flight from Vienna this morning, Frankfurt early afternoon, Dusseldorf at seven. But it seems crazy to go from Berlin to Bolzano via Dusseldorf.

She stood and paced the room. He was bullshitting you. Oh fuck! She flung open the door. The cool air rushed in with a sprinkle of rain. Fuck and shit! Don't say anything, Vince warned himself. He was trying to understand. Perhaps the flight was cancelled, he eventually said. What reason would he have had to lie to me? Charters often get cancelled.

Perhaps he's called the campsite, to leave a message. At once, Michela was pulling on her sandals. She hurried off. Vince stood at the door watching. It was pushing seven now. A beam of sunshine lay horizontally across the glacier high over the village. I am afraid even of thinking of the next few hours, he realised.

Nothing. Michela came back. But she seemed pleased. She was smiling. We'll just have to be patient. Why don't we take a look at his laptop, Vince said. Perhaps there'll be some letter or something. The girl was wary. Clearly she is nervous that they will indeed find something. But as Vince expected, the screen demands a password. Any ideas? As he asks, he taps in, 'Michela'. Error! Incorrect password. Then 'No global'. And 'No-Global'. Error! He tried zeros instead of 'o's. Stopper, she said. He likes those river words. Eddy-out. Vince typed in one after another. She was standing at his shoulder watching. Error!

I give up, she suddenly said. What do I know about Clive in the end? Nothing. Vince kept typing. I mean, I know him, but I don't know anything about him. He never said much about his family, old girlfriends, anything. Vince stared at the small luminous rectangle. Come on, he said. Try, think. But how can you ever know the word another person will choose? After all, Vince had never found the password Gloria used for her e-mail. Kyoto, Michela said. Destiny, Vince tried. No doubt there would have been some way of accessing the program, with expert help, but he hadn't bothered. He had packed her computer away and forgotten about it.

Rabiaux, Michela said. That's the name of this mad wave he loved to play on in France. They do rodeo competitions there. R-a-b-i-a-u-x. It's on the Durance. Error! Incorrect password. Rebel then. The girl began to laugh. She is relieved when the error sign comes up. Paddle. Puddle. Ferry-glide.

Break-in. Break-out. The sheer fact. She was giggling. He always says that. The sheer fact is . . . It drives me crazy. Free-style. Rodeo. Vince gave up. She had put a hand on his shoulder. He turned to look at her. Maybe we might go out and grab a pizza, he said. He'll already be here when we get back and I can set out on a full stomach.

They sat in the same pizzeria with the ancient keyboard player and the clutter of kitsch. Vince explained that they had come here after that last trip, when she was in hospital. I booked the bloody place, she told him. And for next week too. They should kiss my feet the business I'm giving them. Then she asked: I hope everybody was properly concerned about me, by the way.

Waiting for their order, Vince ran through people's attitudes, mimicking. He isn't a very good mimic. But suddenly they were laughing together. It's as if we were happy, he thought. Amelia and Tom, he remembered, were both being terribly solemn and self-important, as if they were involved. He described the conversation with Tom. Michela did her characteristic head-shake. I should never have bothered them like that, poor things. At last the girl seemed completely relaxed. I thought she was a happy person! Vince did Amal's high-pitched voice. I really liked Amal, Michela said. She frowned. You don't think he was castrated or anything? Sorry, not funny.

The keyboard guy, Vince resumed – isn't he fantastic, by the way? – was playing 'El Condor Pasa'. You know? I'd rather be a sparrow than a snail. Gloria used to like Paul Simon, he said. My wife. Tell me about her, Michela asked. Having cut up her pizza into slices, she folded each one in long fingers, eating elegantly, with appetite.

Vince talked. He feels strangely at ease, speaking without pain or embarrassment about his wife, about the music she listened to, the sports she did, her rather brusque, efficient ways. We will drive back to the chalet now, he thought, and Clive will be there. I will shake hands with him, say a word or two about the prices they should be asking for their courses, then set off for England, the City. My desk is piled with papers. For a moment it crossed his mind to worry whether his passport was still in the glove compartment.

And your ring, she asked. She still had food in her mouth. Smiling an apology, touching her lips with a napkin, she looked very young, fresh, at ease. Vince explained how he had dropped it into the rapid. The moment seemed far away. It's the strangest thing I ever did in my life. She is attentive again, reflective. Perhaps you should do more things like that, Mr Banker.

Don't call me that, Vince said.

Their eyes met.

But you are, she said. I'll give precedence to the stuff from what's-its-name, she mimicked his phone voice.

If I was just a banker, I would have gone back a week ago.

That's true. Looking away, she said: I'm glad you didn't.

The chalet was as they had left it. Clive isn't back. Again the young woman was on edge. They spread a bin-bag on the damp steps outside the door and sat there together as darkness fell. The evening was fresh and mild. There was still thunder somewhere far away. Lights high up on the mountainside seemed nearer in the clear air, as if the night were blacker and softer than usual. After a while she slipped a hand under his arm. At what point will you decide to go anyway? Vince sighed. Good question. He felt anxious. Then he said: Help me put up my tent somewhere. I'll still be in time to leave in the morning. She didn't move. It's horrible putting up a tent in the wet. You can stay in the chalet.

236

Vince isn't happy with this. Michela, he said firmly, I am not, repeat not trying . . . Clive slept on the floor, she said, in his sleeping bag. If you've got an inflatable mattress, you can use that.

Every time headlights turned into the campsite, there was a moment of tension and expectancy. But the cars never came this far. Towards midnight she asked: Assuming it was him, I mean, you know what I mean, do you think he would have done it to prove something to me. Am I responsible? Or would he have done it even if he had never met me?

What kind of answer is she after? There are a hundred and one reasons, Vince said, why a guy comes back late from a trip, or doesn't come back at all for that matter. The car, he suddenly thought, their Jeep! The thing to do would be to find out where the Jeep was, whether it had been abandoned. Though even that wouldn't actually prove anything. Out loud, he said: Whoever blew themselves up like that, it was their decision and no one else's. He paused. Like it was your decision to go down the rapid the way you did. You can't blame Clive for that. On the contrary, you put his life and mine at risk. That's true, Michela said. Keith and Mandy, Vince went on, kept talking about a community experience, and it was, I suppose, but that doesn't mean people aren't responsible for themselves, does it? This car, he thought, as headlights swept into the site, this will be the one. Here he is. The headlights were in fact coming their way. They were passing the bathrooms. He felt her hand tense under his arm. The lights stopped abruptly and went out two chalets away. She sighed. She is shaking her head. It's so weird, not knowing if he's alive or dead. And no one to phone. There's no one I can ask.

When Vince went to the car for the inflatable mattress, she called, Vince! He already had it under his arm. You may as well sleep with me.

I told you— Vince began.

It's not an invitation to have sex. She was giggling. It's a big bed. Keep your clothes on if you like.

I'll be waking you up. I always go to the loo a couple of times a night. He was pleased with himself for having admitted this.

I don't think I'll sleep anyway, she said.

And when Clive arrives . . .

He won't. She seemed quite certain now.

But if he does.

You're not doing anything wrong. You slept in the same tent as your daughter last week. Anyway, he doesn't own me. He wasn't even sleeping with me.

There were still cars pulling into the campsite from time to time. Headlights swung across the curtainless windows. The wooden walls whiten and spin. Vince had lain down on the bed fully clothed, his hands behind his head, his legs crossed. She had changed into pyjama shorts and top. She didn't hide when she took off her clothes as his daughter did, and even his wife in her way, but she was quick and discreet. She got under the bedclothes. He glimpsed the long legs, the lithe stomach. She too turned on her back and lay still, listening to the last of the campsite noises, a tinkle of low music, a drunken voice. Vince's mind had just begun to drift, when she said: I'm afraid. At once he was awake.

What of?

Afraid he'll come back, afraid he won't come back. She sighed. Afraid he's dead. Afraid he just left me without even the courage to say so. She sighed again, turned and found Vince's hand. Afraid in general. What will I do now? I was so sure of him, she whispered, so sure. It was like, everything was decided. Then first he cuts me off. He won't sleep with me. Now he disappears, right when this group is arriving. I don't even know if he has disappeared.

Again there came the sound of a distant car. They waited. Then a door slammed, there were low voices. She laughed softly. Her fingers squeezed his unresponding hand. When I heard you on the phone earlier, talking about your job – this, that, give precedence, we can rely on so and so – I felt so jealous, the way you know who you are. You have a place. Her voice was a thread now. I'm not even the romantic girl who killed herself. After all, if I'd really wanted to die, I wouldn't have done something so useless as trying to drown myself within a hundred yards of a guy who's spent his whole life teaching white-water rescues. She laughed. She is on the brink of tears.

Vince opened his hand and let hers slip into it.

I'm afraid of everything really. The dark and the intimacy had freed her to speak. I'm always afraid something won't happen, you know, and at the same time I'm afraid it will. I was afraid Clive would want children right away, and afraid he would never want children. I'm afraid the planet will burn up and afraid they will prove us wrong, it won't burn up, and we've wasted all our lives protesting for no reason. She paused. I'm afraid of being weak, and terrified what it would mean to be strong, to take the lead. Clive always said, Be strong. Be strong. But I was always following. I think that frightened him. When we were paddling he would invent little tricks to make me go up front and take a rapid first.

Again headlights crossed the room. This time they didn't even listen carefully.

Maybe, in the end, we weren't really that different. Again she laughed softly. She lifted her head from the pillow. You're being very quiet, Mr Banker.

239

I'm listening, Vince said.

You're dirtying my sheets with those jeans, she said. Take them off. What are you afraid of? It's the woman's supposed to be afraid. I know you're not going to rape me.

I'm afraid of giving the wrong idea.

Take them off, she told him. Don't be uncomfortable.

Vince let go of her hand, climbed out of bed, removed his jeans. She was curled towards him. It was disturbing. He climbed back in.

I think, she resumed, so many of these people who do dangerous things on rivers and mountains are afraid. It's funny, but I'm pretty sure. Afraid of dying, afraid of settling down. Afraid of life beginning really, and afraid it will never begin. These sports are something you do instead of life. Suddenly, she propped herself up on an elbow. Do you see what I'm trying to say, Mr Banker? They're things people do instead of living. Really, you should tell your bank to invest in all these high-risk sports because it's what every-one really wants. Hang-gliding, deep-sea diving. To feel they're really living, when they're not in danger of living at all. She lay back on her pillow. Clive's problem was, he had seen through it. It didn't work anymore. That's why he was so sad. But you should invest your money in these kinds of things, she finished. You could get rich. Now she was running a finger softly back and forth in the hair of his forearm.

Vince said: How would you like to run the upper Aurino with me. Just us two.

The finger stopped. You what?

Tomorrow. We could run the upper Aurino again. You do the shopping early. I sort out the paddle and the guide at the rafting centre. We should have about four hours before the party arrives. If we don't take any breaks, we can do it.

After a thunderstorm?

It can't be any worse than it was last time.

She was intrigued. You have to drive to England, she reminded him.

If I drive through the night, tomorrow, I'll still be back Saturday morning.

In fine condition for a sixteen-hour working day.

Right, Vince laughed. Let's do it.

Suddenly, she threw an arm across his chest and snuggled towards him, her cheek was on his shoulder, her lips only inches away. My old banker wants to kill himself.

I want to run that river. With you. You lead.

You really don't want to go back at all, do you?

Vince was silent.

At that point, we may as well just make love, she said. Her arm tightened round him.

No, Vince said.

Why not? It's not so dangerous as running the upper Aurino, and it'll eat up less of your precious time. You can leave as soon as we've finished.

I can't.

She laughed. I know you've grown old counting all that money, but not that old.

I'm terrified, Vince said.

The girl's grip softened a little, but the arm stayed where it was. After a minute or two, he said quietly, I would like to run that river again.

You can count me out, she whispered. I've chosen to live.

The minutes ticked by. The air coming through the window was chill now. Soon someone would have to close it.

Listen, Vince eventually said. Are you listening?

Ye-e-e-es.

If Clive doesn't turn up, tonight, before lunch tomorrow . . .

Which he won't.

I think he probably will.

Let's say he might.

Well, if he doesn't, what about . . .

Ye-e-e-es.

Vince hesitated.

Mr Banker will try to make love to me?

No. No. What about . . . if I stay. He stopped.

What do you mean?

I stay and run these summer courses with you. I phone the bank, tomorrow, and tell them I'm resigning.

Again she lifted herself on an elbow. She was looking down on him. You're not serious.

I wouldn't say it if I wasn't. He smiled. I'm always serious.

Well, you're mad then. You're more suicidal than I am.

The only thing I want to know, he said, is whether you would like me to stay, or not.

Don't make me responsible, she objected quickly.

It would always be my decision. You haven't forced me to do anything. You haven't even invited me.

Where would you stay? she asked.

I have my tent, Vince said. My airbed.

You can't spend the whole summer in a tent.

Why not?

Not at your age.

Go to hell. Now, would you like me to stay or not?

And afterwards? When summer's over?

I don't know. I haven't thought. I want to do something different. I've got enough money in the end. I don't need money. I've decided I want to do something different. Work for a cause even. I don't know.

Not because of me?

Vince hesitated. Maybe partly because of you. Does it

242

matter? I know there can't be anything serious between us.

Why not?

You're in love with Clive. He'll be back in the end. You just said how old I am. And there are thousands of nice young men.

Michela sank back on the bed. She shook her head, then giggled. Funny if he arrived now.

So? Vince asked.

I won't say, she said. It's your decision, regardless of me. But you won't stop me.

I'll tell you after you've phoned the bank and resigned.

Vince thought about this. Fair enough, he says. I'll call as soon as someone's in.

They lay in silence for perhaps five minutes, then Vince got up to go to the loo. He closed the window and let himself out. The night was bright with stars and the gleam of a crescent moon. The glow of the sky made the mountains loom darker. Vince stopped and gazed. Was it that all life until now had been a tired spell, from which he was suddenly released? Or was it this situation that was snatching him from reality? The lights of the bathroom came on as he approached. He emptied his nervous bladder. Or each state was a form of enchantment, worth as much or as little as the other. Every place is its own spell, Vince thought. Walking back, something again forced him to stop and look around. The sheer bulk of the mountains imposes a sense of awe, he thought, looking away to the jagged silhouette of the peaks. I'm impressionable, he decided.

Entering the chalet, he found to his surprise that Michela had fallen asleep. She has invaded his side of the bed. He climbed in and lay beside her. He is cramped. I'll never sleep. What if Clive had killed himself. It must be so horrible for her. Very lightly, he allowed his fingers to push her short fringe across her forehead. We haven't really taken this in yet. The skin round the eyes tensed, wrinkled, relaxed again. Michela, he whispered, not to wake her. It is impossible to imagine the girl will ever be his lover. She is playing with me. She likes to mock. To lose such a woman would be terrifying, he thought. Yet, Clive had thrown her away. Clive, Clive, Clive. His mind drifted. You were always awed by men like Clive . . .

Then, towards dawn, there was a sudden explosive clatter and the door banged open. A hot wind rushed in. Vince is sitting up, rigid, staring. Clive! The man seems appallingly dishevelled, grizzled. Wally is swinging from his neck. Vince, what the hell are you doing here? Vince looks down. The girl is still asleep. Vince can't open his mouth. He shook his head. We haven't. It's not . . . Clive swung off his backpack and banged it on the floor. He was laughing, a loud, booming laugh. Well, you should have, mate. While you had the chance. And he began stripping off his clothes. He is going to get in the bed too. There is a strange smell in the room, Vince noticed. Rather boldly, he said: So you didn't blow yourself up, then? Clive stopped. Yes, I did. Of course, I did. Vince stared. What do you think that smell is? It was burning. Clive's hair is smoking. Wally too. The air is full of ash. *Gefährlich!* he shouts. *Draussen!* His clothes are black. His legs slipping out of his jeans are charred stumps. There is ash on the floor, ash on the bed. You throw a handful of ash in the river and it comes back in clouds. Vince can taste it on his lips. Do you think, Clive laughs, I'd be afraid of blowing myself up? Thrust close to him now, the face is blackened bone around gum-less, grinning teeth.

Vince! For Christ's sake. His waking eyes met Michela's. She's leaning over him. God, I thought you were having a heart attack. Vince breathed deeply. Stupid nightmare, he told her. What about? He collected himself. Nothing. The usual angst. She is on her elbow, smiling. Without thinking, he said, You're beautiful. I beg your pardon? Beautiful. She laughed: No sooner do you show a man you trust him than the flattery begins! Vince shook his head. I'm sorry, if I woke you. No problem. She resumed a sleeping position, turned her back to him. Then she said softly: I do know you're only after a nurse for your decrepitude. Yes, I'm ancient, he told her. Like the planet. Well, she was still teasing, I can't look after both of you.

Vince lay still. Outside the light was brightening. What time was it, five, six? Soon the bells would ring. In just a few hours he would have to make that call. The fact is, she went on, an old guy like you could pop off any minute. I could wake up with a corpse in the bed. He found this too cruel. Don't worry, I'll be in the tent tomorrow. Oh I don't mind, she laughed. Better than a man who sleeps on the floor. After a moment's silence, thinking of his dream, Vince said: He probably just had a problem with the car or something. I don't know, a flat tyre. Please, she said. Please. Let's sleep.

Vince knew he wouldn't sleep now. Again he found himself looking at her. Above all, the long neck, the soft V of glossy hair growing on the nape. How careful, it suddenly occurs to him, how careful I've always been! With what caution his life had been planned, his career. How they had gone back and forth, back and forth over the business of Louise's school, the possibility of a move to London. Then Gloria was taken. She was there one minute and gone the next. Just the one phone-call. Those thirty seconds of intimacy. I'm so, so sorry, she said. They had blocked out everything that came before. Vince gazed at this white neck, the wonderful pattern of that cropped hair. It is a miracle. Do you think, he asked then in a low voice – do you think it would be crazy of me if I asked if I could hug you? She didn't reply. She must be sleeping. Michela? he whispered. After thirty seconds or so there came a low chuckle. Sorry, I thought you must be talking to someone else. Well? Hmm. On reflection, yes, I think it would be crazy. The light was growing steadily now, sharpening the angle of her shoulder, colouring her hair. Yes, it would definitely be crazy, Mr Banker. You promised to stop calling me that. Only when I see you've phoned the office and resigned. I'm a sceptical modern girl. Hug me, he said then. She lay still. Oh, did you say something? Hug me. Sorry, what was that? *Hug me*! Just a hug, mind, he added. She turned and all at once her arms are round him, her cheek pressed against his. Vince held the girl quite tightly and waited.